MISTER ZERO

Geordie Gilman

This is a work of fiction. Names, characters, places, and incidents are products of the author's imagination or are used fictitiously and are not to be construed as real. Any resemblance to actual events, locations, organizations, or persons, living or dead, is entirely coincidental.

World Castle Publishing, LLC
Pensacola, Florida
Copyright © Geordie Gilman 2018
Hardback ISBN: 9798891263833
Paperback ISBN: 9798891263840
eBook ISBN: 9781629899138
First Edition World Castle Publishing, LLC, April 30, 2018
http://www.worldcastlepublishing.com
Licensing Notes
Cover: Karen Fuller
Editor: Maxine Bringenberg

Table of Contents

PROLOGUE

He stood in a field on the outskirts of town proudly looking down at his handiwork, cursing at the bloody corpse as though it could hear his ranting. It was early in the morning, the sun behind him barely cresting the horizon, a good hour before showing above the tree line. If he bothered to look he would have seen a beautiful sunrise, a thin layer of pink-painted clouds drifting above the coming day.

Of course none of this mattered to him — he had been roaming in circles and cursing in the dark all night since taking the young woman's life. The knife he used to do the horrible deed still hung loosely in his bloodied hand, now dried dark, crimson-red. His blood-splattered clothes he knew needed to be destroyed. He was glad now that he'd had the withal to remove the only jacket he owned and his prized camouflaged hunter's cap before plunging the knife into her soft flesh. Over and over again he'd stabbed away, destroying what he thought to be a demon in disguise of a teenage girl.

His worries of underestimating the complexity of the task, his brief surveillance work that amounted to no more than making sure she was alone, were greatly exaggerated. It was easier than he had imagined. She had been silently sitting in her car texting on her cell phone, unaware of her surroundings. He simply opened the passenger door and slipped into the seat, brandishing a knife. He stuck the tip of the long thin blade against the flesh under her chin, not pressing too hard to cause penetration but hard enough to be felt, telling her he meant business. Then, in a gruff sounding voice, he told her not to be scared. All he wanted was a ride. He then added, in an attempt to calm her shaking nerves, that if she complied with his demands and did not cause any disturbance to attract attention, he would release her when they arrived at his destination. He could see in her green eyes that she knew his words were all lies, but he could also sense she held out hope he would let her go without harming her. This he knew from past experience; basically they were all the same.

***

The girl was scared, mentally and physically, shaking as she tried to control the steering wheel with the knife still wedged under her chin. She was so terrified she hadn't even noticed the downtown stores' bright lights as she slowly drove by. Tears streaked black down her cheeks from too much mascara she'd applied to appease her peer-pressing friends and defy her mother's demands. The girl was pretty — green eyes and long blonde hair with a soft, unblemished complexion. She was chubby in middle school when she'd first began applying makeup, lipstick first then mascara. Her high school years had brought the beauty out of her, not the makeup.

On the outskirts of town, just beyond a farmhouse, he told her to turn right, which she automatically did without thinking of the consequences of being alone on a dark desolate road with

6

a deranged man. A short distance down the dirt road he told her to pull over in a small turnaround and park. It was the end of the ride. For her it was only a seventeen-year ride, one enjoyable ride filled with love and laughter and a promising future.

***

She was still crying when he told her to get out of the car, pulling her across the console and over the passenger seat. He didn't want her to exit on the driver's side in case she decided to split and disappear into the dark night. He gripped her arm tightly, tight enough to cause bruising by morning, but he knew she would not care. Her major concerns would come soon enough, well before morning.

Just beyond a grove of alders and a scattering of immature pines, he pushed her to the ground in an open field and sat on her mid-section, holding his hand over her mouth to keep her from wailing like a spoiled brat not getting her way. He imagined she was thinking he was about to rip her clothes off and rape her, taking her precious virginity away. Something she was saving for the young man in her dreams, not some monster from her nightmares. She'd be wrong though; her precious cherry was the furthest thing from his deranged mind.

Rape had nothing to do with her abduction. It was her youth and eyes that had attracted his interest. Even in the dark he could see her green-emerald eyes glaring up at him. There was so much terror in her eyes he thought they would pop out of her eye sockets on their own. To help, he slipped the long thin blade in her left eye socket under the eye and slowly, painfully for her but rewarding pleasure for him, rotated the knife all the way around, cutting the optic nerves from the forebrain. Then, with little effort, he popped the bloody horrified eye out.

***

She terrifyingly kicked and screamed when the point of the blade slid under her eyelid, more from the horror of watching it than from the pain, and instinctively kept on screaming into his sweaty hand, unaware of its foul smell. She also hadn't realized her left eye was missing. The one remaining eye saw nothing, forced helplessly into a world beyond all reason.

***

For a moment he stared at the round object, rolling the slimy thing in his hand, wondering if it could still see; but he knew that was impossible, even for a demon. Then, without hesitation or the thought of what he was about to do, he popped the bloody organ into his mouth.

***

Her horror and the excruciating pain were only just the beginning of her nightmare. As she screamed she had no idea she was the only person hearing her muffled cries. With each scream she thought help was on the way. Surely somebody would come along and pull the beast off her, save her life. Tomorrow life would be back to normal; but first she had to fight back. Don't give up; a lesson she'd been taught but never experienced. If she had fought back it wouldn't have mattered anyhow. No amount of life-protecting measures would have been enough to prevent what was happening to her.

She dug deep inside to a place where her willpower was stored for one last push—one last attempt to live. Her chest heaved, trying to push his weight off her, causing his knifed hand to zigzag through the incision, stopping abruptly against a bone.

***

His bloodied hand slipped down the long, sharp blade cutting his palm just below his fingers. Though the cut was minor, this was not good, her tainted blood mixing with his. He should have expected her to react. After all it was his second kill this week, third since arriving the previous month, and they all fought till the end.

**

In the moments before his fatal blow, the one that would open her center cavity to the dark universe above her, she thought of her mother sitting impatiently on the couch by the phone wondering what was keeping her daughter. Only a mere hour ago, just before her abduction, she'd told her mother in a text message she was on her way home. She wanted to call her mother now, no texting this time, and tell her not to worry, everything was going to be fine, and most of all, that she loved her. But no matter how hard she tried she could not reach her cell phone.

Her delicate, nail polished hands that she had used to claw at the evil man's face, without much success, were more than an arm's reach away. And even if her hands were still attached they would have been useless anyway; her cell phone was on the floor of her vehicle.

The only precious things she had left were her hopeless dreams, and they died with her. A short while later she silently prayed for her death, which came instantly when he pulled her pounding heart out of her chest.

**

At about the same time the farmer's rooster awoke the sleeping family, the monster disappeared without a trace of his existence, taking his knife and bloody clothes with him. The only things he left behind were the girl's vehicle and her decomposing bloody remains.

CHAPTER 1

She crawled into her bed naked, giving her freedom to move. After fluffing her pillow she slipped the cloth sheet over her, leaving the comforter down by her legs for later when the cool of the night crept in through her open bedroom window. She then reached over to the nightstand and turned the clock radio on, and as always, she tapped the sleep button to give her an hour to fall asleep.

The same station she had been listening to for over a week came to life. The voices on the radio helped her fall asleep, putting her mind at ease from all the stress of her first fulltime job since graduating from Redmond High two years earlier. Before the hour was up and the radio came to a dead silence, she'd usually drift-off into a deep sleep. But if the hour failed to accomplish its purpose she'd tap the button again...and again, until either her wish for sleep was fulfilled or the harsh daylight, peeking through the narrow outline between the window and aged shade, intervened. Those long sleepless nights of insomnia were infrequent, and mostly caused from over indulging on margaritas.

The female voice on the radio program was soft and gentle with compassion to sooth the listener's mind, which was a far contrast from the voices of those who called in to the host's nightly radio program. Most of the calls were complaints about other people's peculiar oddities, or what they assumed to be odd behaviors compared to their own way of living. And then there were those with guilty consciences that had been buried deep inside of them for years, eating away at their soul and sanity. Those were the most disturbing callers, and also the most intriguing to the listening audience, and those types of calls were what were keeping the program alive.

"Welcome back to the Doctor Nancy program. Hi, I'm Doctor Nancy, and for all you listeners who are just tuning in to our program tonight we are listening to the disturbing story of a troubled man. This man, to keep his identity anonymous, is using the fictitious name of Mister Zero. Now, before the commercial break, Mister Zero was telling us about his troubling, unimaginable world of horror and evil, where demons entered his mind through the voices of beautiful young blonde women...."

"Teenage girls." A low, raspy voice could be heard over the softer voice of Doctor Nancy.

"Yes, you are quite right, Mister Zero. Even though they mean the same, you did say teenage girls. I beg your pardon."

"Good. I don't want to be misinterpreted, so let's get it right, Doctor."

"Okay then, Mister Zero, could you tell our audience what happened next? What happened to the girl's body after she stopped breathing? I think that's where we left off before the commercial break."

Silence filled the airwaves.

After what seemed like the station had gone off the air the raspy voice finally cracked the radio's speakers, breaking the silence. The voice was like the first clap of thunder from an encroaching storm.

"Like I was saying before, I was rudely interrupted by your so-called commercial break to sell junk to your listeners, I heard shallow gasps coming from the mouth so I leaned in closer, pressing my ear upon its face, trying to figure out what it was trying to tell me. But the gasps were only murmuring sighs, none of it making any sense. Then I heard the gurgling sounds rising up its throat and the body started to heave pathetically, violently jerking with spasms. I laughed."

"You laughed?" Doctor Nancy whispered over the radio waves.

"Yes, Doctor, I laughed. There was nothing it could do to me now. I had stuck it hard, very hard. I felt a great satisfaction of relief. Then suddenly, like it was taking all its revenge out on me for my triumphant conquest, like it was my fault it walked into my life, a smelly dark liquid vomit sprayed out of its mouth."

She reached over for the radio's volume knob and turned it louder. Then, after fluffing her pillow again for more comfort, she settled her head back down on the pillow, pulling the sheet and comforter up to her chin and wondering if her friend was also listening to the program. It was the best caller ever, she thought.

"I'm sorry, but that doesn't sound like something to be laughing about," Doctor Nancy disgustingly told the caller.

"Yes, you are absolutely right, Doctor. Believe me when I say I wasn't laughing any more. I stuck it hard again...and again. Then, with great pleasure, I chopped the demon up into a thousand pieces. I should have fed it to the pig over at that farm, but I couldn't do that to him. Not to the pig, I mean. So, do I need

12

to say more...? The filthy thing emptied its stomach all over me."

The radio went dead silent again, and then in the background the trembling, soft voice of Doctor Nancy could be heard. "Should we go to a commercial, Peter?"

"No, we don't want to lose him. This is great for our ratings... say something to keep him on the line!" The male voice snapped in the background, not intended for the listening audience, but he screwed up.

"Okay, so...Mister...Mister Zero, how long has it been since this happened? I mean, this happened before they sent you away, is this correct? You just want to rid yourself of your horrid past, your tortured thoughts, and start over," Doctor Nancy hastily asked, improvising, trying to keep him on the line.

Silence.

She looked around her dark bedroom for movement. Outside her open window she could hear the ocean waves wash up along the rocky shoreline. She was alone, safely tucked in her bed. She wished her girlfriend was listening and would call for comfort to reassure her she was not really alone. In the morning they would joke about it at work, like recounting a scary movie they saw together at the theater.

***

"Mister Zero, are you still with us, or have you ever been with us?" Doctor Nancy patronizingly asked. She was starting to get the feeling he was a fake, calling the program for a little notoriety, or whatever floated his crazy thoughts.

More silence.

"No need for sarcasm, Doctor!"

"I was only trying—"

"Or lies,"

"Right. Okay, now did I understand that you were recently

13

released from a state sanitarium...hospital of some kind? Is that what you told the audience earlier?"

"You can call it by what it is, Doctor, it doesn't offend me. An insane asylum, plain and simple."

"Yes, but we like to be professionally correct, you know. I'm not sure how long you were in the institution, but these days it is referred to as a mental health care facility. So how long ago were you released from the...facility?"

Silence.

"Mister Zero?"

***

"Sorry, Doctor, I was calculating the days. Excuse me for keeping you and your radio listeners impatiently waiting. To be exact, it has been six weeks since I was released."

"Huh...six weeks?"

"Yes, Doctor, six weeks."

"Oh, so...where was I?"

"You were going to ask me when I destroyed the evil demon."

"Oh yes, that's it. So, Mister Zero, you've only been out in the civilized world for a little more than a month, and you were telling me previously that you were performing...an exorcism of the soul. Is that correct?"

"No, it was more like mutilating the demon."

"Oh, yes...well whatever. It must have been a long time ago, and the psychiatrists must have felt you were...cured. Right? And the demons that had haunted you have long since disappeared."

"That is correct...partially correct, at least."

"Partially correct?"

"Yes, the doctors at the institution felt I was fit to live back amongst society and that I was rehabilitated."

"Well, we must trust their diagnosis was correct, and I'm

14

sure you'll fit in your new community just fine. So tell me, where are you residing at this time?"

"I don't think it would be very wise of me to reveal my exact location. I don't want the demons to know how close I am to knocking on their door. Besides my cutting tool, surprise is one of my key weapons. But I can tell you I'm residing somewhere along the northern coast, not far from the quaint little coastal town of Redmond."

"Redmond, you say?"

Silence.

Mister Zero disliked repeating himself, and felt the question was rhetorical, not requiring a response.

"I guess we can confirm that as a yes," Doctor Nancy said, then added her final comments to end the call. "Well, I must say, Mister Zero, it was quite an experience chatting with you, and it's time to let our listeners phone in their thoughts and concerns about what they have just heard. I'm sure our phone lines will be lit up like the night before Christmas.

"So, all you folks living along the coast, and especially near the town of Redmond, how do you feel about this? Do you think that the local authorities should inform the residents when a former mental patient, who had brutally mutilated teenage girls, relocates into their quiet neighborhood? Call in and let us hear your comments. The number here is 1-888-555-HELP."

"Doctor, you are being very rude, you didn't let me finish answering your previous question on when I committed these so-called brutal mutilations." The raspy voice cracked through the radio's speakers and into her dark bedroom.

There was a moment of dead silence before the radio came alive again. In that brief moment it was quiet enough for a feather dropping from her pillow onto her rug to be heard. She hesitated

15

turning the radio off, or at least changing the radio channel to a more relaxing station, to help her sleep. Even though she could not see it, she glanced over at her cell phone on the nightstand, wishing it would ring. All she could hear, however, besides her pounding heart beating against her chest, were the voices coming back to life on the radio.

"Mister Zero, you are still with us. I had thought you were disconnected."

"Disconnected...nice choice of a word, Doctor. However, I believe that word is inappropriate for my state-of-being at the moment, for I am well connected, connected to the thoughts of evilness. I know where evil lives, and I know what I must do to rid the world of its presence. The word I believe you are looking for is deranged. And the so-called mutilation was not committed before I entered the, professionally correct, mental health care facility. It was committed after I was released and deemed sane."

She anxiously reached over to the nightstand and clicked the radio button to the off position. She then pulled the blankets over her head, curling her naked body into a ball, knowing she'd have a long sleepless night ahead of her. Morning, when the comfort of daylight arrived, could not come soon enough for her.

CHAPTER 2

In the predawn hours black ominous clouds slowly crept unnoticed across the western sky. Before the sun crested above the islands in Craggs Bay and winked its morning eye upon the old church's towering steeple, one of three similar white churches that adorned this tranquil New England coastal town, the sun was quickly consumed by the angry clouds and would not be seen again for three long rainy days. The three days of rain and terror would forever place a black mark on this once peaceful town.

The old church was built on a location high above the town, an ideal spot easily seen by all the residents of Redmond, and all those who were out at sea steering home from a long day of fishing. It was also an ideal location for the town's official cemetery, a large stretch of rolling landscape behind the church.

Back in the early days when the cemetery was first constructed, before a new entrance was made to accommodate vehicles and the large equipment needed to maintain the property, visitors had to enter the cemetery through a black, iron-gated entrance.

Venturing beyond the black gate in those days could be very intimidating in daylight, and especially so on cold dreary days, but almost forbidding for human souls to enter its confines at the edge of nightfall. Old decrepit monuments, which protruded out of the ground like signposts inching their way across the traveler's path, along with the silence of the dead they swore could be heard whispering from their graves, sent shivers down their spine.

At this ghostly time of day, when the day began to turn into dusk, eating away the protection of the daylight, there was something else more haunting than the spooky old monuments and the creepy silence surrounding them. It was the gnarly trees growing in the lower section of the cemetery that frightened them the most.

Before the spring foliage gave them coverage, long bony branches from the tall leafless oaks spread their way across the path like painful looking skeletal fingers of the living dead. Those menacing fingers alone could pump hot blood through a traveler's veins and threaten to explode one's heart. But the most menacing of all the gnarly trees was the giant conspicuous blue spruce pine, with its long portentous branches looming like a living creature ready to swallow you whole if you passed under its arms when the winds began to howl and darkness crept in, which sent the spooked visitors turning on their heels and screaming madly back through the iron gates.

On stormy days the gnarly pine tree was even more frightening, as a flock of ugly black crows could be seen huddling along the low-lying branches like vultures waiting for the dead to appear. But in all actuality the crows were as innocent as a sparrow and were only preparing to stay dry from the onslaught of heavy rains, and could care less who suspiciously walked

18

beneath them.

Most everyone who felt an urgency to visit the dearly departed, even in daylight, most often were seen in the company of others; safety in numbers was their thinking. But then there were the undaunted. The brave humans, the ones who were not intimidated by the unknown and strolled along the grounds of the graveyard as though they were walking through a city park on a fine Sunday afternoon.

One of those undaunted humans was the town's gravedigger, and he—if you happened to chance a visit—could occasionally be seen wandering about the graves like it was his very own backyard. On this day the chubby balding man sat on a backhoe excavating a six-foot deep grave, in which a newly deceased would be buried next to four other graves, the graves of four family members who had long ago died and been laid to rest in holes the chubby man himself may have dug. He had dug too many graves to remember which ones were his unless he cared to glance at the departed date, which he had no interest in doing. To him the dead were only old bones in a casket. If the subject of reincarnation was ever brought up in conversation he would snarl and grunt about the dead person's bones in a casket six-feet under the ground, and that's where they'll be forever, unless some crazy fool decided to dig them up.

Grave digging wasn't a demanding job, only requiring a few hours to dig a hole one day and another hour's work the next day to fill it in. Any fool could have accomplished the task, but for the last thirty years the chubby man had been the only gravedigger. When his time came to kiss the only world he had known goodbye, who would have the honors? Or would he know in advance when his death would come and dig his own grave? For now, however, this was not on his mind, only the job at hand,

and he wanted to finish digging the hole before the heavy rains fell, cover the grave with a tarp, and then the next day plop the poor soul's decaying carcass into it.

As he glanced up from where he was digging, David Graham could see two men slowly ambling down the dirt road toward him. Clayton Daniels, the taller of the two, was carrying a blue tarp in one hand and nothing in the other. The other person, walking next to him with his hands hiked in his pockets, was average in height and thinly built, with a blond mop of long scraggly hair. This man was twenty-one years old, but his youthful facial features made him look much younger. Before David had hired the guy the previous day he'd almost thrown him out of his office, thinking he was about fifteen years old, too young to be working at the cemetery.

"Nice hole, David. Who's the unlucky stiff being buried in it? I suppose it's some old bastard who finally met the Grim Reaper," Clayton joked. He always had some wisecrack to say when he arrived at work. It was his way of setting a somewhat relaxing mood for the day he knew could be stressful working under David Graham, a hard working boss. Some of his wisecracks were funny, but most of them were corny. David thought they were all corny and unoriginal, having heard them more often than once, and wondered if Clayton got his jokes from the *Readers Digest*.

Today, however, wasn't the best of days for Clayton to be cracking jokes, as his boss was in a grumpy mood, mainly because of the dark clouds overhead. David Graham hated rainy days even though he was considered an outdoorsman, working outdoors for the town for over forty years; thirty years digging graves, and running the town's maintenance garage. Whenever the day was gray his mood was equally gray. He didn't mind rain, knowing it was extremely important, he just didn't like working in it, having to put on raingear that felt uncomfortable. Therefore, today he decided to forgo the raingear and, if need be, work in wet clothes.

"Jeepers crow, is that all you have to say? Your day's coming, wise guy, maybe sooner than you think. So don't go making wise cracks about the dead."

"Sorry, Dave. So who's the guy being buried?"

"Not a guy. It's the Webster girl being buried next to her grandparents and a couple of other relatives."

"The girl that was murdered? Damn, that sucks…she was so young, and real hot looking. Damn, what a horrible way to die."

"How did she die?" the new guy asked, staring down at the empty hole, picturing a casket inside the hole with a couple of flowers placed on top.

"She was stabbed to death. It happened last weekend. I heard when they found her the knife was still sticking out of one of her breasts, right around the old nipple area. They say she was stabbed at least a hundred times," Clayton answered with a stabbing motion.

"Don't believe a word he's saying. Clay exaggerates everything," David interrupted. "She may have been stabbed to death, but they never found a knife."

"Well, maybe they didn't find the knife sticking in her breast, but she was definitely stabbed over a hundred times. That was for sure."

Still believing Clayton was over dramatizing how Callie Webster was murdered, David added, "I don't know about that either. There wasn't much left of her to examine after those coyotes feasted on her, so why are you so sure she was stabbed over a hundred times? Unless you know more about it than you should."

21

***

"Well, that's what I heard anyway. I can't remember who told me, but that's what I heard," Clayton bitterly answered. He was feeling somewhat defeated. He didn't like being called a liar, and that's what it seemed David was implying.

***

"Okay, enough of that shit — let's get to work. We need to get this hole covered before it starts raining. Clay, you were supposed to bring the cement blocks with you. I left you a note by the time clock back at the garage. We need something to hold the tarp down. Jeepers crow Clay, how long have you been working here, anyhow?" David harrumphed.

"Sorry, I forgot."

"Well, you'd better go get them, the rain's coming soon and I don't want this hole to be filled with muddy water. How about you? Why don't you do something and go get the blocks?" David demanded of the other worker, whose name he could not remember.

"I don't know where they are — today is my first day on the job."

"Don't you think I know that? I'm the one who hired you. So what is your name anyway? And don't tell me its Clay; one Clay's enough."

"It's Malcolm Dangil."

"Dangil! What kind of name is that?"

"I don't know; English, I suppose."

"Well, whatever. See that barn next to the duck pond, Dangil?" David asked, pointing up the hill. "The cement blocks are stacked out back of the barn."

Malcolm looked toward where his boss was pointing, wondering where the barn was. All he could see were trees and

22

gravestones, nothing beyond the hill. "I don't see the barn."

"Well, you can't see it from here, it's on the other side of the hill. But you must have seen it when you came in. The tarp Clay's holding was inside."

"I must have missed it. The only thing I saw was the garage. Is it up near there?"

"That's the barn. We call it the barn. So when I say go get something out of the barn, that's where you go get it. Okay?"

***

"I forgot what you told me; how many blocks did you say we needed?" Malcolm asked, feeling slightly embarrassed he had to ask. It wasn't a good start to his first day on the job.

"I don't know," David said, thinking, looking at the hole. "You better bring at least a dozen—it's supposed to rain hard. I don't want the wind to blow the tarp away."

"A dozen. What do I use to carry them in?"

"Use the truck. Jeepers crow, you do know how to drive, don't you, Dangil?"

"Of course." Malcolm answered with a smile, happy to be asked to drive. Even though his license had expired and he hadn't driven much, never having owned a vehicle, he raced up the hill and disappeared out of sight.

***

David shook his head at Clayton, feeling frustrated with his new hire. "Where the hell did you dig this guy up from? He's more dimwitted than you are, and that's saying a lot."

"You're the one who hired him, I just met the guy this morning. He seems bright enough to me—he found the time clock all right. I think he just needs a few days to get familiar with the work routine."

"Well, I hope you're right, Clay. We sure need the help this time of year, especially with some of the older guys getting ready to retire. Come on, let's get this tarp over the hole, it's already starting to rain," David said, feeling a few raindrops fall on his bare arms. He then looked up at the sky and noticed dark clouds were overtaking the overcast sky. It didn't look good, and he wondered if the weather forecasters would be right for once, calling for two days of heavy rain. If they were, it was going to be a long weekend for the town's maintenance workers, which he was in charge of.

After covering the hole with the tarp, the two men stood looking at each other, waiting for Malcolm Dangil to bring the cement blocks. He had been gone for a good twenty minutes, and Clayton could see David was getting anxious. His breathing seemed heavy, taking deep breaths to calm his temper. To make it worse, the rain was beginning to fall harder.

"Maybe we should go stand under that tree," Clayton said, glancing over at the gnarly pine. He noticed the large black crows were already starting to gather on the branches, but the sight of them wasn't going to stop him from staying dry.

"Forget that, you won't melt. Besides, I see you finally had enough sense to wear a hat. I noticed even the new guy wears one, and he doesn't seem to be too bright. You know, Clay, some friendly advice — you should always wear your hat. You're never too young to get melanoma."

***

Clayton looked older than his thirty-nine years, the last ten working outdoors under the sun without wearing a hat. The years under the hot sun had bleached his natural blond hair to an almost non-color. Today, under the cap he wore, his thinning hair was cut short. He liked the bristle feel when he rubbed his hand over the top.

Clayton grabbed the tip of his cap and pulled it off his head. After glancing at the Cabela's name embroidered into the front of the camouflaged cap, he then placed it back on his head. "Got this free at the Cabela's store over in Benton last weekend for buying a new fishing pole. I plan to do some fishing this year."

"Well, that's great news, Clay. Now go up there and find out what's keeping him. Jeepers crow, I can't stand around here forever," David snapped.

Before Clayton had the chance to start up the hill he noticed the old green work truck slowly cresting the hill, heading in their direction. The sounds from the old truck rattling down the path sent a couple of crows scattering, only to fly back to their perches a few minutes later. This was their turf, where they hung out in inclement weather and in the dark of night. A body being buried close by didn't bother them much; they were use to it.

CHAPTER 3

The precipitation fell lightly during the Friday morning rush hour with an unconvincing warning of what was to come. By mid-morning the sky broke wide open. The light drizzle quickly turned into a downpour accompanied by a loud clap of thunder, scattering pedestrians to take cover. Windshield blades went from intermittent to the fastest speed. Puddles on the roadside quickly formed into deep pools, causing traffic to stall.

Having the pleasure of not being scheduled to work until nine o'clock on Friday morning, Kelsey Mickelson avoided having to travel during the morning rush hour. Unfortunately, she arrived during one of the downpours, and awkwardly ran from her vehicle to the bank entrance with only her handbag held over her head in an ill attempt to cover her hair. She wanted to look professional in both the outfit she chose to wear and her overall outward appearance, which meant perfect hair and perfect attitude—a disposition greatly affected by the weather. But since she had no umbrella or raincoat for protection against the rain, her meager handbag had to suffice.

Once Kelsey stepped inside the bank her first stop was the employees' lady's room to freshen up in front of the mirror. She sighed at the sight of her disheveled hair, and stubbornly ran a comb over the areas that stuck out the most. Her blonde hair was thick with curls at the ends, but today, because of the wet, humid weather, her hair was frizzy, making the chore difficult using a comb. She wished she had thought to bring a hairbrush. She made a mental note to toss one in her handbag when she got home that night. While looking in the mirror Kelsey also noticed raindrop spots on her dark-colored blouse and attempted to brush the wet spots away, to no avail, so she decided to let them dry on their own. It was the best she could do.

After a last glance in the mirror, feeling somewhat satisfied, she exited the lady's room and took her place behind the counter in the window next to her co-worker, Pamela Hays. Kelsey could tell by the smile on Pamela's face that there was still something wrong with her hair.

"What? Why are you looking at me like that?" Kelsey asked, knowing full well what she was looking at.

"You need to buy an umbrella. Want to borrow my hairbrush?"

"I can't afford to buy an umbrella; and besides, even if I did I'd probably never use it anyhow. It can't look that bad, does it?" Kelsey asked as she lightly touched her hair.

"No, you look fine. Just smile a little more, show off your pearly whites, and nobody will notice," Pamela said flashing her bleached-white teeth.

Pamela was the same age as Kelsey, and the two had been close friends since the day they met, having now passed the fourth year of their friendship. When a teller position opened at the bank, Pamela talked Kelsey into applying, which she immediately did knowing she needed to find a job that paid a descent wage to pay her share of the rent. Not the meager employment she had held at Stinson's variety store since her junior year, a job with no possible advancement.

Even though a teller position at a bank was considered low level in the financial world, Kelsey figured the job did have its rewards — basically, more money. Besides the extra money in her paycheck, she would also be working with her best friend. That alone, working with Pamela, would make the job more enjoyable, as common interests always helped with passing the time at work. This morning, with the heavy rains keeping most customers away, Kelsey and Pamela had plenty of time to chat.

While setting up her workstation for business, which included counting the money in her drawer and gathering needed supplies, among other insignificant tasks, Kelsey and Pamela idly chatted amongst themselves. Their conversation was mostly about the lousy weather and wondering how long the rain would last.

"I hope it doesn't rain all weekend," Kelsey disappointedly said as she looked out the front window, seeing black umbrella's passing by and the miserable raindrops splashing against the window. "I just dread the thought of having to stay indoors all weekend, especially after being stuck in here all week when the sun was shining. It just doesn't seem fair; it seems to rain every weekend. Winter was bad enough, and now it looks like we're not going to have much of a spring."

"Oh, Kelsey, stop complaining. Besides, when did you ever let the lousy weather interfere with your weekend?" Pamela teased.

"Yeah, that's true," she said with a laugh. "What was the latest weather report you heard? Did they say it was going to rain all weekend?"

28

"No, the weatherman on the morning news said it was going to rain hard today and possibly tomorrow morning. Sunday, he said, was going to be partly cloudy. Whatever that means. You know how accurate the weathermen are."

"I hope they're right this time. That doesn't sound too bad, and at least we'll get one good day off. Besides, we have to work tomorrow morning anyway," Kelsey added, hoping that was true and that Sunday would be a decent day. She smiled, thinking about sitting out on her porch on Sunday morning, taking in the ocean breeze and looking out over the harbor. She liked her rented house. She liked the smell and feel of the ocean breeze, cool and refreshing all summer long when muggy weather invaded the inland areas. She wanted to live the rest of her life out there. Maybe not in the same rented house, but one she could someday afford to buy for herself.

While thinking about the house on the beach that she would someday own, it suddenly reminded Kelsey of the radio program she'd listened to the previous night, remembering the horrible man saying he lived in the area near the ocean.

Did he mention living near Redmond, near the ocean? Or had she misunderstood him and only thought he had said he lived near the ocean? She definitely remembered hearing him mention Redmond. There was no denying that.

As Pamela went on about not caring about the weather one way or the other because she wouldn't let a little rain ruin her weekend, Kelsey kept thinking about Mister Zero. Thinking about what he might do to her if she happened to be unlucky enough to run across his path of terror. His graphic account of how he disposed of the demon was sickening — cutting the victim into pieces.

Kelsey looked at her nameplate, seeing her name bold against

29

the gold-colored plate. She was proud to see her name in bold letters, and wondered if the murdered girl, the girl Mister Zero mutilated, had a job. And if the girl did have a job, did she have a nameplate similar to hers? Or was the girl's name only visible to the public via the newspaper, printed in small black lettering, not large and bold against gold? She thought not, thinking the girl was too young to enjoy the spoils of having an important job with a nameplate, and turned her nameplate around to face the customers.

"Did you listen to Doctor Nancy last night on the radio? It was just awful. I couldn't sleep a wink after I turned the radio off. The man who called into the program scared me to death," Kelsey said, thinking everyone in town must have felt the same way. Surely Mister Zero had to be the talk of the town, mentioning he was living near Redmond.

"No, I don't usually listen to the radio except during the daytime or when I'm driving in my car. I don't even know who Doctor Nancy is. I'm a country loving music girl. What channel is she on?"

"I'm not sure, but I do know it's an AM station, 960 or 980, or something like that. I know it's somewhere in the 900's. I listen to her radio program almost every night. It helps me fall asleep. But last night there was this weird guy on her program who scared the shit out of me," she said sounding serious, and then added, "And he said he lived near here."

Pamela stopped what she was doing, which was basically wasting time till a customer came in, and listened to Kelsey's story with intent. At times during Kelsey's brief overview of last night's program, Pamela's expression looked horrified, especially when Kelsey described how Mister Zero gruesomely murdered his victim, stabbing the victim hard over and over again. The victim was a teenage girl with her whole life in front of her, a presumingly wonderful life with a loving husband, children, a nice big house, and a job with a nameplate.

But when Kelsey finished her recount of Mister Zero, Pamela could only force a smile. She then stared at her friend with a blank expression, seemingly waiting for the punch line that never came.

"I was scared to say the least." Kelsey went on to explain her apprehension. "Samantha's gone for the weekend, out of town visiting her parents, and it's pretty dark out there on the point with no streetlights. Our closest neighbor is down the road. I don't even know them. I've only seen them a couple of times, some old man and his wife. If something happens I don't know if I'd want to go down there and knock on their door late at night. For all I know he has a gun and would shoot me."

"I don't know. It sounds phony to me, Kelsey. I wouldn't worry about it at all. Do you think the program was fabricated to get people to listen?" Pamela skeptically asked.

"No, not at all. I've been listening to the program regularly for over a week, and it's mainly people calling in complaining about other people or addictions they have. You know, drinking or drugs or gambling problems. But last night was weird. I have never heard anyone on the program like that. He was real scary. His voice I'll never forget—it was very low sounding and deep, like what a big, ugly, bald guy would sound like."

"Well, if it was real I wouldn't want to meet the guy you're describing. Personally, if I was going to get raped I'd want the guy to at least be good looking."

"I'm not kidding, Pam, and he didn't say he raped them. He said he stabbed them and cut them up in pieces. And he also said he was from around here."

"Yes, you mentioned that. But did you mean he said he lived

in Redmond?"

"He didn't actually say he was living in Redmond, but he did say he was living on the coast near the town of Redmond. So he might as well have said he lived in Redmond."

"Hey, you're not changing your mind about going out tonight to the Crow's Nest just because of the weather, are you?" Pamela asked, changing the subject to something less disturbing. "Don't forget, there's a live band playing there tonight."

After briefly entertaining the idea of not going out because of the weather, and also because she had to work in the morning, Kelsey said no, she was still planning on going. Besides, today was payday, she told herself—how could she say no to a fun night of entertainment? Plus, she didn't want to be home alone with her roommate gone for the weekend. She also didn't want to go to bed listening to the Doctor Nancy program if it was going to be another weirdo calling in.

"I need to get out of the house and have some fun. It's been a long week, I can't see myself sitting home alone and listening to it rain all night," Kelsey said, still thinking about the evil man she'd heard on the radio.

A few seconds later, hearing the door open to the outside weather, she looked toward the entrance and noticed a heavyset man quickly entering the bank. The man slouched in like he was ducking from trouble, and to Kelsey he looked like trouble. He had a gloomy appearance, like bad news was coming in through the door. Her feelings about the man changed a bit when she noticed rain dripping down from his balding head, and attributed her initial assessment to the foul weather.

Kelsey watched as the man walked over to the kiosk counter and filled out a deposit slip. Before taking the slip to the counter, a normal procedure one would be expected to do, he hesitated a moment, glancing around the bank, then set his eyes upon Kelsey, direct eye-to-eye contact.

Not wanting to be rude and look away, Kelsey gave the man a friendly smile. She then lowered her head, making like she was busy, hoping he would go to Pamela's window. Her hopes, however, were quickly dashed when he stepped up to her window, pushing the deposit slip and an employment check toward her with stubby, dirty fingers.

His eyes were dark as tar, scary looking, and beads of rainwater were still dripping off his balding head. Seeing him up close and personal, she thought the man could be Mister Zero.

CHAPTER 4

With the rain pouring down harder than it had all morning, David Graham carefully steered the backhoe up the now slick, muddy road. Up ahead he could see the cemetery's work truck struggling to make the hill. The problem, he quickly surmised, was with the rear tires spinning helplessly in the mud, spraying mud all over the place and making the dirt road worse than it already was. Knowing the newly hired employee had driven the truck down the hill David figured he was the person doing the driving now. But it wasn't Malcolm Dangil spinning the tires, it was Clayton Daniels.

"It's four-wheel drive, you idiot!" David yelled out loud, aiming his frustrations at Dangil. He was starting to get agitated and feeling uncomfortable, having been drenched by a quick downpour.

"Jeepers crow, twenty minutes! That's all I asked for. Twenty minutes!" he continued to yell. If the rain had held off for twenty minutes longer he wouldn't have been drenched and in a miserable mood, but the rain gods were not with him today.

Nothing was going according to the schedule he had planned to accomplish for the day. To get the most out of a day's work was all about planning ahead, something he prided himself on doing. Today, besides the grave he had to dig for the next day's funeral, he'd planned on having the new guy use the weed trimmer around the gravestones and Clayton riding around on the lawn mower. He didn't, however, blame it on anyone but himself for not taking the weather into account and not hiring good help.

He shook his head at hiring Dangil, thinking he should have known the guy was a dimwit just the way he walked into his office the other day applying for the job. The interview for the job was scheduled for four o'clock in the small office wedged in the corner of the town's maintenance garage, down the road a mile from the cemetery. When Dangil strolled in, standing slightly cockeyed with his hands stuffed tight in his front pants pockets, David glanced at his watch, which showed fifteen minutes past the hour. Not a good way to start a job interview.

Dangil wore a pair of baggy jeans and a dark colored jacket, compliments of the Salvation Army thrift store. David was not impressed to say the least, and if there were any other candidates worth hiring he would have ended the interview immediately, but Dangil was the only one to apply.

***

The reason for his tardiness and awkward entrance was that Dangil had no self-confidence. He wasn't well versed in interviews, having never applied for a job before. This was the first time for him, and he almost changed his mind about the job thinking it was a waste of time, knowing he probably wouldn't get hired anyway. The lack of money forced him to make the hike to the town garage and knock on the office door.

Earlier in the day, Dangil had filled out the application at the town office, which was located on Main Street near the Redmond Street Bridge. Feeling uneasy about answering some of the questions, he left a lot of them blank — the most important ones, like his employment history and his last residence. After handing the partially filled-out application back to the town clerk, the nice elderly lady told to him to wait a moment. The clerk then placed a call, punching one of the speed-dial numbers.

Dangil sat back down on the same chair he'd used previously when filling out the application, and looked around the one-room town office, bored. Besides the town clerk's desk, the only other furniture in the office was the four chairs lining the wall near the entrance, one being occupied by Dangil. The door directly behind the clerk, Dangil figured, must be the employee bathroom. Another door, off to the side in the back, was marked an exit only door. The office did offer a great view of the bridge and the waterfalls off in the distance.

A few minutes later the clerk told Dangil she'd scheduled him an interview with the town's maintenance manager for four o'clock at the town maintenance building. Unfamiliar with the area, Malcolm asked where the building was located. The clerk politely gave him directions, telling him the building was actually a large garage and located a mile beyond the town cemetery, up on Route 4, a good two miles from where he now stood. With a blank look Malcolm tried to picture the area — all uphill was what he pictured. This didn't bother him much, not as much as the interview itself. He looked at the clock in the town office and noticed he had five hours to kill before the interview; plenty of time to get ready, and also plenty of time if he was inclined to change his mind.

After thinking about his pitiful savings account he knew he had to give it his best effort, which was lackadaisical at best since he had no faith in himself. He figured no one would want to hire a guy with no work experience.

A half-hour before his scheduled interview Dangil hiked up to Route 4, passing the old church and the town's cemetery where he hoped to be working, arriving fifteen minutes late. He would have arrived earlier, maybe even on time, if he hadn't stopped to gaze out over the gravestones and the sloping landscape. He was feeling excited with the possibility he may be working there, and gazed a little longer than he'd expected to.

When he finally arrived, he walked into a silent building and looked around for an office or someone to point it out. The place seemed abandoned; all he could hear were creaking sounds like mice running around scurrying for cheese. In the far corner he spied a partially open door. After a polite, low sounding rap, he creaked open the door without hearing a response to his knock. Inside he saw his future boss staring angrily at him.

The man's expression said everything. If Dangil wanted to make a good first impression it was too late. He'd screwed up.

"It's mostly manual labor, you know, landscaping and occasionally helping with the graves. Your application is pretty vague on your work history. In fact, you failed to add it to your application. Have you ever done this type of work before, cemetery work?" David asked him after the customary brief introductions.

Not wanting to screw up any more than he already had, sounding stupid by bumbling his words, Dangil answered all the questions politely in short sentences.

"I've mowed lawns."

David stared at the interviewee seated in front of him, waiting to hear his other qualifications. A moment later, after taking a couple of sips of cola, he finally figured that was Dangil's complete answer.

"Well, that's a start. How about a driver's license? You have one, don't you?"

"Yes, I do," he answered, and pulled his license out of his wallet for proof, hoping David wouldn't noticed the license was not valid, as Malcolm had not renewed it do to his incarceration. He had planned on doing it but lacked the money, and didn't see any sense in it anyhow since he didn't own a vehicle. If he got the job and was required to have a valid driver's license, renewing it would be his first priority.

David handed his license back to him and only nodded. Basically that was the end of the interview. After a quick handshake Dangil walked back home, wondering what it would be like finally having a job with a decent income.

Now, two hours into his first day at work—more listening and watching than actually working—Dangil started to feel comfortable. When he'd first arrived he felt nervous, as anyone would on his or her first day. The only job he was asked to do was load the cement blocks on the truck and help Clayton secure the traps over the open grave and dirt pile. Then the rain ended his first day early.

David advised his two workers they'd be knocking off early due to the inclement weather. He also advised them they'd most likely be requested to come in the next day, Saturday morning, to help the city maintenance crew with storm drains and other cleanup duties, work that was not mentioned in the interview but was expected.

***

Hearing they would be getting off work early, Clayton was eager to go and sped up the hill in two-wheel drive, thinking if he got enough speed he'd easily make the hill. He was wrong.

Unfortunately for him, the truck's worn tires were too slick for the slippery mud. Still, being stubborn, he hit the gas pedal one more time. The truck spun its tires without gaining traction, then abruptly stopped.

***

A moment later, just as David was about to blow a gasket, the truck crested the hill and disappeared. At that, David suddenly remembered Clayton was driving and cooled his temper. He liked Clayton, having worked with him for ten years. Most likely, he figured, to Clayton's credit, Clayton was demonstrating to the new guy how four-wheel drive worked.

***

"The truck has four-wheel drive. The shift is right there," Malcolm Dangil blurted out in a condescending voice, as though anyone but an idiot would know the truck had four-wheel drive. However, he hadn't meant it to sound demeaning; they were the first words out of his mouth in a while. He had been quiet since they finished securing the trap over the grave David had dug for the Webster girl, and having to get more cement blocks to hold a second tarp placed over the dirt pile for refilling the grave.

While sitting in the truck waiting for Clayton, Dangil had been thinking about the money problems he was having and how much more was left in his savings account. The spinning tires brought him out of his trance just long enough to remind Clayton the truck had four-wheel drive, not that Clayton hadn't known. Malcolm was just trying to be helpful, but Clayton could care less.

Clayton gave him a detesting stare, then angrily told him he knew the truck had four-wheel drive but wanted to try making the hill without the use of all four tires, which was the truth. Malcolm figured it was a macho thing to impress him, and let the comment slide. He didn't want to make any enemies, especially with his only co-worker besides the boss man.

After parking the truck in the barn, Clayton asked Malcolm if he wanted to meet him at a bar later that night. He told him on Friday nights the Crow's Nest Tavern was packed, with plenty of young women to pick up. Malcolm was interested, having heard of the place when he first arrived in town the prior month, and wanted to check it out sometime. Now just didn't seem like the right time, especially with his limited funds. He politely refused Clayton's offer, saying "thanks," but he need a good night sleep with work in the morning. He also said he didn't want to make a bad impression with a poor performance. He wanted to arrive at work fully rested.

***

Clayton wasn't buying the lame excuse, thinking Malcolm may still be a little upset at him for his angry outburst about the truck. Or maybe the reason was that he didn't want to associate with him outside of work, since there was almost a generation separating the two. Clayton was nearing forty and Malcolm was in his early twenties, having turned twenty-one the day of his release from his incarceration.

"Sleep! You don't have to stay all night, just go out for a couple of beers. I'm not staying late myself, because I'm sure we'll be working tomorrow. David will let us know back at the garage before we leave today, but I'm sure we will."

***

Malcolm thought for a moment before changing his mind. In reality, he wasn't sure he had any extra money to spend. He was planning on stopping by the bank on his way home to find out how much money he had left in his bank account. Maybe withdraw a few dollars and stop at the grocery store to purchase

40

a few groceries. Or maybe not, since he still had food left over in the refrigerator, from his last trip to the community food pantry, that would spoil soon if left uneaten.

"Maybe I'll show up. I'll have to check my finances first."

"Yeah, I know what you mean. When I was your age I use to think that someday I'd have plenty of money and own a lot of land. That never happened, the land thing, but I'm having fun enjoying my life. You see, it's not all work and no play. You still have to think of yourself first. So take it from experience and let me give you some advice. You might as well go out and enjoy your life, because the only land you're going to own is the ground above your head when someone like us fills your grave in. So I'll see you there, right?"

"Yes, maybe I will go. But if I don't show up don't hold it against me."

"Great. See you there, buddy," Clayton said with a nod, and ran out into the rain toward his vehicle, something Malcolm lacked in his impecunious life. If this job worked out, the first thing he was going to buy was a vehicle of his own.

Malcolm watched the truck disappear, thinking it would have been a nice gesture if Clayton offered him a lift back to the garage, having given him a ride from the town garage to the cemetery. But he didn't. Malcolm shook his head, deciding right then and there he was not going to the Crow's Nest Tavern. He then waited for his boss to park the backhoe and give him a lift back to the garage. On the ride back he was informed by David he'd have to work in the morning, and to be at the garage no later than seven.

CHAPTER 5

After a brief mid-morning rush at the bank business slowed considerably, making the time go by tediously slow for the two tellers. The heavyset man — the customer with the gloomy look who'd caused Kelsey to gasp with disconcertment, thinking he may be the mysterious Mister Zero — had come and gone. The customer had been the last person Kelsey waited on, and that was almost an hour ago. Pamela waited on only two during that slow time, two in and quickly out the door customers depositing checks.

Now they were bored.

As the morning wore on, Kelsey began tinkering with non-essential tasks to pass the time. Numerous times she glanced at the large clock anchored to the wall directly in front of her, watching the minutes tick by closer to lunchtime. Before long, which she would have said took forever if someone cared to ask, she noticed it was only a few minutes till noon. Her lunch break, she knew, was just what she needed to stave off the monotonous day even though she wasn't hungry, especially since she only had a plain tuna sandwich on inexpensive white bread to look forward to. Tuna was not her favorite, but it was cheaper than cold cuts and she was tired of egg salad, so tuna was what she'd made herself for lunch. The sandwich and the thirty-minute break, she knew, would put her in a more favorable mood heading into the weekend.

Just as Kelsey was about to lock her money drawer and take her lunch break, a rain-drenched man wearing only a light jacket and cap walked into the bank. He stood quietly near the entrance, hunched-over, wet, with his jacket collar pulled up around his neck. His face was angled down, hiding his facial features. His conspicuous hesitation could have indicated he was unfamiliar with the bank, or he could have entered to come in from the rain. Or something else most bank employees held worriedly in the back of their mind.

If not for the fact that he removed his cap and shook the rain off, exposing himself to all the cameras aimed at his every move, a bank employee might think he was about to rob the place. That's exactly what Kelsey thought the moment she set her eyes on him, the same thoughts as when the heavyset man entered the bank earlier. With the lack of a police department, Kelsey figured it was only a matter of time before someone tried robbing the bank. During her first day at the bank, Kelsey had asked Pamela if their bank had ever been robbed. Pamela said no, but then added that if it ever did happen, just hand the money over and flash the robber a smile — the money was insured.

Pamela quickly set Kelsey's mind at ease about the customer. "I know that guy. He came in the bank last week on your day off. I've also seen him a couple of other times before. To me he seems kind of strange, but an interesting kind of strange at the same time, if you know what I mean."

Kelsey said nothing, and only watched as the man made his way toward the kiosk counter in the center of the room. It was a counter for customers to fill out bank slips — deposit and withdrawal slips.

**

"I wonder what he would be like to go out with," Pamela continued, thinking about spending a night in bed with the mysterious man. Seeing his thin but tight body, Pamela imagined he could go all night long — satisfy her fantasy with someone other than her current boyfriend, Matt Burger.

**

"No, I don't think I've ever seen him before," Kelsey said, trying to remember if she had.

"Hey girl, look at the time; it's time for your lunch break. Get going. I'll take care of the customer," Pamela said with a wink.

Kelsey hesitated, and watched the man as he stood over the kiosk counter, noticing he grabbed a yellow slip, which meant he was making a withdrawal. "Pam, can you take your lunch first? I'd like to wait on him."

**

Pamela smiled, thinking it was probably the first time Kelsey had paid any attention to a costumer other then the sweet little kids cuddled in their mothers' arms. Not the ones running around the bank causing disruption, of course. Those bratty kids no one could tolerate, except most probably their mothers.

"Have at him, see you in thirty. Oh, by the way…if I didn't have Burger draping all over me every night, I'd have said 'no way sweetie, he's all mine.'"

**

Seeing how Kelsey's window was the only one available, the man walked up to her, his soaked cap in one hand and the withdrawal slip in the other. His expression was stoic, as though he were staring into emptiness, too many things on his mind to see reality; mostly money, or the lack of it, and going home to his shabby apartment with nothing to do but listen to the miserable rain.

***

"Good morning; or is it afternoon? I never know what to say when it's exactly noon," Kelsey said with a weak laugh, and then paused, expecting a response, but none came.

The man said nothing and slapped the bank withdrawal slip on the counter. He then placed his wet cap back on his head and stood staring down at the slip, not wanting to look directly at Kelsey.

"Well, by the looks of your jacket and hat, it looks like we're having nasty weather," Kelsey added, trying to make light of the man's soaked clothing, hoping to get some kind of response from him other than banking business.

***

"Yeah, it's raining heavy out there," he said, turning his attention toward the entrance, thinking about how miserable it was walking the two miles from the town garage, and having to walk another mile back to his apartment when he finished his banking business.

"It does look miserable out there." Kelsey responded.

"I didn't finish filling this slip out, and only wrote my name down because I first wanted to find out how much money I had left in my bank account. I'm not too good at keeping records," he said, now looking directly at Kelsey.

His voice was low and gruff sounding. It was a voice that should have been coming from a much older man—one surrounded with a life of hard times, no affection of love from

45

family, and two packs a day since high school. His voice gave Kelsey a nervous chill, as it was very similar to the voice she'd heard over the radio the previous night on the Doctor Nancy program—the voice of Mister Zero. It was a voice Kelsey thought should have been coming from the heavyset man who'd come into the bank that very morning to make a deposit. But that man's voice wasn't even close to the guy on the radio.

Kelsey thought no more about the comparison to the voice on the radio, thinking he was hoarse from the miserable weather. Maybe he had a cold coming on, nothing for her to fret about.

Kelsey took the slip and looked at the man's name, Malcolm Dangil, noting the first name would be easy to remember, if she desired to. Kelsey's favorite teacher, a compassionate man who taught history and counted his days till retirement, was a Malcolm—Malcolm Kilpatrick. Kelsey, and most of her other classmates who liked the teacher, called him Mister Malcolm.

She then punched this Malcolm's name into the computer and pulled up his account. Not meaning any harm, she giggled at the total amount of his savings. The paltry amount wasn't much to brag about, but it was comparable to her savings, which was the cause of her playful response.

***

"I know it's pitiful," Malcolm Dangil said, responding to her humiliating reaction. He knew the amount was embarrassing. Someday, he thought, he'd have a bank account to brag about. Now he just needed to survive until payday.

"Oh, I wasn't laughing. It looks just like the amount I have in my savings account. Your balance is seventy-two dollars and fifty-two cents."

"Actually, that's more than I thought I had. How much can I withdraw from it?"

46

"Well, if you show me your I.D. you can withdraw as much as you want. You can actually withdraw it all and close out your account if you have a mind too, but I wouldn't recommend it. Better to have a little than nothing. Don't you think?"

Malcolm thought about it for a moment. He really didn't want to close the account anyway, because he needed one to cash his checks. Then again, seventy-two dollars wasn't much money these days, and he wasn't going to receive his first paycheck for another two weeks.

"Forty. I'll withdraw forty dollars," Malcolm said, and then handed her his expired driver's license. "I'll keep the rest for an emergency. Not that thirty-two dollars will do me any good."

"Don't forget the fifty-two cents." She smiled and quickly glanced at his driver's license, noting the name and photo matched.

"Oh yeah, fifty-two cents. What does that buy nowadays? Probably nothing."

"Well then, forty dollars it is," she said, pulling out two twenties from her money tray, and then handed him the two bills and receipt for the withdrawal, along with his driver's license. "By the way, what are you going to do with all this money?" Kelsey teasingly added, hoping their conversation would go on a little longer since there was no one standing in line waiting. So far she thought it was going well, better than the way it had started out.

With the limited amount of light coming in through the bank's two picture windows, the overhead lights did little to brighten the interior of the bank, but it was enough to bring a sparkle to Kelsey's eyes. To Malcolm, their color was a shade of green that resembled an emerald. He hadn't meant to stare at her eyes, but he couldn't help it, they were enchanting.

"I'm not sure," he said, taking his eyes away as he tucked his wallet in his front pocket. It was a safer place to keep it than in his back pocket, something he'd learned living on the streets of Portland. "I was thinking about maybe going out tonight for a few beers to celebrate my new job. I'm new to the area and haven't been out to enjoy the nightlife. Any suggestion on where I should go?"

Hoping for the opportunity to suggest the idea of meeting up with the man in front of her, Kelsey jumped on the question without hesitation.

"There aren't too many places to go for the young crowd in this town. Everyone I know goes to the Crow's Nest Tavern. The tavern's right down the street at the edge of downtown. You can't miss it—the old bowling alley is across the street. I'm actually going to be there tonight myself. Maybe we'll meet up. I'll be with my girlfriend; she's the one who works right there," she said, pointing to the window next to hers.

Malcolm said nothing and looked at the nameplate next to the vacant window. Seeing it, he then thought to look over at Kelsey's nameplate.

"Her name's Pam—she's at lunch in the back room. Probably spying on me," she laughed.

"Oh yeah, I think I saw her when I came in."

"You could have...she just left for lunch when you walked in."

"Well, thanks for the money. I hope to see you tonight, Kelsey," Malcolm shyly said, hoping she didn't mind him using her name.

"I'll definitely be there, around nine, Malcolm."

Malcolm Dangil walked out of the bank feeling much better than when he'd entered. The only thought crossing his mind was he hoped the rain would stop so he wouldn't look like a drowned rat when he arrived at the Crow's Nest Tavern, but unbeknownst to him, the rain had no plans of stopping any time soon.

CHAPTER 6

His living room was not unexpectedly dark; even in the light of day shadows were hardly noticed. The only natural light was the dim, gloomy light coming in through the one film-covered window the room offered. Unfortunately for Malcolm Dangil, however, the window was facing west away from magnificent ocean view the two other tenants on the eastside of the apartment house enjoyed. His view of the ocean could only be seen from the small window in the kitchen of his second floor apartment if he angled his head slightly, but not today. Today the windswept rain and ocean fog blocked any possible view.

Malcolm spent most of his time in his dingy apartment lying on an old, two-cushion couch that also converted into a bed. The couch was the only comfortable piece of furniture in the sparsely furnished living room. Besides the couch, there was only enough space for a non-functioning recliner with the upholstery on both armrests worn down to the wood frame, and a disgusting looking coffee table with noticeable coffee rings imbedded in the cheap wood. A closer examination of the coffee table revealed decayed food crumbs in the gouges made by tenants before him, plus the new ones created by Malcolm. There was also an empty three-shelved bookcase up against the wall.

The bookcase served him no purpose at all. The only thing it held was a good layer of dust on top. Malcolm was not into cleaning; in the two months he'd lived there the only cleaning he did was wash the dishes and brush the crumbs off the kitchen counter with the same cloth he used to wash his dishes. The closet-size bathroom had no air vents, so Malcolm kept the door closed to limit the musty smell from entering his living room. An air freshener was on his list of items to purchase the next time he was in the grocery store. The next time being when he received his first paycheck.

The reason the bookcase held no books was because Malcolm owned only one book, which was sitting face up smack in the middle of the coffee table. The book was titled *20th Century Ghost* written by Joe Hill, who just happened to be the son of Stephen King. He'd acquired the book from the Salvation Army thrift store, the same store where he'd acquired his jacket. Not knowing the author or who his famous father was, Malcolm picked it up because it was a hard cover and about ghosts. He liked ghost stories, and he believed in ghosts as well as other immortal creatures like vampires and demons. He also preferred short stories to novels because they were easier for him to stay focused on, attributed to his short attention span.

Besides the jacket he wore every day, Malcolm owned very little clothing, all donated by the Salvation Army thrift store in Portland, where he'd spent a good amount of his teenage years living on the streets. Someday, when he had to eventually move, he wouldn't need any help, or even a vehicle to move his stuff — one box for all his belongings would do it.

He also owned a jackknife. It was his prized possession. His knife was longer than normal jackknifes, and felt uncomfortable in his pants pocket, so he mostly left it at home, using it often to carve into the coffee table. The carvings were shaped symbols—nothing of significance, just things that came to mind as he carved. He only defaced the coffee table because he noticed others before him had vandalized the table with their initials. His carvings, he felt, improved the table.

Malcolm switched on the standing lamp next to the couch and sat in silence, wondering if he should stay home for the night or go out. He was debating on whether to save his remaining money for food and emergencies, instead of spending it at the tavern. He was hedging toward going out, spending time with the girl from the bank, but knew if that didn't work out, in the morning he would regret having spent the money—another disappointment in a life of choosing to take the wrong path. Just when life started to turn his way, an obstacle would always block his path. And why would this time be any different?

He reached in his pocket and eased out the thin, fake leather wallet he'd purchased for six dollars at the local Walmart store. Inside he found the folded bills, two twenties and a one. He tossed the bills down on the coffee table next to some loose change, wondering if what he was looking at would be enough to go out. If it wasn't, which was his first thought, he'd stay home and forget about the lovely girl he'd met at the bank—for now anyway.

He knew the forty dollars he'd withdrawn from his bank account and the one-dollar bill he had left over from his previous trip to the bank would be enough for his night's entertainment, but he doubted very much he'd have enough money if he wanted to impress the girl from the bank. To have any chance of winning her favor, he knew he'd have to pay for her drinks as well as his; every guy knew that.

There was also the other problem. How would he approach her, and what would they talk about? They had nothing in common except their age. Their worlds, he was sure, were completely different, with him growing up in foster homes and her most likely being raised by a loving family.

He was nervous just sitting there in his living room wondering what he would say to her, not wanting to be embarrassed by saying something foolish. It had been a long time since he last talked with a girl, and not knowing what subjects to talk about could be a turnoff. The wrong thing could cause her to lose interest in him, thinking he was just another jerk. Telling her his life story would also be a turnoff. There was nothing in his twenty-one years on Earth that would interest anyone, especially a beautiful young woman with a seemingly good job and growing up in a quiet, friendly town. A conversation with intentions of romance was what he wanted to talk about, but would she? If she did have the same intentions as he did, how would he start the conversation? Or would he just sit there and wait for her to bring it up?

Yet the whole idea of going out was doubtful. Most likely he wouldn't be going anywhere, and would end up spending another lonely night at home. It all hinged on the weather, and by the sounds he was hearing outside his window it didn't look good. The rain seemed to be coming down harder than it had all day.

While pondering his decision, Malcolm stared with discontent out the window, watching the miserable rain pounding heavily against the windowpane, and listened despondently to the howling wind and rainwater dripping from the gutters to the tin porch roof below. The weather alone should have been enough to make the decision of going out easier, but the thought of staying home bored to death weighed heavier.

Malcolm didn't own a television and had only a radio, which he listened to every night while reading or just thinking about a future he hoped would be much better than his life now. He didn't want to think about his life before, the one in which he ran away from his last foster home into the streets of hell. And mostly that other matter, the one that was a constant nightmare, the one that drew him to listen to the Doctor Nancy radio program every night, listening to other's disheartening phobias, trying to fit in a world that crucified the meek.

Feeling hungry, he boiled a pot of macaroni pasta. After putting the drained pasta back in the pot, he added a good amount of margarine and mixed in a pinch of salt and pepper, and a lot of ketchup. On the side he ate enough bread to make three sandwiches. The pasta and bread were compliments of the food pantry. He ate the meal sitting on his couch while rereading the only book he owned. Malcolm was not an avid reader by any means; he read out of boredom. It was something to pass the time being alone in a sad room.

By four o'clock, having read for a couple of hours with frequent breaks to reflect on what he had read and his dilemma on the evening ahead, he finally made up his mind to stay in for the night. Stay out of trouble and save his money. He'd listen to the radio and fall asleep till his alarm went off in the morning.

Outside he could hear the raging rainstorm getting worse, pounding winds against the windowpane. The noise was driving him insane. The only good thing about it was he was home, staying dry.

The rain caused him to reminisce about the days he'd spent on the city streets of Portland in such weather. The long cold nights hanging around lowlifes in rundown buildings, trying to stay awake all night with one eye open. He was young and naïve back then, and before long he was becoming one of them — a drug-starved lowlife. His life on the streets eventually landed him in one of the state's mental institutions. His confinement in the institution reminded him of the orphanage he'd grown up in and the foster homes that had given him no love, which was a world apart from the life of a normal childhood. The only difference between the childhood homes he grew up in and the institution was that there was no escaping the nuthouse.

Malcolm couldn't blame his incarceration on his misfortune of having to live on the streets, or even on one particular person, even though both of those were the main reasons for his wrongdoings. He blamed it on himself for lacking a strong willpower and sensibility.

His last night of freedom in the homeless world was the night he met Cherry, a young runaway like him. He was seventeen at the time, a year of homelessness behind him. Cherry was only fifteen. The night he met her the temperature was extremely cold, nearing zero degrees — almost certain death for the old and weak spending the night outdoors.

That very morning while sitting at a table in a soup kitchen, and before meeting Cherry, Malcolm had overheard a seasoned homeless man telling another about sleeping in a church. He heard the man bragging that he'd found a warm, quiet sanctuary lying on a pew bench. All he needed to be comfortable was his blanket, and the sack he used to carry his clothes for a pillow. How he found the particular church was by happenstance. Because of the cold weather he checked the door to see if the church was still open, and found the door was indeed unlocked. After waiting until later in the night, the man then slid in with his small bundle of clothing and curled up on the pew. He said he was gone before anyone became the wiser. He'd stayed there three nights in a row during the recent cold spell, and was planning on going back that night.

Later, when Malcolm met Cherry, he remembered what the man had said about the church. So, instead of trying to stay warm outdoors, he talked Cherry into going with him to the church.

It was a mistake. In hindsight he should have found shelter elsewhere.

Sometime during the night the man, who had been drinking heavily, attempted to sexually assault Cherry. Her loud screams awoke Malcolm, as well as three nuns who were living in the convent on the other side of the church.

The man turned violently crazy and attacked the nuns, killing one and badly injuring the other two. Malcolm had tried to intervene and help the nuns, but the courts saw it differently and charged him with accessory to the crime. He was so distraught and uncontrollable in court the judge had no choice but to incarcerate him to the state mental facility until his twenty-first birthday. The day of his release went uncelebrated. He wanted nothing from the state's welfare system, and only accepted help from the community services the town of Redmond provided for the down-and-out.

Malcolm knew it was time to stop reading his only book when he started losing his concentration thinking about the girl at the bank. He had read the same paragraph three times and still didn't understand what was written on the page, even though he had read the book before. He kept thinking about her, seeing her facial features in his mind. Her blonde hair and dazzling emerald-green eyes stood out. He said her name over and over again—sometimes out loud, sometimes in whispers, and constantly in his head. He wanted her badly—not like how he'd wanted Cherry. His feelings for Cherry were different. She was something his hormones were throbbing for. She wasn't even pretty—chubby, with the beginnings of acne. Kelsey was different not only in looks, but also in maturity. She was a woman, not a girl one year removed from giggling at boys in the middle school hallways.

Noticing the rain had somewhat subsided to a damp drizzle, Malcolm took the opportunity and began the two-mile walk across town to the Crow's Nest Tavern. It was nearing nine o'clock, and he felt if he was going to go out it was now or never. The change in the weather, he figured, was also a sign telling him his luck was about to change for the better. He knew for sure his luck couldn't get any worse than it already was. If he'd felt any sense of premonition he would have stayed home, but he lacked that forewarning power.

Locking his apartment door, Malcolm strolled out into the dark stormy night.

CHAPTER 7

The telephone he used was conveniently located two blocks from his apartment in the back corner of a rundown pool hall. The pool hall's phone also suited his need for privacy, with only a few patrons lazily playing pool and an unkempt fella nursing a beer at the bar. The only other person in the place was the proprietor, who was a hearing-impaired old man content with smoking his cheap cigars and reading paperback murder mysteries. The phone was free to use as long as the caller dialed a local number, which was on the honor system. Most kept to the policy — most of the regulars, that is.

Mister Zero, however, was not a regular, even though he had used the phone once before, the previous night. Tonight he dialed the same number, a radio station located outside the local exchange. He knew the proprietor wouldn't mind, thinking he was dialing locally. The bill from the phone company would not reflect the long distance call until the next month's statement, and he would be long gone by then.

Like he had the previous night, Mister Zero ordered a root

beer soda, tossing a dollar bill and four quarters on the bar; a generous tip, he assumed, in an attempt to show he was not the type of person to be unappreciative of the service.

***

The proprietor, Ralph, would have thought differently if he cared about tips, since that was the exact price for the drink, and nonchalantly picked up the bill and the four quarters. What Ralph was thinking about the strange looking character was his low, gruff sounding voice. The voice, he thought, should have been coming from the mouth of someone much older. But then again it was a miserable night outside—maybe the man had a cold coming on.

***

Without thanking the proprietor for the soda, Mister Zero walked around to the backside of the bar toward the phone. He took the phone over to a corner table away from prying ears, stretching the cord to its limit, and dialed the number he knew from memory, having dialed the number the previous night. He didn't have to wait long for his call to be answered, because Peter Willey, the program manager for the Doctor Nancy program, answered it immediately.

***

Willey, the lone person managing the incoming phone calls, promptly informed the caller he had dialed into the program. He then screened the call by asking who was calling and what the call was about. Willey wanted to make sure it wasn't a prank call, which happened more often than one would expect, or some ridiculous complaint like a woman's husband is possessed because he snores and talks in his sleep. Those types of calls would surely lose most of the listening audience.

The caller on the phone tonight with Willey only grunted at

the request for his name and reason for his call. His only words were his demand to talk with the host. Willey, recognizing the caller's voice, told him to hold. He then frantically waved his arms to grab Doctor Nancy's attention, and was greeted with an annoyed response.

***

Doctor Nancy disliked being interrupted when she was on the air. To her the interruption was unprofessional. Whatever the concern was, she always felt it could wait until a more opportune time. She used her hand in a waving motion to let Willey know she was being interrupted, and continued talking to her audience over the airwaves.

This did not stop Willey from opening the adjoining door to the soundproof room.

Seeing Willey's intrusion, Doctor Nancy removed her headphones, placing them down around her neck. Her unblinking eyes glared up at Willey.

"It's him, I'm sure, same haunting voice." Willey mouthed the words in a low whisper, not wanting his voice to be picked up over the air.

"What?" Doctor Nancy asked after clicking the mike off.

"It's him. No mistaking that guy's voice. I told him to hold, but I don't want him to hang up and take a chance of losing him," Willey answered in his normal sounding voice with a hint of excitement.

"What are you talking about?" she asked, sounding annoyed, wondering whom the hell he was talking about.

"The guy from last night. You know, the demon slayer. The guy who called himself Mister Zero."

"You're definitely sure it's him? It could be a prank call. We had two prank calls last night. It's just the nature of the program," she skeptically asked, hoping it wasn't him.

After last night's horror show she'd hoped she'd never hear from the wacko again. The man had haunted her night's sleep, and the dark, swollen rings under her eyes proved it.

"Yes, it's him. We'll go to commercial, then you can talk to him. See if he wants to go on the air," Willey anxiously told Doctor Nancy.

Doctor Nancy said nothing, thinking about the crazy man from the previous night's program. His raspy voice telling her in graphic detail how he mutilated young women he thought to be demons. The horrible images he'd described of unmercifully torturing them before snuffing out their young lives caused insomnia for anyone listening to the program, including Doctor Nancy, who seriously considered quitting, but was coaxed with increased monetary incentives by Peter Willey to continue.

Those incentives Doctor Nancy knew were only false promises, as they were out of Willey's control, but the compliments he threw at her were building her already inflated ego. However, in her line of work, talking to the most mentally disturbed people, how much could a woman living alone take? How many more psychopaths could she endure listening to? After last night's caller, she felt she was already on the fringe of losing her own sanity.

Now the horrible man was back, waiting on the other end of the line, somewhere outside in the dark night. Maybe he was somewhere nearby, or closer, she worriedly thought. Maybe he was outside the studio talking on a cell phone, sitting in his parked vehicle right next to her Mercedes, waiting for her to leave—alone. After all, she did have blonde hair and green eyes. The only criterion she lacked was her age, no longer being a teenager.

61

***

Willey's thoughts contradicted those of Doctor Nancy. Ratings, he was sure, would skyrocket. His status as a program manager would also rise, increasing his chances to land a more lucrative job in a big city market. Maybe even working for a major cable news broadcast.

***

"Go!" Willey nervously demanded, awaking Doctor Nancy from what was most likely a self-induced trance. "Go to commercial!"

Doctor Nancy despised Willey, thinking he was immature and arrogant, but she also liked the notoriety she was receiving, a reward much greater than the money she was being paid, which was considered small change in most media markets. To her it was all about self-satisfaction, so she painfully tolerated his arrogance.

Hearing Willey's urgency to go to commercial, Doctor Nancy shook her unprofessional trance off and steadied herself for the dreaded call. "Sorry for the interruption listeners, but we need to go to a commercial break. We will be back momentarily."

Doctor Nancy slowly removed her headphones from around her neck, placing them on the desk in front of her. If her manager was wrong, and this wasn't the same person from the night before, she'd pull his beaded eyes out of his snot-nosed head. On the other hand, if it was the same person, she didn't want to talk with the monster. She wanted her manager to do the right thing and hang up on the caller, tell him not to call back. Either way she didn't want to talk to the scariest person who had ever called into her program.

Dealing with a very disturbed caller, like the weirdo from the pervious night, was not worth any rewards. Last night's caller was a nightmare, and she didn't want to lose another night's sleep — it wasn't worth any amount of money or notoriety. If this was the same caller, she contemplated grabbing her briefcase and going home, drinking heavily, and waking up with a head-pounding hangover. That would be better than listening to the weirdo calling himself Mister Zero.

She looked over toward Willey, who was now sitting in the chair reserved for a visiting guest, right next to her, no more than two feet away.

"You sure it's him? Did he tell you his name?"

"I'm sure it's him. Talk to the guy."

"Peter, please, I don't think we should; the guy is crazy. Can't you just tell him there are other callers in the queue ahead of him? Maybe he'll just go away."

"No, Nancy. This guy is good for ratings. Now put your headphones back on and talk to the guy."

Doctor Nancy hesitated to place the headphones back on her head, and for a moment only stared at Willey with a look of shock. When she finally did relent she hit the phone button and took a deep breath of stale air. Trying to sound as professional as possible, she introduced herself to the caller and asked whom she was speaking to.

A moment later, after a slight pause, the man responded. There were no salutations. He got right to the point for his call, which caused Doctor Nancy's heart to skip a beat.

"There is another demon lurking amongst us. She has to be destroyed tonight or there will be hell to pay. I'm going to rip her heart out while it is still beating, and cut it into a thousand pieces."

There was a long silence before Doctor Nancy finally responded. The silence was like the calm imbedded in the eye of the storm, creating hope that the worst of the storm was over. But it was only just beginning; the worst was yet to come.

"Are you the same person who called into the program last night?" Doctor Nancy asked, knowing full well he was. His voice and insane words were unmistakable.

"You know I am. I told you last night I'm the only demon slayer. If I don't destroy her no one else will."

Willey was anxiously tapping his finger on her desk to get her attention. The two-minute commercial break was over, and he wanted to tell her they were going live.

"We're back from commercial, I'm putting him on the air," Willey whispered, now hunched over her shoulder, and hit the On Air button.

This startled her for a moment, but she quickly managed to regain her composure. "Welcome back, listeners. The caller on the line tonight is a man who calls himself Mister Zero. He called into last night's program telling us some bizarre story about slaying demons.

"Mister Zero, before we indulge any further into your strange ideological theories, would you like to tell our listening audience why you call yourself Mister Zero?"

"My name speaks for itself. When I have finished eradicating all the demons from this planet, there will be none left...zero. After tonight there will be one less."

"Well, that would be a relief to all of us. But really, how do you know this person you were telling me about while we were off the air is a demon?"

After a short pause his raspy voice entered her earphones, and the ears of anyone tuned into the program. This time his voice was filled with annoyance.

"I told you before, Doctor, and anyone who was listening last night, I can hear the demon in their voices. If you had listened to me last night I wouldn't have to repeat myself."

"Yes, I'm sorry, you did tell us that. Believe me, I do listen to every word you say. I just wanted you to repeat it so the folks at home can get a better understanding of where you're coming from. So, to continue, this woman who you suspect to be a demon—have you talked to her? Did you have a conversation?"

"Yes, we did, however brief. So you could say we had a conversation."

"What was the conversation about? Where did you meet this young woman?"

"Happenstance. We just happened to meet at her place of employment."

"Maybe you were mistaken. Maybe you only thought she was a demon. Was she rude to you, and is that why you thought she was a demon?"

"On the contrary, Doctor, she was very pleasant. That's what they do. They try to trick us, make us believe they are our friends. But I know better—I know their evil ways."

"Surely there must be other indications—besides their appearance and hearing it in their voices, whatever that means—as to why you know this woman is a demon. You can't just go around murdering innocent people."

"I told you all this last night. Do I need to reiterate it?"

"That would be nice for all the folks at home who were unable to tune in last night. I'm sure they'd like to know. As I recall, you mentioned they are teenage girls with blonde hair and green eyes."

Mister Zero sighed and then went on, sounding irate. "Their eyes are not just green—they sparkle, like green emeralds. Have you ever held a green emerald in your hand?"

"Yes, yes I have."

"You remember how it sparkled? I've held their sparkling eyes in my hand."

"There must be some other indications. You just can't assume every young woman with blonde hair and eyes that sparkle like gems are demons in disguise. That would be just plain preposterous."

"If you must know, they also have imperfections."

"What do you mean by that? Facial blemishes, things like that?"

"Yes, something like that, I suppose. Those are noticeable imperfections, however, not really relevant. The imperfections I'm talking about, like facial expressions that give you away when you lie, those are the hard ones to detect. Believe me, they're good at disguising their lies, and I'm good at seeing through them."

Doctor Nancy paused, trying to come up with a plausible response. She knew, being a psychologist, it was her responsibility to convince the madman he needed to seek help, and what he was thinking of doing was insane.

"You know, you could be destroying a young innocent girl's life. How would you feel if you killed an innocent girl who was only trying to be polite to you?" she professionally said, hoping her words would convince him that he was wrong. Maybe her words would give him pause to think about what he was about to do. That is, if he really did murder them and was not just fabricating a wild story, something delusional people did for attention.

"No Doctor, I never make mistakes identifying demons. I am never wrong. I would also like to inform you I could see the demon in her eyes. There is more to the eyes than just their sparkling color. Those green eyes are the color of envy. You see,

Doctor, the demons are jealous creatures. They want to take over the world, but before they can they must destroy all humans. I, however, will defy them. Tonight is one more step in my quest. I'm heading out as we speak, and before midnight the demon will be destroyed."

With those defiant words the call abruptly ended, leaving Doctor Nancy speechless. Peter Willey smiled with contentment, and went to a commercial break.

CHAPTER 8

It seemed every time Kelsey Mickelson arrived at Pamela's apartment to go out somewhere for the evening, Pamela was never ready, and tonight was no exception. On her drive over — which was a mere five-minute ride across town, since the town of Redmond didn't have a traffic problem and only needed the one traffic light where Route 4 intersected with Main Street — Kelsey was hoping tonight would be the exception. She had been thinking about Malcolm all afternoon, and was anxious to see him again, and too nervous to hang around Pamela's apartment waiting for her to get ready.

But Pamela wasn't even close to being ready. To Kelsey's dismay, the only thing Pamela had accomplished in preparing to look her best was showering. Even that simple task had not been completed, as she was still in the process of drying her hair when she answered her door, wearing only a towel wrapped around her mid-section, and barely above her nipples. She still had to get dressed and apply her makeup, and knowing Pamela's meticulousness, it would be a long tedious process. At least another hour, Kelsey figured, and she was not exaggerating.

***

Pamela Hays always wanted to look perfect when she went out for a night on the town. She wanted to be the hottest looking girl in the place like when she'd roamed the halls in high school, being head cheerleader and homecoming queen. It was her legacy to be homecoming queen, her mother had said, and being the prettiest girl attracted the most popular guys, the guys with the brightest futures. Pamela only had to look at her father to know this was true. Her father just happened to have been the quarterback on the Redmond High football team, and was now the president of the Redmond Savings bank where Pamela worked.

When her father had given her the bank clerk position, it was only to be a temporary position for the summer. After that she'd be off to college. Supposedly, that is. But some plans that seemed to be etched in stone just didn't work out.

Pamela had planned to continue her education, even having been accepted at the state college, but she fell madly in love during the summer and told her disapproving father she wanted to take a year off. Her comment to her father was "Everyone is doing it." Taking a year off before starting the rest of your life was the new thing, according to her logic. And to add to her father's disappointment, she moved into a one-bedroom apartment with her boyfriend.

Two months into their lusty romance Pamela dumped her boyfriend, saying she needed her space, which basically meant she had fallen out of love. Then came another boyfriend with a similar ending — don't let the door hit your lazy ass on your way out. It wasn't long after he was thrown out that Pamela met Matt Burger.

Attending college was not going to happen anytime soon for Pamela Hays.

***

"It's getting late. Are you almost ready?" Kelsey anxiously asked, thinking about Malcolm already being at the tavern and flirting with other women. She was sure other women would be attracted to the new man in town. How could they not be? After all, someone with a mysterious, interesting appearance, a look she'd noticed when Malcolm first entered the bank that morning, could not be overlooked. Even though he lacked the muscular physique young women drooled over, Malcolm definitely made up for his physique in the looks department. Plus, with most of the good-looking bachelors already attached, the pickings were slim, and he would surely attract a few wandering eyes.

"There's no sense in hurrying, no one gets there until after nine," Pamela answered from the kitchen, banging cupboard doors.

Kelsey glanced at her watch and sighed as 8:45 stared back at her. She then slowly walked into the kitchen to see what Pamela was doing when she should have been in her bedroom getting dressed.

"What are you doing?" she asked, knowing full well what her host was doing, seeing a bottle of tequila on the counter—along with several other ingredients to mix a batch of her favorite drink—next to a blender.

"I'm mixing us a couple of margaritas. It's a lot cheaper here than paying for them at the tavern."

"I was kind of hoping to get there earlier tonight. I don't want to miss Malcolm."

"You mean the weird looking guy from the bank today?" Pamela teasingly responded. "Don't worry, I'm sure he'll be

70

there. The guy liked you, I could tell. I noticed you two were having quite the conversation. When I waited on him he never spoke more than two words to me. Believe me, Kelsey, he'll be there waiting. Best to have a little buzz on when you go; it will relax you and you'll have more fun," Pamela said, then smiled as she handed Kelsey a salted margarita.

"What, were you spying on me?"

"What do you mean?"

"You said you saw we were having, and I quote, 'quite the conversation.'"

"So, I was only looking out for my girl," Pamela said with a laugh.

"Anyway, I hope you're right about him liking me."

"I know I am," Pamela proudly answered, and took a seat at the table.

Kelsey didn't sit and leaned against the counter, licking the salt off the rim of the glass before taking a sip. She liked margaritas almost as much as Pamela, and Pamela made the best, with plenty of tequila.

"What about Burger? What time are you meeting him?"

"Matt? Oh, he won't be there until after ten, most likely. Matt and his lowlife friends are probably getting drunk at the Holy Mackerel before going to the Crow's Nest. Which is fine with me—I hate that dive bar. No bad wishes for the owner, but I hope it washes out to sea someday during a hurricane. Besides, maybe I'll meet someone interesting tonight. It will serve him right, the cheap bastard," Pamela said, then paused, taking a good sip before continuing.

After sexually licking the salt off her lips, thinking of rolling in the sack with her boyfriend, Pamela then added, "Men are all alike. They think they can do anything they want when they have a girlfriend wrapped around their little cock. Well, he'd better think twice if he thinks he has me wrapped around his cock. Just because he's black, it ain't much bigger than some other cocks I've seen."

"Yeah right. You guys will probably be married by this time next year. Besides, his cock can't be that small, is it?" Kelsey said with a laugh, wondering how big Burger's penis really was. Other than seeing a man's penis in *Playgirl* magazines, Kelsey had only seen one in person, and that was in the backseat of a dark vehicle parked out back of the Crow's Nest Tavern when her date attempted to have sex with her. Kelsey jumped out of the vehicle and told him to jerk-off if he was that horny, and went back inside the tavern. She wasn't going to waste her virginity on some guy she knew she'd never go out with again.

"It's smaller than you think, but that's not the reason I wouldn't marry him. I'm waiting for someone down the road, and I have plenty of time before that happens. Till then, I'm playing the field," Pamela unconvincingly responded.

"Oh, Pam, you love him. You know you do."

"No, I don't. Well, not that much; not enough to marry the guy."

With that fragile comment, Pamela finished her margarita and stood to pour herself another. "You ready for another margarita? I'm sure Malcolm, or whatever his name is, is doing the same thing we are."

"Sure, what the hell—why not? As you suggested, I'll be more relaxed when I see him. So, where's Theodore? I don't see him anywhere. I wanted to say hello to him. He's so cute and cuddly."

"Sleeping. If he's not sleeping he's probably looking out the front window watching it rain, wishing he were out in it. He only comes around when he wants something, just like all men. The horny thing."

"Remind me to say goodbye to him before we leave. Someday when I have my own place, I'm going to have a cat. Samantha says she's allergic to cats — that's why I can't have one now."

Pamela grabbed her margarita and headed for her bedroom to dress, leaving Kelsey alone in the kitchen. The apartment was suddenly quiet. She sat alone and sipped her drink, thinking about how the night would play out, hoping for the best but also trying not to get her hopes up in case Malcolm wasn't there. In her thoughts she could see him smiling at her as she walked into the tavern, smiling like he wanted to lick every inch of her body. Wishful thinking, she thought as she shook the image away for later when alone in her bed, trying to sleep. She then glanced around the kitchen with boredom, seeing the radio on the counter.

Sometimes, if they were planning on staying awhile, Pamela would have the radio turned on, tuned to a country station, but tonight it was silent. The silence reminded Kelsey of the previous night, when she'd laid in silence listening to the Doctor Nancy program. She wondered now if the same horrible man would call back again tonight. Inquisitively, as though a force took control of her mind, Kelsey turned on the radio and tuned into the WBLG channel, which broadcasted the program.

At first she heard nothing, only silence, then loud static.

"How's your reception?" Kelsey shouted over the annoying noise. "I'm trying to find WBLG, but there's no reception."

"Should be fine, must be the weather," Pamela mockingly shouted back. She could hear Kelsey fine; her bedroom door was open and only a few feet away from the kitchen.

Kelsey tried again, wiggling the tuning knob slightly in both directions until she heard the unmistakable voice of Mister Zero.

"Oh shit, he's back on. Pam, come listen to this. The guy's back on the radio."

Pamela came into the room half dressed, buttoning her blouse. "What are you talking about?"

"The awful man I told you about from last night. He's the guy that mutilates young women he thinks are demons. Just listen to him."

After listening for a few minutes Pamela said, "He's all full of shit. No one would call the radio station and say that. It's all about ratings — the more gory, the more people will tune in. Change the channel; let's listen to some music."

Reluctantly, while Pamela finished dressing, Kelsey changed the channel back to the country station and slowly sipped her margarita. Her thoughts, however, were on Malcolm being at the tavern surrounded by groping women. She couldn't get there soon enough.

CHAPTER 9

After hanging up the telephone and placing it back on the bar where it belonged, Mister Zero headed out the door and into the rainy night, not caring to thank the pool hall's proprietor for the use of the telephone. The only thing on his mind was completing his mission, which was to destroy the demon. He already knew where she was going to be, having found out earlier in the day. He wasn't sure, however, the exact time she would be arriving there, so his plan was to arrive early and wait, as he always did. His sudden appearances and the looks on their faces were the most rewarding of all, even though he enjoyed the killing part. Surprising them took finesse, cunning maneuvers to get the best, surprised expressions.

With plenty of time before executing his plan of attack, he would first go home to his dingy apartment to prepare himself, mentally and physically, to avoid any potential mistakes that might occur if he was not fully prepared.

A few hours later, with the rain coming down harder, along with increasing gusts of wind, Mister Zero held onto his cap and walked briskly toward his destination. He felt no displeasure because of the inclement weather. To him his task was daunting enough and meant to be. Therefore he felt there was no use in making his job any harder by worrying about something he had no control of. It was the demons' way of discouraging him from fulfilling his responsibility. But no matter what obstacles they threw at him, he knew they could not prevent him from completing his crucial task.

He smiled as he walked along the sidewalk, thinking of seeing the surprised horror in her emerald green eyes. Like on his previous kills, he would cut her eyes out first, one at a time, so she could watch him devour the first one. She'd hear the second eye pop as he bit into it, maybe visualizing it in her mind. He wanted her to suffer — it was what the demons deserved.

Along his walk through the downtown area he stopped for a moment under an awning in front of a corner convenience store, for no known reason other than to catch his breath and relax his anxiety. He could feel his heart rate increasing the closer he got to his destination.

A sign posted on the glass door told him the store was closed for the night, which, at that late hour in the evening was not uncommon, as most stores were closed. It was not a large sign, but large enough to notice if you happened to look while attempting to gain access.

Seeing an inside light was still on, he curiously peeked through the glass and saw a man sitting behind the counter counting money. From where he stood looking in, Mister Zero could see there were four short stacks of paper money. One for each denomination, he surmised, the highest value being twenty dollar bills. He also noticed a pile of coins along with a few rolled coins. The coins he would leave behind. To him they were useless, weighing heavy in his pocket, and would only hinder his quest.

Money, however, was essential to his job, and with no viable income it was necessary to improvise. His motto for furnishing his livelihood was "It's only money, they can always get more." Besides, he truly believed he was doing everyone a huge favor — dipping into the money-well once in a while should not be frowned upon. Everyone had to pay the piper. In this case the piper was the Demon Slayer.

Mister Zero looked at his watch to check the time. The inexpensive watch he owned was digital and glowed in the dark when he pushed the button. Seeing the time caused him to smile, which was a rarity. He still had plenty of time, he assured himself, seeing he was only five minutes away from his destination.

Pretending not to see the closed sign, Mister Zero twisted the knob and pushed the door open to the sound of a bell hanging overhead. The man behind the counter looked up and told him the store was closed for the night, come back tomorrow.

"Sorry for intruding," Mister Zero spoke with earnest. "I noticed your light was on and assumed you were still open."

"No, you assumed wrong. Like I said, we're closed. I hung the closed sign in the door. Same time every night for the past fifteen years. Guess you must have missed it."

"Not to embarrass a customer, perhaps maybe next time you should lock the door as well," Mister Zero responded as he stepped inside, eyeing the bills on the counter.

There seemed to be enough money sitting there to support him for at least another month. His needs for survival did not require much money. The last time he relieved someone of their funds was a pitiful amount totaling no more than a hundred dollars, and that meager amount lasted him for two weeks. The man he'd robbed was a pathetic drunk who drowned his sorrows of heartbreak on Mister Zero as they shared a booth in the dark corner of a seedy, rundown bar. Mister Zero felt he deserved the money, having had to listen to the man as he slobbered all over him. Besides, he also helped the man to his vehicle, a dark parking lot where the man spent the night sleeping it off.

Seeing the direction of his stare, the proprietor slowly removed the bills, placing them on a shelf below the counter. "You're right about locking the door, mister, but I'm expecting my friend to join me any minute now. That's why I left it unlocked."

Mister Zero turned and glanced outside, noticing it was pouring harder, and there was not much traffic to speak of, foot or vehicle. Now seemed a perfect time to relieve the man of his day's receipts. Make it quick, he figured, and he'd be long gone before the man's friend arrived. That is, if there was a friend coming, and it was not something he'd fabricated in an attempt to ward off any potential problem. It was a tactical defense, but didn't often work when dealing with a professional criminal.

Without saying anything, Mister Zero cautiously walked up to the counter, mindfully eyeing the proprietor, hoping there wasn't a weapon nearby. As he stood quietly in front of the counter, pondering his next move, he spotted a black cat resting comfortably in the man's lap. The cat seemed to be sleeping, but a closer examination revealed its eyes were slightly opened.

***

"Like I said, we're closed," the proprietor repeated, hoping the man would leave and stop scaring him.

The scary man lurking over him really unnerved the proprietor, acting like he intended to cause havoc. He couldn't help but think of the night he was robbed at gunpoint, and didn't want to experience it again. It was the first and only time he had been robbed, and had been scared out of his mind, having a gun pointed in his face. A week had passed before he dared to reopen the store. And even then, he never wanted to work alone, hiring a helper. Tonight his helper was home sick.

The unwelcome customer was giving him the creeps. His eyes were dark and scary looking, as though there was no life inside of them. The only thing he could think of doing to defuse a potential catastrophe was to be nice to the man, not like the time before when he'd yelled at the robber to leave. If he was polite, he worriedly thought, maybe the man would change his mind. That is, if robbery was his intention.

"Well, I guess I could wait on you if you make it quick and have the correct change. I'm really in a rush to finish closing as I have company coming." The more people he mentioned coming in the store may deter any illegal thought the man may have.

Eyeing the rolled coins, Mister Zero picked up one of the rolls of quarters, rolling it in his palm. "From what I can see, and it's quite obvious, you have plenty of change. But, I happen not to need any change tonight."

Just as Mister Zero was about to add "What I really need are those bills you stashed under the counter," the bell above the door chimed. The interruption caused a moment of pause for both men.

The proprietor behind the counter exhaled the breath of air he had been holding when he saw his significant other strolling through the door. It was good timing, he thought. Just a second before he'd felt as though he was getting ready to have a nervous breakdown and crawl under the counter.

***

Mister Zero was also somewhat relieved, blessing his good fortune that he hadn't made his move yet. It could have been an untimely moment, possibly ruining his plan for the night. Or then again only an inconvenience, for no task was unattainable for the Demon Slayer.

"I only wanted to inquire about using a phone, no change required," he quickly explained, and set the roll of quarters back where they belonged. He then turned to face the newcomer. The man seemed to be no match for the Demon Slayer, Mister Zero surmised, seeing his meek facial features — small eyes matching his small nose and thin lips. Surely the man was no more than an equal to the one behind the counter, both meek looking. A match made in heaven.

"I'm sorry, we don't have a phone. Try the pool hall down the street a couple of blocks. I'm sure they have one you can use," the proprietor said, sounding confident and more direct. To add emphasis, he pointed his finger out the door.

Disregarding the proprietor's recommendation, Mister Zero looked around the store, panning for any potential hazard. From what he could tell taking the money was still viable. Two wimps and a cat did not pose much of a challenge.

***

"Really, the pool hall is just a couple of blocks north of here," the proprietor reiterated, thinking maybe the man didn't believe him. He did have a cell phone right next to the stacks of bills on the shelf below the counter, but that was not a store phone and that's what the man was asking to use. He had only asked to use a phone, which implied the use of a store phone. Therefore the proprietor had convinced himself that he was not lying when he said he didn't have a phone.

The proprietor's friend was now joining them, coming around the counter and placing a delicate hand on the proprietor's shoulder. "Hey Milton, did you have a nice day? Business must have been good today, I see you still have a customer."

80

***

Mister Zero thought about how easy it would be to take their money. A little intimidation was all he needed and the money was his. He had his knife—a long, shiny knife. What else would he need to persuade them to turn their money over to him?

But, he didn't want to mess up the chance to slay the demon, just in case something went wrong. It had to be done tonight. Tomorrow would be too late.

"He wanted to use the store's phone, but I told the gentleman we don't have one," Milton Crosby told his boyfriend.

"Oh, is that all," Roger said with a smile as he reached inside his sport jacket and pulled out a cell phone. "Here, use mine. Just punch in the number and hit send."

Before grabbing the cell phone, Mister Zero took a moment to think. He had no use for a phone right now. There was no one to call. No family and no friends; he was alone in the world.

"I'm not sure of the number to dial. I'll need to look it up in the phonebook," he said, stalling.

"Sorry, no phonebook. I'm sure they have one at the pool hall I mentioned. They'd be glad to oblige you," Milton informed him.

At that Mister Zero thought it would be a good idea to get the phone away from them. Take it out of the equation so they couldn't call the police for help when he made his move.

"I don't need a phonebook after all. The number has just come back to me. It's my mother I want to call, and I had forgotten her number because it's been awhile since I last dialed her. I only want to let her know I'm fine."

Roger handed him his cell phone, then turned toward his partner. "Oh, Milton, what a nice son he is to go through all that trouble to find a phone to call his mother—and on such a miserable night to boot. There should be more sons in the world like him, then there'd be less violence."

Milton Crosby did not respond. He was pissing his pants staring at a long shiny knife.

CHAPTER 10

When Malcolm Dangil entered the Crow's Nest Tavern's foyer he was greeted by a bearded, heavyset man blocking the entryway to the bar area. The tavern's owner had hired the bouncer mainly for his size rather than his intelligence, to make sure everyone entering the bar was at least twenty-one years of age. Those who weren't of legal age, the owner figured, would not put up much of an argument with a man twice their size, and would quietly leave. He was an impressive deterrent for minors attempting to enter the tavern—even Malcolm felt intimidated.

To limit the redundant activity of checking everyone's identification card, the bouncer only checked the ID's of non-regular customers, which were few. Malcolm was one of those few first time patrons, so the bouncer scrutinized him with a firm eye then asked if he was twenty-one. Malcolm confirmed he was of legal age and pulled out his license for verification. The bouncer took a quick glance at the license, noting his date of birth, and then let him pass by with a friendly smile.

Once inside Malcolm removed his cap and gently shook

the rain off, not wanting to get anyone standing near wet. He then replaced it on his head and scanned the crowded tavern for Kelsey. He was sure he'd recognize her in an instant, having her image imprinted in his brain for most of the day, but that was not the case. The place was crowded and crawling with mostly young women. For a town with a small population, Malcolm wondered where they all came from. For the two months he'd lived in Redmond he'd seen few people his own age. He then remembered the town of Benton, which was much larger in population than Redmond, was nearby, and Malcolm assumed most out-of-towners came from there.

It was difficult locating Kelsey in the crowd because most of the women, he noticed, were about the same age she was. And to add to his dilemma of recognizing her, a lot of those same women wore the same hair color, and also had a similar build as Kelsey.

Trying not to draw any attention, Malcolm inconspicuously strolled around the tavern, taking quick glances at the women he thought might be Kelsey. Not finding her, and feeling slightly uncomfortable being there with no one he knew to converse with, Malcolm was leaning toward calling it an early night and heading home before the rains picked up again. There was always next week, he consoled himself. And, if he waited another week, he'd have a few more dollars to spend since he would be receiving his first paycheck.

Just as he was about to give up on Kelsey and leave to head back home, Clayton Daniels walked up behind him with a shit-eating grin. Clayton was the last person Malcolm wanted to see at that moment, and there he was standing right next to him, smelling and looking like a drunken bum. Not having shaved in days, his stubble beard showed signs of graying and his eyes looked like they were made of glass.

"Sorry I'm late, guy, I had a minor accident to deal with."

Malcolm had totally forgotten all about Clayton mentioning he was planning on being at the tavern and inviting him along. Seeing Clayton tonight was the furthest thing from his mind. He was only thinking about Kelsey. If he hadn't coincidentally met her, and been invited to join her at the tavern, he wouldn't have come out in this miserable weather in the first place. And even if he had remembered Clayton mentioning he'd be here, and been invited by Kelsey, Malcolm felt he still would have stayed home. That's how much he disliked Clayton, even after only knowing the guy for a few hours at work.

Clayton was not someone he wanted to hang out with, but he would never mention this to Clayton, or anything concerning how he felt about the man for that matter. Malcolm knew how to keep his feelings about others to himself. From his past experience living on the streets and dealing with different types of characters, he knew you could never tell how one would retaliate when they were being insulted. Especially if the person was the conceited type, and Clayton definitely fit that category according to Malcolm's limited experience with human nature.

Malcolm was not the kind of person to criticize someone for his or her impolite upbringing or social status, which, in Clayton's case, was at rock bottom. Not to say Malcolm felt he was any better off. The difference was, Malcolm wanted to change his life around, be a better person; whereas, knowing as much as he did about Clayton, which was very little, Clayton seemed to be the type of person who was satisfied being what he was—a loser.

Hanging around Clayton would only hinder the new lifestyle he planned for himself, a plan he'd visualized while incarcerated in a state mental facility. He'd had his fill of dealing with lowlifes like Clayton Daniels, listening to their idiotic ideas on how society should be run and how society should treat the less fortunate better. Even though Clayton was not one of those homeless persons, having a job and a place to live, there was something odd about Clayton that resonated with him. At home that afternoon, while sitting on his couch listening to the rain, Malcolm had thought about his first day working with Clayton and David Graham. David Graham he liked, but he couldn't figure out why he disliked Clayton other than knowing from the first time they met, that very morning, that Clayton was a loser.

***

What Malcolm didn't know was that he was correct in his assumptions about his coworker. Clayton had no chance for a gratifying life. Clayton was a loser from the day he was born, which could be attributed to being the son of a lazy, good for nothing alcoholic loser. His father had been a loser, working the same job as Clayton was now, only back then it was part-time work, working only in the spring and summer seasons, mowing the grass around the gravestones and helping David Graham with the back-aching job of digging and filling the graves before the town purchased the backhoe. His father died relatively young, having just turned forty-four, from overindulging in everything, with smoking and drinking being the main culprits. Clayton was on a path to most likely die the same way.

"No problem, I just got here myself. What was the accident?" Malcolm asked, not expecting an answer, figuring it was something insignificant like spilling a beer on his kitchen floor.

"Ran over some fucking cat. I tried to swerve out of the way but ran the critter right the fuck over, and then hit a parked car. Not too bad, but almost bad enough to ruin my night, though just a fender-bender."

"Yeah, not to mention ruining the cat's night," Malcolm said in jest, but Clayton didn't get the humor, as alcohol had a way of distorting one's mind.

"What, don't tell me you're one of those fucking animal rights activists? It was only a fucking cat, for crying out loud."

"Yeah, I guess you're right—the owner can always get another cat."

Sensing the sarcasm, Clayton unconvincingly tried defending his actions. "Yeah, well, it's raining like hell out, and you can't see a damn thing driving in this shit. Besides, the thing shouldn't have been out in the middle of the goddamn road. So fuck that cat. We've got some partying to do, my friend, and that means getting laid. See anything entertaining in here? There's got to be at least one ugly slut in this joint hoping to get laid tonight. There's no place else to go in this mothball town but this joint to pick up sleazy women."

"I can definitely see there are a few women in here, but I don't know any of them, it's my first time here," Malcolm said. He wasn't the slightest bit interested in picking up sleazy women. He was only interested in one woman, and she definitely wasn't sleazy.

"Oh, they're here, believe me. Just give it some time and you'll see what I mean."

"I was hoping to meet up with the girl I met today from the bank, but I haven't seen her yet. I guess maybe she must have changed her mind. Did you stop to see if the cat was all right?" Malcolm asked, wanting to change the subject.

"No, I didn't stop at all, kept right on going. I got him real good though; no way he survived. With all this rain he'll probably get washed down the sewage drain and out to sea," Clayton proudly explained.

"What about the parked car you hit?"

"What about it? He shouldn't have parked in the street. Enough about the goddamn accident—I've had worse. I do need another beer though," Clayton said, then waved the bartender over like he owned the place and ordered a draft beer. "What about you, are you drinking?" Clayton asked Malcolm.

"You buying?"

"Hell, no. I'm a little tapped out at the moment, and I'll need all the money I have to get my truck fixed. I don't have collision insurance to pay for the damage. How about you, you buying? You're the new guy, and new guys are always suppose to buy."

"Sorry, Clay, that makes two of us—I don't have much to spend either," Malcolm told him, but he actually did have enough to buy Clayton a beer. He just wasn't willing to waste it on him.

When the bartender nodded his way to take his order, Malcolm ordered a bottled beer. He pulled out his wallet and grabbed one of his twenties, holding it away from Clayton's view.

As he waited on his beer, Malcolm turned his attention toward the door, watching the rain-drenched customers strolling in, hoping to see Kelsey. His immediate thoughts were, if she didn't show soon the beer he ordered would be his last for the evening.

"Here's your light beer, pay the bartender," Clayton said, handing the bottle to Malcolm.

Malcolm handed the bartender the twenty. While waiting for his change he sipped his beer. The beer tasted odd, not what he expected it to taste like. He couldn't remember the last time he had a beer. He only knew it was a few years back when he was living on the streets and under the legal age to drink alcohol.

"How's that light beer tasting there for you? I can see you're a real gusto man," Clayton sarcastically said.

"Not bad—I guess its okay. I do prefer regular beer, but I'm supposed to be meeting a girl in here and I don't want to get too drunk. I've been looking around for her, but I haven't seen her yet."

"Yeah, you did mention that. Who's this girl you're looking for?"

"She's a girl from the bank I met today; her name's Kelsey. She told me she'd meet me here tonight, but I don't see her anywhere."

"The night is still young, my friend. By the way, she got any girlfriends?"

"Yeah, she said she's going out with her girlfriend," Malcolm answered, but quickly wished he hadn't.

"Oh, she's bringing her girlfriend. Well, old buddy boy, how about you fixing me up with her friend?" Clayton rhetorically asked as he pushed his index finger into Malcolm's chest, emphasizing he was the buddy he was talking to.

Malcolm frowned at the remark of being called his buddy, but mostly his disgust was at the thought of fixing him up with Kelsey's friend. Even if the friend Kelsey was planning on coming with was in the same class as Clayton, which he knew was next to impossible, he'd never fix him up with her, fearing he'd want to go on a double date sometime. Working with the guy was bad enough, even though it had only been half of the workday.

"Gee, I don't know. I hardly know Kelsey myself, and I don't know her friend at all. I only know they work together at the bank. Maybe she has a boyfriend."

Malcolm could picture Clayton slobbering all over Kelsey's friend, ruining any chance of furthering his relationship with her. He was now thinking it was a bad idea coming here, and was anxious to leave before she showed up. That is if she was still coming. The only bright spot in the evening so far was that the band started to play, which distracted Clayton for the moment.

Malcolm looked at his beer, seeing he had hardly drank any of it. He then took a hardy gulp, washing it down with a bit of displeasure. He glanced at the large mirror behind the bar and didn't like what he saw. The person staring back at him was not the person he was planning to be, drinking in a crowded bar with the likes of Clayton Daniels. He had his plans for his future, and the man standing next to him would only hinder his quest.

CHAPTER 11

Mister Zero made quick work of it, leaving the store a bloody mess, as he did not want to arrive late and take a chance of missing his target when she was leaving the confines of safety to go home. The only thing he bothered to do, which he knew was necessary, was to wash the sticky blood from his hands and the tiny splatters that dotted his face and neck, plus he cleaned the blood dripping knife thoroughly so as not to contaminate his next kill with human blood. The spots of blood on his dark clothing, he figured, would most likely go unnoticed in the dark. Tomorrow he'd wash them at the local laundry. His only regret was not having the withal to grab a roll of quarters for the washing machine and dryer.

Funny, he thought as he strolled along the sidewalk in the pouring rain, how shocked a person could be watching a loved one being ripped apart and knowing they were next, unable to help or even scream. Even the cat had whimpered, disappearing into a dark corner of the store.

He'd taken the knife to Roger first, the man who had

unfortunately entered the store at an untimely moment, grabbing the back of his head and plunging the shiny blade deep into the side of his neck, then ripping it across his narrow throat. The man died instantly, slumping to the floor behind the counter in a heap. Milton was still pissing and shitting. Mister Zero almost felt sorry for the wimpy little man, but then remembered the man didn't have one ounce of generosity in his soul.

***

At about the same time Mister Zero was stuffing the cash in his pants pockets, Kelsey Mickelson was watching Pamela drain the last of the tequila in the blender. The whizzing sounds and spinning alcoholic mixture had a hypnotizing effect on her. Her thoughts drifted to an imaginary life with Malcolm, living on the seashore in a house with a white picket fence and a couple of kids running around the yard. Many nights she dreamed of living a life she'd never had growing up, one with a handsome husband and happy, beautiful children. Malcolm, she thought, could be the one to make her dreams come true.

When Pamela shut the rotating motor off Kelsey was still lost in her imaginary world. Her unblinking eyes were staring beyond Pamela at a dandelion colored wall.

"Dreaming of getting laid tonight? Here, drink this. It will help you get laid, I'm sure," Pamela said, bringing her back to the real world with a teasing smile, placing the margarita next to her.

"No, I'm just hoping I'm not too drunk and make a fool out of myself in front of him." Even though Kelsey knew next to nothing about him, to her, Malcolm seemed like a young man who had a destination ahead of him, someone conservative about his money and future. Those were the two most important attributes for her ideal man. Most of the guys in Redmond had no planned future. They lived for the moment, spending their weekly paycheck every Friday and Saturday night getting intoxicated, and most likely other nights of the week as well. Kelsey didn't want one of those guys — ones like Pamela was attracted to. She wanted a guy like Malcolm, or who she hoped Malcolm to be.

"Trust me, you won't make a fool of yourself."

"Well, what if I do? You always hear that making a first impression has the greatest impact on a relationship, and I don't want to make a bad first impression on him."

***

Pamela shook her head in amusement. The guy wasn't even in the same league as Kelsey. To her, he was at least two levels below anyone she'd ever consider having a long-term relationship with. She figured Malcolm was someone who grew up on the wrong side of town, and was trying to fit in with the better class citizens without putting in the required effort. Kelsey could not see this. The reason was that she most likely was love struck, blinded by passions that affected normal thinking.

Pamela herself had been love struck before. Several times, including with her current boyfriend, Matt Burger, who was "serious" boyfriend number three. Like her previous two boyfriends, she'd fallen in love with Matt before knowing the guy. Matt first attracted her attention because he was black, a rarity in this small town. She noticed him when she visited her mother on a day when Matt's landscaping company was grooming the spacious yard her parents owned. She spent more time talking to Matt than she did with her mother.

Pamela's previous two serious boyfriends had lasted less than two months, the latter being the longest. Now Matt was the longest, and the way their relationship was going he would soon be replaced with another. The novelty of him being black was wearing off. Plus, she quickly found out the notion that all black men were well endowed was a rumor. It was no more a fact than saying a prayer would grant you your wish, though some wishes snuck through the fabrics of reality.

The first time she'd seen Matt's hard penis was brief—just for the time it took him to undress and stick it in her. She'd felt his penetration inside her love-nest was slow in reaching its depth, thinking it was still growing larger inside her—a feeling that was only imagined. The next time he let her stroke it. His penis was big, but not the ten inches she expected a black penis to be.

Maybe, Pamela thought, Kelsey saw something in Malcolm that she'd missed. Maybe he could be her next conquest after Matt's allure wore off. She'd really never had a long conversation with Malcolm, only the two times she waited on him at the bank. Kelsey, on the other hand, did have a long conversation, and most likely an interesting one, as she was adamantly smitten after he left the bank. Maybe it was worth pouring Kelsey another margarita before heading out. If he lost interest in Kelsey…well, there was always room for the possibility of another intriguing encounter, even if for only one night. After all, Redmond had a shortage of interesting men.

"Drink up, girl, you're lagging. You've got to get in the right mood."

"What mood is that?"

"A better mood than you are in now. It's Friday night, time to have some fun. Explode some of that horny energy you've been saving up all week, I'm telling you, because your boyfriend is doing the same thing."

***

Knowing Pamela was right, except for the boyfriend remark, Kelsey showed her acknowledgement by hoisting her glass before taking a good sip. She had to loosen up and relax, show

Malcolm she was a fun person to be around. Two long sips later the drink was gone.

"Any more?" Kelsey proudly asked, holding up the empty glass. She was starting to feel good and seemingly in a better mood, not tight and nervous.

Pamela reached into the cupboard over the sink and produced another bottle of tequila. "Plenty. Tonight is going to be a night to remember. Oh, by the way, just to remind you, don't forget you're driving. I'll be going home with Matt and not coming back here."

"Great, and here I am going on my third margarita before even making it to the Crow's Nest. Just my luck Malcolm won't even be there, and I'll run into that weirdo on the radio, Mister Zero."

"Don't worry about him—that weirdo won't be there. The guy would be too conspicuous looking. He'd stick-out like a sore thumb if he were there. I'll bet he's a big ugly guy missing most of his teeth," Pamela said, and switched the blender on high for ten seconds.

"On the radio tonight he did say he was going out tonight to find another demon to kill. I wonder if he rapes the girls before he kills them. He never mentioned anything about raping them on the radio—he only said he killed them and mutilated them, slowly cutting them up into pieces. Oh my God, you should have heard him. He was awful. What a horrible person." Kelsey visualized the man cutting up one of the victims with a large knife, grinning with pleasure as he cut away.

"I think it's time to leave, Kelsey. You're getting a little weird. No more tequila for you, girl. Well, at least not until we get to the tavern, and after you drink this one." She handed Kelsey a margarita.

95

"Yeah, you don't have to care. You don't have to worry about the creepy guy, you're not a blonde."

"Sorry Kelsey. I just can't imagine the guy on the radio is living in this tiny town, or even that he really exists."

"What about the girl who was murdered last week? Callie Webster was brutally murdered, cut up into pieces. And she had blonde hair. They found her not too far from here in a field. The guy who killed her is still out there, and they have no idea who he is."

"Look, I hear your concern, but it's probably only a coincidence. Maybe the guy on the radio used her murder to get some notoriety. I mean, come on, he's using the name Mister Zero. The guy's a wacko. Come on, drink this up, and let's have some fun tonight."

CHAPTER 12

The three margaritas Kelsey drank in Pamela's apartment only slightly impaired her driving; it was the driving rain and Pamela's constant distractions that made it difficult for her to navigate the dark, rain-slicked road. Pamela, on the other hand, was feeling a little more inebriated than usual. She never stopped talking for more than five seconds the whole way over. Kelsey figured her friend had started drinking well before she'd arrived at her apartment.

When they arrived at their destination, Kelsey parked her Ford Focus in a parking lot across the street from the Crow's Nest Tavern. The large parking lot had previously belonged to a bowling alley that had closed a few years earlier. The parking lot, with a large For Lease sign sticking haphazardly out of the ground, had remained vacant since the bowling alley closed. Patrons of the tavern were now unofficially using the vacant lot, since the tavern's parking area was small in size and inconveniently located in the back of the building. The bowling alley's gravel parking lot, however, was prone to potholes, and tonight those holes were full of rainwater, causing Pamela to utter profanities, saying they should fix the damn parking lot.

Of course the never satisfied Pamela also had her complaints about having to walk across the street in the pouring rain, complaining that the rain was messing up her hair. Kelsey had worn a Red Sox cap, something she hadn't done that morning going to work, and told Pamela she should have been prepared for the weather. After all, she'd had plenty of notice — it had been raining all day.

The first thing Kelsey did when she entered the tavern was to look around for Malcolm. While the bouncer was checking her and Pamela's fake driver's licenses — which he barely glanced at, and only checked to keep them hanging around the entrance longer for no other purpose than to check them out — she spotted Malcolm standing at the bar chatting with some guy she disliked. Seeing the two together hit her with a wave of melancholy.

Kelsey had no idea what the man's name was and hadn't cared, even though he must have told her a dozen times — each time he strolled over to her table in an attempt to start a conversation with the intent of scoring with her. He was a disgusting person with no manners whatsoever, and what made it more disgusting was that he was old enough to be her father. If the man had children, which Kelsey doubted since she could not fathom why any woman would ever want to sleep with the disgusting man, she would have felt sorry for them, having the misfortune of being born with his genes.

Now, the disgusting man was chumming with the man she was hoping to plan a future with.

"Look at this hair, it's a mess," Pamela moaned, bushing her hand over the top trying to smooth it out. "I'm going to head to the bathroom; I'll only be a minute. You going to wait here or are you coming with me?"

Kelsey was anxious to meet Malcolm. There had been nothing else on her mind all day but him, and there he was, only a few feet away. She wanted to walk up to him right at that moment. Walk right up to him and grab his hand — but not until the man she despised went away, disappeared forever. So, reluctantly, she opted to follow Pamela to the bathroom.

Surprisingly for the amount of people patronizing the tavern, they were alone in the bathroom. Pamela stood slightly hunched over in front of the mirror, gently brushing her hair. Kelsey was leaning against the sink counter looking away, thinking about what she was going to say to Malcolm. Mostly she was thinking how she would approach him and start the conversation.

"How's it look?" Pamela asked, staring at her hair, touching it lightly here and there, making sure there were no hairs out of place.

"How's what look?"

"My hair. What did you think I was talking about?"

"It looks great," Kelsey answered without looking. "It looked great anyway, before you dragged me in here."

"I didn't drag you in here, it was your choice. Sounds to me like you're in a bitchy mood tonight. We probably should have had at least another margarita at my place before we left."

"No. I guess I was just thinking of something else."

"You mean someone else, don't you? So, are you excited to see your boyfriend?" Pamela teased, still looking at her image in the mirror, not completely satisfied at what was staring back at her.

"He's here. I spotted him at the bar. He was talking to that weird old guy who keeps hitting on me every time I come here. I swear to God, the guy is here every time I'm here. It's like he's

99

stalking me or something."

"What guy's that? Do I know him?"

"That gross old weirdo who looks and smells like a homeless person. I can't remember his name, but I think he works for the town over at the cemetery. He's old enough to be my father, for God's sake."

"I'm not sure, but I think I know the guy you're talking about. If it is that guy, what's your boyfriend doing talking him?"

"I don't know, and stop saying he's my boyfriend. He's not; I hardly even know him," Kelsey answered, sounding annoyed.

"Don't get huffy, Kelsey, I'm only kidding with you. By the way you're fantasizing about him, it sounds to me like he's already your boyfriend."

"No, I'm not fantasizing about him," Kelsey unconvincingly said. Then, after a short pause, she asked, "Should I wait till he comes over to me, or should I just walk up to him and say hi?"

"Why are you asking me?"

"You're supposed to be the expert. At least that's what you keep telling me. So tell me, what would you do?"

"Professionally speaking," Pamela proudly said with a laugh, "if you're asking me, I'd wait. But you also might want to try getting his attention. When he looks over, and I'm sure he will, just smile. Maybe lick your lips and look sexy. That should work—it always does for me."

"Lick my lips. Are you kidding me?"

"Yes, I'm kidding—just smile at him. Let the evening flow, and I'm sure it will work out fine. Come on, girl, let's go have some fun; the party is waiting." Pamela stuffed her hairbrush into her purse. She then hooked her arm through Kelsey's, leading the way.

They headed straight for an unoccupied table, which was

near the band but not so close they'd get drowned out by the music. With the table situated on the far side of the tavern, it made for a good spot for viewing the crowd and anybody coming through the door.

CHAPTER 13

When Malcolm glanced over toward the entrance for the umpteenth time since arriving at the Crow's Nest Tavern, in anticipating of spotting Kelsey, he noticed the heavyset bouncer sitting on a stool checking someone's driver's license. The license, he assumed, belonged to the young woman standing in the entryway wearing a blue Red Sox cap. Seeing the woman caused him to hold his breath. The woman was about the same size as Kelsey and, striking his enthusiasm even more, she wasn't alone. There was another female standing with her, a tall brunette in the process of attempting to fix her hair. Both her hands were nervously working in tandem, one on each side of the head.

Malcolm started to get excited at seeing the women, thinking one could be Kelsey and the other her friend from the bank. His excitement was short lived, dissolving quickly when the woman he thought was Kelsey turned in his direction. Her face just didn't match the one he had visualized all day, and there was no recognition in her expression when she seemed to glance his way. She actually looked disappointed, frowning with a squint of her eyes. He was sure the woman, who disappeared into the lady's bathroom behind the brunette, wasn't Kelsey, and was most likely someone else's dream girl.

Trying not to show his disappointment, Malcolm took a long slug off his beer, feeling the suds wash down his throat like warm piss water. He then looked around for a clock, finally noticing one above the cash register behind the counter. Seeing the time on the digital clock, he realized he had only been there for about twenty minutes. He thought it had been much longer, but figured time goes by at a slower pace when waiting. He decided he'd give himself another twenty minutes, and then if she didn't show, he was going to slip out the door and go back to his boring apartment. He'd tell Clayton he was going to use the bathroom, which was conveniently located near the exit, and leave without saying goodbye.

"As for myself, I only like watching football," Clayton was saying, more to himself since Malcolm wasn't paying attention.

Clayton had been telling blonde jokes loud enough to be heard over the music, but when he told a couple of his favorite ones it seemed Malcolm was uninterested, never even cracking a smile. So now he was on to sports, a subject that disinterested him but added to a weak conversation, like talking about politics. "I think baseball is boring and golf is worse. What about you, what sports do you like? And don't tell me you like tennis. Tennis is the worst."

"What's that?" Malcolm asked, realizing the question was directed at him.

"Sports. What kind of sports do you like to watch?"

"I don't know. I really don't watch any sports. I did play baseball when I was younger," Malcolm said, thinking about the pickup games he'd played in the streets of his old neighborhood in his early teenage years. He was never a very good player, and was always picked last or completely left out if the teams had an even number of players. If he was left out he'd wait until someone quit and went home; or, after becoming bored with sitting and waiting, he'd go home himself—a home that did not feel like home, where the family he lived with was not his family.

"I hate baseball. I don't know why everyone seems to be wearing those baseball hats. Check this one out," Clayton said, pulling his Cabela's cap off, handing it out for Malcolm to get a close look. "Now this is a real hat, camouflaged."

"Yeah, that's a nice hat," Malcolm said, not wanting to touch the dirty thing. What he wanted was to find Kelsey.

"You like it? I got it free last week. Do you hunt?"

"No, never been hunting."

"Hey, we ought to go hunting together this year. I know some really good hunting spots."

Malcolm didn't want to answer one way or the other There was no way in hell he would ever go hunting with the guy. So, not to be rude and ignore Clayton, he changed the subject, but the only thing he could think of at the moment to say was to ask Clayton about the cat he'd run over earlier. In hindsight he wished he'd remained silent.

***

"So, do you think you killed that cat you ran over?" he asked.

"I don't know, maybe."

"Have you ever run one over before?"

"You still on that subject?" Clayton asked, sounding annoyed. He was still disappointed Malcolm hadn't laughed at his blonde jokes. What was he, some kind of queer? he thought. But just as the thought crossed his mind, he quickly decided Malcolm wasn't when he remembered he was waiting for a girl to show up.

"Just wondering. I was wondering what your perspective was on what happens to animals after they die. Like, do they go to Heaven?"

Clayton did not entertain the idea of answering the ridiculous question. He wanted to get drunk and pick up women, not talk about animals. Especially he didn't want to talk about religion, but part of the question angered him. Death was a subject he was well versed on since his job revolved around the dead. Clayton was not a religious person, and had a difficult time believing in Heaven and all the other crap that went with it. He figured if and when he was lying on his deathbed, he'd think about it then. Before answering with a generic no, he thought about giving the question a more descriptive reply. He suddenly remembered a dog he had run over once.

It wasn't his fault, actually. It was dark, nighttime, with no streetlights on the road he was driving along, and the dog was running alongside his owner's vehicle on the driver's side. Clayton didn't see the dog until it was too late because of the glare from the oncoming vehicle's headlights. When he got out to check on the dog, he saw the dog was still alive, though barely. He could tell by looking at the dog's eyes the animal was in a state of shock, and seeing the dog's guts spilled out in the middle of the road, still wiggling with heat, he knew the dog wasn't going to live much longer. A moment later the dog had stopped moving, its eyes frozen in time.

"I don't believe in that Heaven shit," Clayton said, shaking his head as though the subject tasted sour. "Have you ever seen a dead squirrel in the road, flat as a pancake? The squirrel gets run over, blood and guts splatter all over the road. Then another car runs it over, then another. After a couple of days of being run over and laying in the hot sun, the thing is flat as a pancake.

Now, let me ask you, do you think some bubble of energy rises out of that flat pancake in the middle of the road and magically floats to Heaven? I don't think so. Hey, by the way, where is that girlfriend of yours, anyway?"

"She's not my girlfriend, I only just met her today. She told me she was coming here tonight and invited me to meet her. But who knows, maybe something else came up. Maybe because of the weather she changed her mind. I don't know, and it really doesn't matter because I'm not staying here much longer. We've gotta work in the morning, anyhow."

"So do I, I've got to work too. It's still early, my friend, so drink up. She'll be here, so don't worry about it. What about those girls over there? Is one of them her?" Clayton asked, pointing toward two women strolling past the grinning bouncer, who was checking out their butts, something Clayton was all too familiar with as it was his favorite activity. "Stretching the eyeballs," he'd say to anyone in hearing distance. But most paid him no mind, and either turned their backs toward him or moved on to a more desiring location.

"Not her," Malcolm said, knowing immediately neither of them was Kelsey.

"What color hair does she have? Personally, I like blondes myself. I think a girl looks prettier with blonde hair. I don't care if their hair is bleached or natural, as long as it's blonde. I don't even care if their bush is black, but I'd rather it was shaved. What about you? You like shaved pussies or what?"

Malcolm had no comment.

"So what about it, what color hair does she have?"

Malcolm was about to say he didn't remember the color, which he did but didn't care to tell Clayton, when he felt someone standing a little too close to him, almost rubbing his side. Thinking the person was only someone squeezing in to order a drink, Malcolm moved over a bit to let the person squeeze in without turning to see who it was. The counter was overcrowded, and the only way to get a drink order was to squeeze in between someone, making a space, and a wave of the hand for the bartender to notice.

"Hi, remember me?" the person pleasantly asked in a voice that was definitely female.

Malcolm turned to see Kelsey smiling at him. It was like she'd materialized out of thin air, just popped up next to him. She was standing so close he could smell her perfume, an irresistible scent he wanted to inhale deeply. She looked prettier tonight than in the bank, a sexy enticing glow emitting from her green eyes. He fumbled nervously on what to say, and could only muster a "Hi" in response.

"I was watching you from over there," Kelsey said, pointing over at a table where her girlfriend, Pamela, sat smiling at them. The smile had a hint of mischief, like the recipient was in for an unforgettable night, a look that would thrill any young man looking for a night of excitement. When Malcolm acknowledged her by smiling back, he suddenly realized she was the girl attempting to fix her hair when they entered the tavern, and the other girl wearing the Red Sox cap was Kelsey. Only now the baseball cap was no longer on her head. "I was hoping you'd notice me and come over. But sadly, you didn't, so I had to make the first move."

"Oh, sorry, I apologize for that. I was looking for you, really, I was, but I never saw you come in. How long have you been here?" Malcolm answered, not wanting to tell her he didn't recognize her when she arrived.

"Not long. We've only been here for about ten minutes. I

noticed you right off. You guys were talking so I didn't want to interrupt, but I couldn't wait any longer," she told him, and then in a whisper that tickled his ear, she added, "I want you to come over and join us. Just you though."

From behind his back, Malcolm could hear Clayton making grunting noises in an attempt to be noticed. Malcolm paid him no attention, wanting him to go away, but knew that wasn't going to happen. Not the way his luck was going. Ever since the day he was born, when his mother gave him up for adoption, he'd had bad luck. If his life were going in the same sad direction, Clayton would surely be the person to ruin his night, ruin his only chance to make a good first impression.

"Hey buddy, you going to introduce me to your friend?" Clayton said, tapping Malcolm on his shoulder.

Not wanting to introduce them, but also not wanting to be rude and have Clayton do something stupid, Malcolm knew he had no choice but to introduce his obnoxious coworker to Kelsey. Make it a quick introduction, then go off alone with her before Clayton started telling her his stupid blonde jokes, or asking her if she was a natural blonde while staring at her crotch.

The problem he was facing, though, was that he wasn't good at making introductions. Especially when introducing someone he hardly knew, and disliked, to a girl he also hardly knew. Whenever he did make introductions, which was almost never, he'd get nervous, not wanting to offend the person by not using their proper name. Tonight, he wondered if he should introduce his coworker as Clay or Clayton.

***

Unbeknownst to him, even Clayton's parents had a hard time with his name. Clayton was born with only a last name. His mother wanted to name him after her father, Edgar. Clayton's father wanted to name him after his own father. Two days later, after a one-sided argument, his father won the battle. Their two-day old baby boy was now Clayton Edgar Daniels. His mother, however, refused to call her only child Clayton, or even Clay, and addressed him as Edgar. His father called him Clay, except when his son needed scolding, which was often. On those occasions he called him Clayton.

"Oh, this is Clayton, we work together."

"Hi, Clayton," Kelsey said, looking away slightly, not wanting to make eye contact with someone she despised.

"Call me Clay, all my friends do. My father, when he was still alive, called me Clayton, and I hated it."

"Well, Clay it is," Kelsey said without a hint of earnest.

"The pleasure is all mine. I've seen you in here before, but never had the opportunity to introduce myself," he fibbed, knowing full well both of them knew each other, though not personally. "It's nice to finally meet a beautiful young girl in this dive. I also have to say, your eyes are remarkably beautiful. You're the sexiest girl in here."

He meant every word, thinking dirty thoughts as he complimented her looks. He instantly pictured her nude, with perky breasts and succulent, firm brown nipples like his older sister had, before they drooped, when he peeked in her bedroom as a teenager. He then reached over to shake her slender hand, the hand that rested on Malcolm's arm.

***

Kelsey hesitated at first, wanting to keep her hand planted where it was, but then reluctantly lifted it and lightly shook his hand. His grip was tight, and she could feel the roughness of his labored hands. Before she could pull free of his grasp he placed his other hand over hers and smiled. His teeth were uneven and stained a yellowish-brown. His breath, however, was more disgusting, as a repulsive odor of tobacco and beer began to drift her way just as she was able to pull free.

"Is that your girlfriend over there?" Clayton asked, knowing she was, seeing both of them were regulars and always together.

"Yes, she's waiting for her boyfriend. He should be here at any minute," Kelsey wisely said, even though she knew Burger would not be arriving for at least an hour. She told the lie so he'd get the hint that he was not invited to join them at the table. She did want Malcolm to come over, as she had whispered to him, but there was no room at the table for the man she highly detested. Clayton would not be invited to join them, not ever.

"Malcolm, why don't you come with me and meet my girlfriend, Pam? She's dying to meet you," she said, grabbing Malcolm by his arm with a light tug.

***

Clayton knew exactly what she was doing. She was ditching him, just like the other times when he'd attempted to strike up a conversation with her.

Angrily, Clayton watched as Malcolm followed Kelsey over to the table. He felt snubbed, like he was dirt, and didn't like it one bit. In an effort to calm his anger, he looked around to see if he could find someone he knew to talk with, but it seemed, like always, most of the people in the tavern were much younger than him. There was no one he recognized close to his age of forty. There were some he noticed who were his age, but not acquaintances he could just walk up to and start a conversation with.

Guzzling the rest of his beer and then wiping the dribble off his chin with his coat sleeve, Clayton waved to the bartender and ordered another draft beer. Like all Friday nights, as the night wore on, he knew his chances of scoring grew higher because the women would be intoxicated. But in all reality the percentage of him scoring was still historically low. There was no one less likely to score than Clayton Edgar Daniels.

***

The table where Pamela sat was small, with four chairs pushed in a tight circle. Pamela sat facing the stage, where the band was wrapping up their first set. Her eyes, however, were glued toward the bar, watching Kelsey flirt with her new friend. Kelsey was performing expertly — a fast learner, Pamela thought.

At the table, Malcolm was introduced to Pamela and sat with his back to the bar, still feeling Clayton's eyes staring at him. He'd had that sixth sense of being watched embedded in his brain ever since his stay at the mental facility. There was always someone watching him besides the staff. The creeps he watched out for mostly were borderline geniuses. The ones who really belonged in a prison for the crimes they'd committed, like ripping someone's face off with their teeth, but were not sane enough to be sent to prison. They were the scariest of all.

Pamela immediately quizzed him on his background. She seemed to want to know everything about him, and was more thorough with her questions than the interview Malcolm had with David Graham at the town's garage.

Like his interview with David, his responses were brief. When asked about his job he couldn't give much detail, having only worked one day. When asked where he'd lived before coming to Redmond he only told them Portland, not wanting to mention his incarceration in the state mental facility. The one question he answered thoroughly when Pamela asked what he'd like to do with his life — something Pamela herself had no idea about for her own future — was his ambition of being a writer. He

111

sounded sincere, telling them he wanted to write ghost stories, and working in the cemetery could give him some inspiration.

Hearing this Pamela quickly became uninterested, thinking he was living a pipe dream, and turned her attention to Kelsey. Malcolm sat quietly and listened to Pamela and Kelsey talk about the good old times they'd shared. They talked about the exciting nights going out drinking and the different guys they'd dated. Their conversation didn't interest him much, mostly the parts about the guys they dated, but he enjoyed listening, and enjoyed just being at the same table with the two of them.

Suddenly their conversation took a change of direction and centered on the weird psycho they'd heard on the radio. Pamela was the one to bring it up, saying Clayton almost fit their perceived description of Mister Zero. They had both figured Mister Zero was most likely to be big and ugly with a few missing teeth. Kelsey, however, disagreed about Clayton resembling Mister Zero, saying he wasn't big enough and he didn't have the low raspy voice. Her interpretation of Mister Zero was that the guy was most likely heavy and bald.

"That may be true, but he might have disguised his voice on the radio. And from where I'm sitting, that guy standing over there at the bar is one ugly fucker. Oh, sorry Malcolm, I forgot he's your friend," Pamela giggled.

"No, I just happen to work with the guy. I just met him today."

"Have you ever listened to that radio program, the Doctor Nancy Show? It's on every night at nine o'clock, Monday through Friday," Kelsey asked Malcolm.

Malcolm hesitated, not wanting to say he did. He didn't want her to think he liked listening to other people's depressions, which helped him cope with his own.

"No, I only listen to music on the radio," Malcolm lied, but immediately felt guilty that he had, wishing he could take it back. He wondered if Kelsey could see his deception.

"What, am I the only one? Everyone I ask if they have listened to the program says no. I think it's pretty interesting. This guy that was on last night and also tonight said he goes around killing demons. Chops them up in tiny pieces. I think he said he eats them, but I'm not sure. What scares me the most, though, is how he said the demons are teenage girls with blonde hair and green eyes. That scares me. He could be a customer I've waited on at the bank. He could be in here now, right here in this tavern."

"Why do you think that?" Malcolm asked. "He could be calling from anywhere. Isn't this a syndicated program, broadcast all over the country? I mean, the guy could be living in California, nowhere near here."

"How do you know it's syndicated? I thought you said you never heard of the program."

"Oh, I'm not sure—I could be wrong. I was just thinking that most of those types of programs are syndicated."

"Well anyway, he said he lived on the coast, near Redmond. Honest, that's what he said, and my house is right on the coast. You can hear the waves crashing on the rocks at night on high tide. It's pretty scary when you're all by yourself and there's a storm out there. My roommate is out of town for the weekend."

Before Malcolm could formulate a decent question to ask if her roommate was male or female without being too obvious, Pamela interrupted his thoughts.

***

"And here he comes. I was wondering how long it would take him to find his way over here," Pamela said, watching Clayton as he made his way over toward them.

When the band took a break, Pamela had angled her chair to face the bar. She had the best seat for viewing, facing him, with her back to the wall. It was her favorite spot to sit. She could see everything from there. She could see the bar area and the entrance, where the bouncer sat high in the stool looking bored. She could see anyone approaching from every angle. She even had a great view of the stage.

Kelsey glanced over her shoulder and saw the man moving toward them. She braced herself, hoping he wouldn't stop and would continue on to bother another table. But her hope instantly faded when he stood tall next to her, close enough her shoulder touched his hip.

Not wanting to sit before being invited, Clayton stood drooling over the vacant chair. He had been eyeing the chair for a long while, wondering if he had been made a fool of when Kelsey told him Pamela was waiting for her boyfriend to arrive.

"Hi," Clayton said, looking directly down at Pamela. "My name Clay. I'm a good friend of Malcolm; we work together. I happened to notice everyone laughing over here, having a good time, so I thought I'd come by and join in on the fun. Is anyone sitting here?" he politely asked when no one offered him a seat.

Kelsey spoke up first, saying the seat was taken. "We're saving it for Burger, Pam's boyfriend. He's a very jealous person, and he should be here any minute now. I don't think he'd like it very much if he saw some guy trying to muscle in on Pam. Maybe you heard of him, Matt Burger. He was the captain of his football team in high school. Oh," she added, intending to humiliate him, "after your time, I suppose."

Not getting the insult, Clayton shook his head. He had never heard the name mentioned before. Sports, especially athletes, were the furthest thing from his mind.

114

On cue Pamela jumped in. "He just called me," she said, holding her cell phone up as proof.

***

Clayton didn't know whether to believe her or not, but not to embarrass himself any further, knowing he wasn't going to be invited to join them no matter if the boyfriend showed up or not, he made his way back to the bar with his tail stuck up his ass. Needless to say Clayton was humiliated, and he didn't like it one bit. Before he walked off, however, he gave Malcolm a bit of advice that he'd better not stay out too late because he was going to work his ass off in the morning.

***

Malcolm only nodded his response, but wanted to tell him he wasn't the boss so take a hike. It was embarrassing enough just being associated with the guy.

When he was out of hearing range Pamela whispered. "You're right, his teeth are disgusting. I wonder if he ever had a dental cleaning or brushed his teeth? Can you image anyone making out with that guy? How gross can that be?"

They all laughed at the remark. Even Malcolm, who was now starting to feel comfortable around his new friends, joined in on the roasting. It was the first time in a long while that he had a long conversation with someone of the opposite sex, though he spoke few words.

"Do you still think he could be Mister Zero?" Kelsey seriously asked.

"No, but do you know what's funny?" Pamela said, directing her question at Malcolm. "When Kelsey first met you at the bank, she thought you could be Mister Zero."

"No, I didn't," Kelsey interjected, feeling a little embarrassed. She covered her face with the Red Sox cap that was on the table, not wanting Malcolm to see her blush.

"Yes, you did. Stop hiding behind that hat. You said he could be because his voice sounded like the man on the radio."

"I didn't say that."

"Yes, you did. You said Malcolm had a low, gruff sounding voice."

"Well, I was only kidding," she said, removing her cap, and then continued to try and explain it to Malcolm. "The man's voice I heard on the radio was real raspy. Your voice is not even close to his. I like the sound of your voice. It's very pleasant."

"Oh good, Matt's here. He's earlier than usual tonight. I wonder what the special occasion is—or did he get shut off at the Holy Mackerel?" Pamela interrupted before Malcolm could respond.

Malcolm was going to tell Kelsey his voice may have sounded raspy because he was nervous, or something on that line, but he didn't get the chance. He then turned around and noticed a tall, beefy black man standing near the entrance, looking the place over like a cop searching for a person of interest. He seemed very intimidating to Malcolm. Trying not to stare, Malcolm turned his attention elsewhere, anywhere but at the man making a beeline for their table.

CHAPTER 14

When Matt Burger spied his target he moved directly toward them, towering over everyone standing in his way. Matt Burger was definitely an imposing figure and he enjoyed it, being somewhat of a bully at times.

As soon as Matt sat down in the vacant chair across from Malcolm he looked directly into the unknown man's face, and then abruptly turned and asked Pamela who he was. He seemed pissed that another man, one he didn't know and had never seen before, was sitting at the same table as his girlfriend.

"Oh, this is Malcolm, Kelsey's friend she met at the bank today," Pamela quickly replied, putting Burger at ease. To Malcolm she added, "And this is my boyfriend, Mathew Burger."

Burger nodded and gave a slight hand wave that he was fine with it. There was no need to shake hands, figuring the guy across the table from him hadn't earned the honor of his friendship, and wouldn't be around long enough to have that privilege. From what he knew of Kelsey, the guys she dated didn't hang around long.

"How long have you been here?" Burger asked his girlfriend with skepticism. He was extremely jealous, and didn't like his girlfriend being in the company of guys when he wasn't around.

"Oh, not long. I guess we've been here for about thirty minutes or so."

"Hi, Burger," Kelsey said, smiling. She liked calling him by his last name, as most of his close friends often did. Burger didn't mind; in fact, he preferred to be called Burger, just not by his girlfriend.

"Hey, Kelsey. You girls look pretty wasted. How many drinks have you girls already had?"

"Just one, but we're ready for another," Pamela answered, holding up her empty drink glass, indicating she was ready for another drink.

"Only one? Ha, who do you think you're fooling?"

"Well, we've only had one here."

"That's what I thought. What are you girls drinking? Margaritas I suppose? I'll splurge, you girls sit tight," Burger said, rising from the table.

"Of course we're drinking margaritas. What else would we be drinking?" Pamela cheerfully replied.

"How about you, what are you drinking?" Burger asked Malcolm, offering to buy his as well.

Money was never an issue with Burger. He owned his own landscaping company, mostly taking care of homeowners' yard work in the spring and summer seasons, snow plowing and roof shoveling in the winter. This time of year he had plenty of work, and he'd have plenty more with the amount of damage the storm outside was creating.

***

Malcolm hesitated at first, wondering if he should accept

118

the offer of a beer. He wondered if he did accept, would he be expected to buy the next round? Was that the protocol when someone bought a round for the table? He did have enough money to buy a round for the table, but that was all he had, and he wanted to save it for more important things, like paying the rent that was overdue and buying food so he wouldn't starve to death. For now he was living mostly off the food he received at the local food pantry, and a lot of those items were perishable, like bread and produce, items that spoiled before he had a chance to eat them. He had no problem with buying Kelsey a drink, as that was his plan, but he'd never figured on buying everyone else's drinks as well. Then again, he didn't want to be rude. Refusing the offer would put him in the category of being unfriendly and send him packing, exiled back to the bar to stand next to Clayton.

"I guess I could have one more. Light beer is fine for me. Thanks, Matt," Malcolm answered after a brief pause.

"Not a problem, I'll be right back," Burger said, then made his way over to the bar, squeezing into the only available spot, which just happened to be right next to Clayton.

***

Clayton had been watching the table with discontent. He was hoping there was no boyfriend coming, which would give him another reason to venture over. Maybe, he thought, after a few more drinks the brunette sitting across from Malcolm would change her feelings toward him. Maybe see him in a different light. Maybe even ask him to give her a ride home. He'd rather give the blonde, Malcolm's woman, a ride home, but that would have to wait until another time. For months, since he'd first noticed Kelsey at the tavern, he had been attempting to score with her, intentionally bumping into her when she made her way to the lady's room or the bar to buy a drink. Trying to strike up

119

a conversation, Clayton would politely excuse himself, and then offer to buy her a drink. Kelsey would always refuse the offer. There was no hesitation in her response, but to Clayton it was a friendly refusal, giving him cause to feel she was beginning to come around. That was before Malcolm arrived on the scene.

Now, seeing Burger sitting at the table where he had hoped to be sitting, Clayton knew his hopes of scoring with the sexy brunette were also dashed. A voice in his head was angry, telling him to take revenge. On who the voice did not say. Clayton figured it was the beer talking, as it always did when he was drinking a little too much.

Burger leaned into the counter, slightly nudging Clayton for a little more elbow room, which he reluctantly conceded. Clayton wasn't about to start something he couldn't finish, like a fight. Picking a fight with someone as muscular as Burger would be suicidal.

***

Back at the table, with nothing to hold in his hand but an empty beer bottle, and nothing to contribute to the conversation the two girls were having, Malcolm began feeling like he was an outsider. Ever since Burger had arrived he'd been trying to think of something to say, to add to their conversation, and not just sit there looking stupid, but nothing came to mind that wouldn't sound like he was interrupting. What made it worse, trying to come up with anything to say, Burger made him nervous. The man was intimidating, more with his being a black man than his large stature.

When Malcolm's beer was brought over he thanked Burger again, who had made two trips to the bar, bringing the ladies' drinks first. Those were the last words Malcolm spoke to him other than saying goodnight when he left to go home. So he just despondently sat there sipping his beer and listened, all the while thinking he should have stayed home, rested up for work the next day, and saved his money.

***

Burger hadn't spoken much either, seeming to be preoccupied with looking around the tavern and not paying much attention to his girlfriend. He was eyeing every woman who walked by the table, checking out her physique. There was one table he focused on the most, where two young female blondes were watching several people dancing in front of the stage, while the band played a crowd favorite country tune. Burger wondered why no one was asking them to dance. Surely they seemed interested, moving in their chairs to the beat of the song. Burger would have asked if Pamela hadn't been sitting next to him.

***

Seeing his inattentiveness, Malcolm perceived Burger's interest in his relationship with Pamela was deteriorating. To him it looked like Burger was scouting for a new plaything for future consideration. If he was in a romantic position with Kelsey, as Burger was with Pamela, he knew he would never treat her like that. He would never set his eyes on another woman.

When the band took a break between sets, Malcolm began feeling uncomfortably nervous. Anxiety was also setting in, taking control of his body like when he was standing in court facing the judge, waiting to hear his sentence. It became worse with every passing second. He had a decision to make, and needed to decide soon. He still had half a bottle of beer left, but Kelsey and Pamela's margarita glasses were nearly empty, and so was Burger's beer. Malcolm was either going to have to buy a round of drinks for the table, or excuse himself and say he was heading home because it was getting late and he had to work in

121

the morning.

He decided on the latter—he was going to excuse himself. One reason was he felt he wasn't making any headway with Kelsey, and staying longer, he imagined, wouldn't change things. Plus, he convinced himself he was bored sitting there.

Since Burger had arrived, even though Burger didn't add much to the conversation the girls were having, Malcolm had started to feel like he was being ignored. He could see no reason to hang around and spend what little money he had left. The right thing for him to do would be to say goodnight and head home.

But something was nagging at him, telling him to stay. It was Kelsey's body. She was sitting close enough for him to smell her enticing aroma. That, and something else was telling him not to leave without Kelsey, not to leave her unattached and available to the young wolves that were there for one purpose only, which was to pick up women. Surely she must know several guys her age in the tavern since the place was her regular hangout, and probably had her eye on one or two she knew from previous nights at the tavern.

His anxiety was getting worse, like a claustrophobic stuck in a broken elevator.

Taking a glance at the clock and seeing the time was getting late, Malcolm decided it would be best for him to leave and not overstay his welcome. After all, he was new to the tavern and also new to Kelsey. To leave on a good note, he'd tell Kelsey he had a wonderful time and ask her if they could do it again. Ask her out for a date, and hopefully she'd say yes. However, he didn't feel comfortable asking her at the table in front of her friends, and hoped for the opportunity to be alone with her. That most likely wasn't going to happen soon, so it was going to have to be at the table with her friends listening or not at all.

Just before he spoke, Kelsey, who had been mulling over the same decision, mentioned having to work in the morning and that she was heading home. To Malcolm's surprise, knowing he was on foot and he'd be drenched if he walked home, she offered him a ride, which he gladly accepted without hesitation. He hadn't expected to be offered a ride, and never would have thought to ask. Suddenly he felt a little luck was on his side — the tides were turning in his favor. The ride, he knew, would give him a good chance to ask her out on a real date without anyone else within hearing distance. There was also the possibility of a goodnight kiss. His anxiety disappeared. He now felt excited, and also a bit nervous.

As they got up to leave, Kelsey said goodnight to Pamela, telling her she'd see her at the bank in the morning. She then flashed a smile in Burger's direction, her way of saying goodnight without words, and then grabbed Malcolm's arm and walked away toward the exit. Burger had his eyes on her the whole way out the door, but he wasn't the only one watching.

***

Clayton Daniels was also staring with envy. On their way toward the exit they walked by Clayton. Malcolm nonchalantly said he'd see him in the morning, wanting to leave on a friendly note. Kelsey could not look in his direction, staring toward the exit door. Clayton returned a two-finger wave and watched as the young couple walked out the door together. Despite the amount of beer Clayton had downed, his eyes did not blink once — they never wavered. A moment later he downed his beer, slamming the empty glass mug on the bar with a thud. He then gathered his composure and followed them out into the stormy night.

CHAPTER 15

David Graham awoke early to the sound of rain. The raindrops he was hearing were heavy, pounding hard against the aluminum siding of his modest bungalow. He looked at the clock radio on the nightstand and noticed the time was ten minutes till five, forty minutes before the alarm would go off. It would be useless for him to try going back to sleep, so he grumpily slid out of bed.

Trying not to wake his wife of forty-two years, he carefully yanked the window shade halfway up to survey the damage from the night's storm. He was hoping to see the sun rising in a light blue sky, but his hopes were instantly dashed, as all he could see out the window was rain. To make matters worse, he noticed the end of his crushed-stone driveway, where a sixteen-inch culvert ran beneath, was sitting under a good two feet of muddy water. From the amount of water he was staring at he knew this was not a good sign. If his culvert was flooded, which rarely happened—less often than a blue moon—he was in for a long day at work. Plus, to add to his misery, being a salaried employee meant there would be no extra money in his paycheck.

His only reward for his hard work would be the satisfaction of a job well done, and even then there'd be the critics complaining about the slow progress in the cleanup.

Before he pulled the shade back down he heard his wife stirring in the bed, wiggling her body up against the headboard. Her gray hair, long and stringy, covered most of her face.

***

"How does it look out there?" Margaret asked, brushing her hair aside in an effort to see out the window. Unfortunately, her husband blocked her view. All she could see were the streaks of gray dim light sneaking around her husband's large frame.

"Not good, not good at all," he replied, then pulled the shade closed, darkening the room. "I'm sorry I woke you up. It's still early, go back to sleep."

"Too late for that, I'm awake now. I'll get up and start the coffee and make your breakfast. By the sound of the rain out there, you're going to need it."

"Suit yourself, but I need to head out soon. I told the guys to be in by seven. I need to be there at least an hour earlier to get things ready."

Sitting at the kitchen table, David quietly sat drinking his third cup of coffee while Margaret cleared the table, setting his plate and utensils in the sink. She'd wait till later, after eating her own breakfast, to wash the dishes. She had her daily routine, mostly revolving around weekly morning TV game shows and the afternoon soap operas she had been diligently watching for years.

"I should have known this weather was coming and would ruin the weekend. It's been awhile since the last time we had this amount of rain, so I suppose it was overdo. I just hope it doesn't last all day and night and I'll have to work again tomorrow."

"Sounds to me like you're complaining—I thought you loved working. Besides, you were going to have to work today anyway for the Webster funeral, so stop your bitching," Margaret said in an attempt to tease her husband, words that usually came from his mouth.

"Only a couple of hours. I was planning on going to the hardware store after to pick up some supplies I need. I guess I can't do that now. I'll have to wait until next weekend if I'm working tomorrow as well."

"What were you planning on buying at the hardware store?" Margaret asked, taking a seat across the table.

"Oh, nothing important, I guess. I was planning on getting a head start on the garden. It's almost that time."

"Well, with all this rain it looks like you're going to have to postpone that idea for another week anyway. But I have another idea."

"What's that; you go to the hardware store for me?" David laughed.

"No, retire. That way you'll have everyday to do what you want."

***

With that comment, David rose from the table and headed for the door, grabbing his hat and raincoat on the way out. They've had this conversation about his retiring many times before, and each time he told Margaret he wasn't ready to retire. Being only sixty-two, he felt he had another good five years left in him, maybe more if his health held on, which was a good probability since he still felt nowhere near his age.

His drive to work, which normally was a ten-minute ride, took him twice as long, having to detour around flooded streets and fallen tree branches. Streets he and his crew would be busy

126

with, unclogging the over-worked sewage drains and removing debris. He had seen these same streets flooded numerous times before, mostly during the late winter months—not as much in spring, like today. The last time they had a severe spring storm and flooding was five years ago, which occurred at the end of a long snowy winter and then unfortunately heavy rains hit the region. The rain he was seeing today was about the same as back then, except today it was still raining. He feared the worst was yet to come.

The latest weather report he saw on the local news channel while he was having his morning coffee called for the rain to continue for at least another day, which previously was only going to last one day. The reason for the changed forecast was that the previously fast moving storm was now going to stall off the coast. This was not good news, not what he wanted to hear. If this updated weather forecast was correct, it looked like he'd be working Sunday as well.

His normal route to the town garage led him past the town cemetery, where he spent most of his working hours. Unfortunately, the cemetery was built on a hill behind the church, where the land gradually sloped down toward the road. This was not good for the road when the weather was bad. David cringed when he noticed rainwater from the cemetery rushing over the road and into a drainage ditch that was already dangerously overflowing. From past experience he knew the ditch could not handle any more water. And since Route 4 was the main artery in and out of town, he also knew they'd have to tackle this problem first, as well as the downtown area, where the Abenaki River was already threatening to overflow its banks.

Finally arriving at work, he parked in his normal spot next to the town's three-bay maintenance garage. The first thing he did, like every morning, was to get the coffee machine going. He then sat on an uncomfortable wooden chair in the small office and booted up the computer. The official home page — which was not actually official, but David felt should be — showed an aerial view of Redmond, with the town's garage in the upper right corner, shown on the outskirts of town. The cemetery and church with its white steeple were not far away, more centered, like they were the town's crown jewels. The two other churches with impressive steeples were also shown, closer to the downtown area and nearer the coastline.

Since David Graham was in charge of the maintenance department, as well as the town's cemetery, one of his responsibilities was to organize the cleanup and repair any damages the storm caused. The first thing he did was gather the equipment his crew would need to repair the damage to the streets, and make a list of what streets were the most vulnerable to flooding.

His next task was to load what he could lift by himself onto the work truck. This task was something he could have done the previous day, in preparation for the coming storm, but if "history repeats itself," as the saying goes, he didn't want to drive off without the hydraulic pump, or some other valuable piece of equipment, and have to return to the garage to retrieve it. More than once one of the maintenance workers had used the pump for personal work without authorization. The employee always returned it the next day, but often forgot to replace it back on the truck. The man who had borrowed the pump both times was only reprimanded, and still worked there. There was no way David Graham was going to fire a good friend.

After taking a short break, drinking another cup of coffee that he didn't need as he was already wired from the three cups he had drank at home, David loaded up one of the two work trucks with the equipment and checked out the dump truck to make sure there was a full tank of gas and that the old thing started. He had urged the town to buy a new dump truck, but the request had fallen on deaf ears. It was the same non-response he received when he inquired about updating the sewage system, which was much older than the dump truck—most likely a hundred years older.

Once he completed all the necessary preparations, David anxiously sat in the quiet garage for the next thirty minutes looking out the window at the pouring rain, intermittently checking his watch. The last time he'd checked his watch it was seven-thirteen; he noticed it was now seven-twenty. He had arrived at the garage just after six, and finished his list of tasks in what seemed like record time. The time now, waiting for his crew to arrive, seemed unbearably long. There were sewage drains to unplug and other street repair work, along with setting up barricades for road closures. If they didn't get started on it soon, he knew he'd hear the complaints from someone on the town's council, and maybe even the mayor himself.

Seeing the torrential rain pouring down in sheets, he began to worry about how much damage was out there, and started to contradict his decision to have only one crew come in today. The earlier weather reports had called for the heavy rains to end by morning, so he'd only planned to have a work crew of five, including himself. This morning the updated weather reports called for all day rains. Now he was thinking he should have had two crews, mandatory for everyone. Since the town employed only seven maintenance workers, besides himself being the boss, he could have had a crew of four, and a smaller three-man crew with himself helping both crews, the most vital one first. That's what the top dog did, drive around making sure the work was done correctly.

The workers were scheduled to be at the garage by seven, but by seven-thirty only one had arrived, his longtime friend and coworker, Morrie Stover. Joe Hobart had called and said he'd be a few minutes late. Considering the weather and Hobart's commitment, David figured he'd arrive soon, so there was no concern for alarm, as he was a responsible employee. The other two, Clayton Daniels and Malcolm Dangil, however, had not called, and this concerned him, more the new guy than Clayton. Clayton wasn't very dependable on his off days, although he always showed up, arriving late and not in the greatest of shape to function normally.

***

When Joe Hobart arrived the three of them moped around the garage with their hands in their pockets, anxiously waiting to get started. Joe had driven to work by way of Main Street, and had seen the fast flowing river tearing away the steep embankment. It would only be a matter of time before the river crested over and onto Main Street, he told David. He'd also noticed the guardrail leading to the bridge spanning the Abenaki River was damaged, with a ten-foot section missing. Pausing briefly to check out the damage from the comfort of the truck, Joe had noticed the missing section was still there, partially intact on one end and only crumpled. Before driving off he made a mental note to mention it to David, figuring they might want to tackle that job first.

"How are we going to tackle this mess, Dave? It's a friggin mess out there. From what I could see the river's about to spill over at any minute," Joe said, hinting at the possibility the problem could become urgent.

"There's not much we can do about the river. I'm planning to clean up the drain down by the cemetery first. Route 4 needs to be cleared immediately, or the mayor will have my ass in a sling. Main Street is the next one we'll tackle."

"Shit, the mayor will complain no matter what. You can never satisfy the guy. If he had a business located on Main Street he'd want that street cleared first," Morrie chimed in.

"Hey, Dave, I almost forgot to mention. On my way over I noticed the guardrail leading to the downtown bridge was torn up. Looks like someone plowed right through it," Joe said, feeling proud for remembering without having written it down.

***

David thought for a moment about the guardrail, wondering what could have run into it. Most importantly, though, he wondered how bad the damage really was. Joe seemed to exaggerate more than most, but just to be on the safe side, he considered calling the sheriff's department to have them check it out, to see if a vehicle had gone through and possibly could have ended up in the river.

"How bad was the damage? You think someone could have gone through and ended up in the river?" David asked.

"I don't believe so. I did take a quick look out my side window, and didn't notice any indication a vehicle could have gone through. The guardrail was actually still intact on one end. I couldn't see the other end," Joe answered.

"Why didn't you get out and take a good look? You could have looked to see if there were any tire tracks."

"No, I didn't, but it wouldn't have done any good anyhow; if there were any tire tracks, they would have been washed away by the rain. The water is gushing down the embankment."

"Well, probably someone just ran into it last night, maybe

some drunk on his way home from a bar. I'll check it out later when we get down that way. No sense getting the sheriff's department involved — they probably have plenty to do themselves with all kinds of nuisance complaints. Although I might mention it to them later, just to be on the safe side."

"Sounds good to me, Dave. Like I said, from what it looked like to me I wouldn't worry too much about it."

"Jeepers crow, where the hell are those guys?" David rhetorically asked angrily.

"I'm surprised Clay's not here, Dave. He's never late, is he?" Morrie asked.

"Not unless he has to work on his off day, then he's always late. So I'm not surprised, especially being a Friday night. I'm sure he'll be here. I'm more worried about the new guy. He didn't look too enthused yesterday. I never should have hired the idiot. I probably should call Clay though…see what's keeping him. If they don't show I'm calling Mickey and Jay, see if they can come in." After a pause he added, "On second thought, I might call them anyway. I think we'll need them to come in, have two crews out there working this mess."

At about the same time David was going to make the call to the two workers who weren't scheduled to come in, Clayton Daniels stumbled in. He looked like an old dog limping home from a losing fight.

"Well, look who finally showed up. The one and only Mister Daniels finally arrives," David commented. He then glanced at his watch and added. "It's nearly eight o'clock — I told you to get here at seven sharp. What did you do, stay out all night? You look like shit. I hope you are in good enough shape to last a full day, because with this weather it looks like we'll be here all day."

"All day! I thought you said we're only working till lunch. I

132

made plans this afternoon."

"Well, it sucks being you. Besides, I don't remember saying any such thing, because I didn't know how bad the weather was going to be. Oh, by-the-way, where's the new guy — what's his name?"

Clayton raised his eyebrows, indicating he had no idea where he was. "When I last saw him at the Crow's Nest he said he'd be here."

"The Crow's Nest; you were there too? So, how late did you guys stay out?"

"Not too late. I left well before eleven," Clayton answered, which was not exactly correct. He had left the tavern drunk at eleven, right after Malcolm and Kelsey strolled out the door.

"What about Dangil? What time did he leave the bar?"

"I'm not sure, but I do know it was before me. I saw him leave with some girl. Who knows, he's probably still in bed with her; she looked the slutty type."

**

Clayton was picturing the young blonde sitting next to Malcolm. He'd had a good view of her all night while leaning against the bar, angrily staring at their table, seeing Dangil practically sitting on top of her. He thought of the way her slender hands delicately held her drink, and her girlish laugh, so young and tender, thinking how much fun it would be to spend the night with her. Ravage her body until both wore themselves to sleep. Then, in the morning, do it again. If she resisted, he'd have more enjoyment looking at her terrified eyes.

**

"Call him. You got his number?"

"No, he doesn't have a phone."

"Jeepers crow, I can't get any good help these days. What

are we doing, raising a bunch of lazy kids nowadays? Well, we can't stay here all day. You guys take the truck and head over to Route 4, where it intersects with Main Street, and close the road if necessary. And don't forget to place the road closure signs in front of the barriers, along with the detour signs. Traffic will have to be rerouted up Hill Road, around the back side of the cemetery. After that, head over to the cemetery and see what you can do about clearing up the drain on Route 4 — it's already overflowing. I'm going to call Mickey and Jay, see if they're available, then I'll meet you there after they arrive."

As David was walking to the office to use the phone, he happened to look out the window and noticed Clayton's truck was all smashed in on the passenger side, from the rear tire well to the headlight. The damage was measurable, and David wondered how he managed to drive it home from the bar in the first place, let alone to work.

"What the hell happened to your truck, Clay? Drive home drunk last night from the bar?" David angrily asked. He didn't condone drinking, especially from his crew.

"No, it was on the way. Someone's fucking cat ran out in front of me. I tried to swerve out of the way and hit a damn rock. Fucking cat — I should have run the critter over."

"You do know my wife loves cats. In fact, she has two, so don't go there blaming a cat for your stupidity." David grimaced. "If it were one of her cats you'd be in a heap of trouble, and not just from me."

"Nope, Dave, I'm sure it wasn't one of hers. I was nowhere near your house. It was downtown on Main Street."

David shook his head. Clayton was either still intoxicated from last night, or just too plain stupid to get what he was saying to him. He was then about to ask if the incident was near the bridge where the guardrail was damaged, but was interrupted when Joe Hobart yelled they were ready to roll.

CHAPTER 16

Elsie Hermann stood in front of her kitchen window despondently looking out toward the backyard at the nearly empty birdfeeder. She knew she'd have to fill it soon or the birds would find another birdfeeder in someone else's yard. Yes, some would eventually find their way back and new ones would arrive, but that wasn't her way of doing things. It was her responsibility to fill the birdfeeder, and she enjoyed doing this simple chore. Filling it made her feel needed, something to give her otherwise mundane life meaning besides caring for her two cats.

On any normal day she'd trot her small frame out her back door to fill the birdfeeder, but it was raining now and not so enjoyable filling it in such miserable weather. The birds would have to wait until later in the day when the rains subsided.

With a sigh she could picture her husband, Claude, tromping out there in his rubber boots to fill it, as he was never deterred by inclement weather. Her husband was gone now, having passed away from pancreatic cancer after fifty years of marriage. Since then, the long-life resident of Redmond had settled into a simple life with simple needs, mainly because her unlucky husband had gambled away most of their savings on horse races and lottery tickets, leaving her with barely enough savings in her bank account to live on. Besides the pitiful savings account, the only other income she received was the monthly retirement check, which, unfortunately for her, was the minimum amount one could receive since she, herself, had never entered the workforce.

Looking on the bright side, if there was such a thing after losing the only person she'd conversed with for nearly half a century and loved dearly despite his faults, the mortgage on her house was paid-off. The only expenses she had to endure now were her utility and food bills, plus the taxes on her moderate size ranch-style home, which were minuscule because the value of the deteriorating home was one of the lowest in the community. She had no phone or television, only a radio to keep her informed on the latest news.

Elsie had no grown children to look after her, so she was on her own. She had no regrets about not having children to share her life with, and had never really thought of having any. She told herself if it was meant to be it was meant to be; therefore only the two of them shared their lives together. Meaning her and Claude, and not counting the numerous cats they'd had running around the house over the years. She enjoyed taking care of cats, thinking of them as her children. She was down to two cats now, and often said, remembering the ones that had previously died, they would be the last. It was too painful, mentally and physically, having to bury the small cuddly critters.

With only the necessities, having no luxury items like a dishwasher or an expensive vacuum cleaner to suck up shedding cat hair and fur balls and such, Elsie was completely comfortable with her living conditions. Although the structure of the house was in rough shape, to say the least, with sagging porches and weathered clapboards and missing roof shingles, it was her home, and had been for over a half century.

The house was located at the end of a long gravel driveway that split two apartment buildings, and quietly nestled virtually invisible amongst a grove of pines and hardwoods, mainly maples and oaks, with a scattering of spiny alders. Among the variety of trees in her backyard stood four tall white birches. Ellie enjoyed looking out at the white birches, as they seemed to attract woodpeckers. Whenever she heard the sound of pecking wood she'd look out toward the white birches and see a woodpecker at work.

Behind the stand of trees twenty yards beyond her property line ran an overgrown railroad track. The track was also virtually invisible. Someone would have to be standing on the track to realize what it was. All it had taken was two decades of abandonment for it to be swallowed by nature.

Her few neighbors, the ones who lived in the two apartment houses, hardly knew anything about Elsie, and hadn't cared to know. They only saw her briefly when she strolled by on her way to town, pulling a two-wheeled cart. Other than that, Elsie was a ghost to them.

Elsie held no interest in knowing any of them either. She had her cats and birds and the voices on the radio to keep her company. And there was always, most days anyway, the noise of the mailman climbing the decaying front steps to look forward too.

In the comfort of her living room, Elsie sat on her recliner listening to the weather forecast. One of her two cats, the one she'd renamed Chubs because of the cat's weight, lay purring on Elsie's lap. Her other cat, a bony calico she called Lilly Bell, sat perched on a windowsill, probably wondering where the pretty birds had disappeared to. The weatherman on the radio was now predicting the heavy, wind-swept rains would worsen as the day wore on, and continue through the night and into the next day.

After the weather report, the local news station reported the funeral services for Callie Webster, the teenager who was brutally murdered, would be postponed until Monday, or possibly Tuesday morning. It was all according to the weather, the news broadcaster concluded.

When she'd first heard of the gruesome murder of Callie Webster, Elsie thought the newsman had made a mistake saying the victim was a local girl. She couldn't remember the last time someone was murdered in Redmond. The murder was closer to home than she'd realized, which she found out later when she overheard two women in the grocery store saying the victim had lived on a street not far from Elsie's, less than a mile away.

A couple of days later, Elsie was still thinking about the Webster girl and wondered if she was going to be buried in the same cemetery as her husband. It was only logical she would be — it was the only Catholic cemetery in Redmond, and just about everyone in town shared the same faith. She also began wondering if the person who committed the horrible crime was her neighbor, one Chester Briggs. He looked the type, in his dark staring eyes anyway — unblinking, like a cat trying to read its owner's thoughts.

***

Briggs was a nice enough man, trying to be friendly with Elsie, but to Elsie's way of thinking he was a little too nice, wanting to walk to town with her one day when the two happened to leave their respective residences at about the same time. She convinced herself to not let his use of a cane fool her into thinking he was a kind old man with hip issues. For all she knew about the man, the cane could have been only a prop to commit violence. Elsie told Chester Briggs he was being a little too forward, and told him to hobble along on his cane and leave her be. Besides, she was on a personal quest; no need to have some noisy neighbor slowing her down and butting into her business.

Elsie was on her way to the cemetery that day to pay her overdo respects to her late husband's grave. Her first stop was to buy a small bouquet of flowers on her way through town, and then make the trek up the hill to the cemetery. The round trip, she figured, was about four miles. A tough hike for someone her age, but she felt obligated — it had been some time since her last visit. It was a nice day for a walk, and she enjoyed the fresh spring air, but after visiting the depressing sight of the cemetery she decided it would be her last time. The next time would be the day she was laid to rest beside him, buried in the lower section of the cemetery near the old gnarly pine. The privileged deceased were buried higher, near the top of the sloping ground, with a better view of the ocean. Even in death the privileged were spoiled.

***

For the first time that she could remember Elsie started locking her doors, protecting her two precious defenseless cats. Later that same day she spotted movement in her backyard, in the woods at the edge of her property. The person lurking amongst the trees scared her at first, thinking he, and not Chester Briggs, was the murderer of Callie Webster — or, at the very least, a peeping Tom. She looked around the inside of her home for a place to hide, hoping to find a secured room. There were none; even the bathroom door had no locks. She then decided her only recourse was to confront the intruder. He was invading her privacy.

Gripping a four-foot long ice chipper she conveniently noticed in the back hallway on her way out to confront the intruder, Elsie plodded her way to the edge of her property, using the ice chipper for support as well as a deterrent. In the loudest voice she could muster, which was more like the shrieking sound of a blue jay, she yelled at the intruder.

To her relief, after a convincing explanation, she determined he was not a peeping Tom, and was most likely not the murderer of Callie Webster. The person in the woods turned out to be a young man living in one of the nearby apartment houses.

The young man was Malcolm Dangil, and she let him know he was venturing a little too close to her home for her comfort. She also let him know she was not happy to have someone trespassing on her property. Malcolm had tried to explain he was only exploring the woods, never having been in the woods before, as he had spent his whole life living in the city. Elsie was sympathetic with his interest, and told him he could stay as long as he did his exploring further down, on the other side of the tracks, and not to disturb her birds.

Other than her encounter with Malcolm Dangil and her final walk to the cemetery, every day of Elsie's life blended in with all the other days. Not one single day stood out from any other day. Her days moved by uneventfully, like the sun rising and setting. She smiled a little more on sunny days, and sighed a bit more when clouds occupied the sky, but other than that her days were simple. She was mostly content with staying at home, watching the songbirds pecking away in her birdfeeder and listening to her favorite radio station while waiting for the mail to arrive, which came infrequently and varying from week to week. The one constant day she could expect a delivery was Saturday, even though it was mostly fliers and other junk mail. The only times she ventured outside her home were to buy groceries at

Bud's Shop and Save twice a week, and the uneventful trip to the bank every Saturday morning to make a withdrawal and check on her savings account; plus the one day a month to deposit her retirement check, which she expected to receive the following Wednesday.

These simple treks to do her weekly errands never changed, leaving her home at about the same time regardless of the weather, the only exceptions being when the weather was too extreme to tempt faith. This morning was one of those exceptions. Even the songbirds that gathered every morning around her birdfeeder had exceptions. They had sensed the oncoming weather, feeding their feathered bellies earlier, and were now huddling in the safety of the trees. Elsie sensed the same urgency and had no intentions of hanging around to wait for the mailman like she usually did before heading off to the bank on Saturday, not after hearing the weather report on her radio calling for heavier rain.

"Looks like I'll have to venture out earlier than usual this morning, Chubs," Elsie said with a sigh, sweeping her frail, liver-spotted hand over the cat's soft black fur. "You be a good kitty while I'm gone, and leave Lilly Bell alone. Don't be a bully."

After snapping the clips on her forty year-old rubber galoshes, Elsie slid into her late-husband's knee-length raincoat and tugged her rain hat on as tight as she could. She then headed out for the bank in her usual slow stride. She looked like a miniature fisherman heading out to sea, expecting a day of foul weather.

CHAPTER 17

When the Redmond Savings bank opened at nine o'clock sharp, a long unexpected line of customers came trudging in through the door, with Elsie Hermann leading the way. The rain-drenched customers shook their wet hats upon entering, and waited in line again behind the same elderly woman, who kept her rain hat on. Elsie had no intention of removing her headgear only having to replace it again when she ventured back out into the rain.

***

At about the same time Elsie was waiting for the bank manager to unlock the door, Pamela Hays found herself standing alone behind the counter wondering where her friend and coworker, Kelsey Mickelson, could be. Normally, except for the occasional Saturday mornings prior to a Monday holiday, when there'd be three counters open, it would only be the two of them waiting on the customers.

Standing alone now, Pamela was having a dreadful feeling something was wrong. It was unusual for Kelsey to be late on a Saturday morning, her only day scheduled to be there before the bank opened for business. In fact, she was always early on Saturday morning, usually the first one to arrive, trying to impress her boss since she was still on her three-month probationary period.

While preparing her workstation, Pamela's mind went through all the different scenarios as to why Kelsey was not at work. The one scenario that kept popping up in her head was maybe Kelsey got lucky with her date last night and was finding it hard to pull herself away from him. It was a reasonable explanation, Pamela thought, but after considering it some more she knew Kelsey was not the type to spend the night with someone on a first date. To get Kelsey into bed with a guy he would have to show promise, someone with a promising future — a lot more than a guy working in a graveyard could offer. A more logical reason was maybe she was nursing a bad hangover. Pamela herself was feeling the effects of a late night of drinking, and had considered calling out of work herself. Burger had talked her out of making the call, saying her father wouldn't approve, and even drove her home early in the morning after a brief round of awkward sex, lasting less than five minutes.

Thinking that Kelsey was home alone still in bed and feeling the side effects of a late night of partying, Pamela started feeling a bit of relief. Then, as she stood alone watching the line of impatient customers entering the bank, the thoughts that Kelsey was home comfortably in bed quickly dissipated when she began thinking the worst again. Maybe there really was something wrong, because if Kelsey had called out sick the bank manager would have already found someone to replace her. The manager would also have told Pamela that Kelsey was not coming in, not ask her if she had heard from Kelsey, which she did ten minutes before the bank opened for business.

When her prep-work was completed, Pamela looked up and signaled the first customer in line. The customer was a petite elderly lady with a round black rain hat hovering just above her sharp dark eyes, which were the last hint of her younger years. With a slow stride the woman walked up to the counter and stretched her bankbook across the counter toward Pamela. She then deliberately waited to be asked her business. There was no need to rush into anything when money was involved.

It took Pamela a moment to recognize the frail-looking woman standing before her. She should have known right off, especially after having waited on her for almost a year now — the woman was Elsie Hermann. Even with the oversized raingear she should have known her immediately, seeing the heavy splash of rose-colored rouge and eyes too large for the shape of her narrow face.

Whenever Pamela waited on Elsie, which was less often now since Kelsey was the teller Elsie favored, Pamela was always very polite toward the woman. The heavy layer of rouge Elsie wore always reminded her of her own grandmother, who had passed away several years ago. Not that the resemblance was the reason for being polite to the woman, but it was one of the reasons. The main reason was her job required her to be polite to all the customers. Some customers were harder to please than others, and most days Elsie was not one of those. Today, however, weather was a main contributor to one's demeanor.

"How are you today, Mrs. Hermann?" Pamela asked with a forced smile.

Pamela was feeling a bit under the weather, and had too much on her mind to be her usual self. Her stomach felt nauseous, like whatever was fermenting down there wanted to come up her throat and out her mouth and land on the counter and all over

145

Elsie. She should have eaten breakfast, she thought, or drank a glass of milk. At least the milk would have coated her angry stomach. But even if she had eaten breakfast she still wouldn't have been her normal, happy self; Kelsey wasn't there.

"Fine, considering the horrible weather we are having. It's raining cats and dogs out there. If I had known it was going to be this bad I would have stayed home, but I needed some money to purchase some items at the grocery store. Not many, mind you, as I don't have my cart with me today. I can only carry so much. But you never know how long this weather will last. I've seen it rain for over a week more than once. Flooding this very building, almost up to the ceiling," Elsie commented, raising her arm as high as she could over her head to illustrate how bad that storm had been.

"Really? I hope this storm doesn't last a week. What can I do for you today?"

"You can take twenty dollars out from my account. I need it to buy a few groceries. I'll be back next Tuesday if I need more," she told Pamela. Then, after remembering her monthly check was scheduled to arrive next week, mumbled more to herself than to Pamela, "probably Wednesday." She then paused to recall the date, now thinking her monthly check was coming the week after. Lately she had been starting to forget things, which didn't worry her much, passing her forgetfulness off as having a senior moment.

***

Keying in Elsie Hermann's account number in the computer, Pamela pulled up Elsie's savings account. After filling out a withdrawal slip for the woman, she then entered the twenty-dollar withdrawal amount without looking at the account balance, knowing the woman's balance always remained about the same, give or take a few hundred between pay periods. Pamela then printed out the receipt and handed it to Elsie, along with the twenty-dollar bill and her bankbook.

"How much money do I have in my account?" Elsie nonchalantly asked as she tucked the twenty and bankbook in her money purse, leaving the receipt on the counter. She then placed the purse in a pocket of her raincoat.

"Oh, it's right there printed on the receipt I gave you. Right below the withdrawal amount," Pamela kindly answered.

Having left her reading glasses at home, Elsie squinted her eyes tight trying to read the receipt. In better light she might have succeeded, but not with the bank's artificial lighting; all she could see was blurry lines.

Pamela noticed she wasn't having any luck and placed her index finger where the total amount of her savings was printed. "Here, Mrs. Hermann, I'll show you. It's right here."

"How much does it say?"

"$1,245.79, just around your average amount," Pamela answered.

Elsie grabbed the receipt back and squinted at the blurry numbers again. "I thought it should be higher. How much is the interest rate these days, anyhow?"

"Not very high, I'm afraid. It's just below one percent."

"Below one percent! I use to get five percent not long ago."

It was evident Pamela's main thoughts were still on Kelsey's whereabouts, as she seemed to be looking beyond Elsie at the main entryway. Someone about the same size as Kelsey had just walked in, closing an umbrella. To Pamela's disappointment it wasn't Kelsey. Then again, why would it be? Kelsey didn't own an umbrella.

"Why am I only getting one-percent interest?" Elsie repeated.

"I'm sorry. What were you saying?"

"My interest rate, for Heaven's sake. Why am I only getting one-percent interest?"

Pamela tried unsuccessfully to explain to Elsie the interest rates had not been that high for years. The petite woman, wearing a raincoat much too big for her size, was not accepting that answer and threatened to close her account, saying she'd had her savings account for over seventy years, well before the young lady was born, and there was another bank right down the street she could do business with.

"I'm sorry. Mrs. Hermann. I'm sure the interest rates at the other banks are the same," Pamela consoled.

***

"Where's the other young lady, the nice one who always waits on me?" Elsie asked, looking around for the other teller, the polite shy young woman who was always smiling like a bright spring morning even on gray rainy days, like the one they were experiencing now.

***

The word "wait" struck Pamela ironically seeing the line of customers impatiently waiting their turn. She wondered why people always seemed to flock to the bank when the weather was bad on a Saturday. She could understand them flocking to the grocery store, but why the bank?

Forgetting how busy they had been the last time the weather was bad, when Pamela arrived at the bank that morning she figured it would be another slow day, like the previous day. If it were to be slow, Kelsey would have had time to fill Pamela in on what happened after she left the Crow's Nest Tavern with Malcolm. The morning, however, was turning out completely the opposite of what she'd expected, and it was definitely for the

148

worse.

The line behind Elsie was getting longer, zigzagging beyond the roped barrier toward the main entrance. Knowing the other bank employees were also too busy with customers to offer any assistance, Pamela hoped the bank manager had enough common sense to call in another teller, which she had. But unfortunately for Pamela, the extra help wouldn't be there for at least another half-hour. Till then she was on her own.

"Running a little late, I'm afraid," Pamela sighed. "Is there anything else I can do for you, Mrs. Hermann?"

"No, you've done all you can, I suppose," Elsie nodded.

After Elsie left with a huff, Pamela knew it was going to be a long frustrating morning, and she was right. When the bank finally closed at noon she drove by Kelsey's rented home, avoiding the worst roads due to road closures. As she slowed by the house, to her disappointment, she noticed Kelsey's vehicle was not there. A call to Kelsey's cell phone also went unanswered.

Still trying not to worry, she assumed Kelsey most likely ended up spending the night with Malcolm at his place and was still there, having too much of a good time to have the courtesy to answer her cell phone. Maybe her extraverted lifestyle was finally corrupting Kelsey, and she'd changed her mind about saving herself for the right guy. If this was so, and she was there at Malcolm's place, Pamela had no idea where he lived. Therefore, the only thing she could do was drive home and make a batch of well-needed margaritas.

There, in the comfort of her living room, Pamela sat all afternoon on her couch, getting intoxicated. Her television was on, but there was nothing that interested her. She scrolled through the channels, eventually stopping on the Home Shopping Network.

Occasionally, between trips to refill her glass, she called

Kelsey's cell phone, and also the phone at her rented house, hoping she'd answer and tell her what was going on. But her calls went unanswered. A couple of batches of margaritas later Pamela started worrying more about her cat not coming home than Kelsey not contacting her. She couldn't remember the last time she'd seen Theodore. The margaritas didn't help her memory either.

Most of the time she didn't show her affection for Theodore, but she loved her cat. Theodore was her first pet, and after living together for a while their fondness for each other had grown. She'd adopted him from an animal shelter after hearing on the news that the shelter had more cats than they could handle. Theodore was the last one left.

The two hadn't hit it off right at the beginning. It took Theodore a couple of days to get used to his new home, coming out of hiding from under the bed. He then started his routine of eating and sleeping and exploring, with the latter lasting no more than a few days, being a one-bedroom apartment. His exploring was replaced with viewing the outside world through the window, watching anything that happened by with curiosity, and wishing to be outdoors with them.

As darkness began to set in, Pamela fell asleep on her couch. When she awoke it was already dark. Knowing she needed to eat, Pamela stood staring at the inside of her refrigerator. Nothing looked exciting, so she closed the door and staggered to her bedroom.

In the morning she awoke with a headache. If she'd had the energy to get out of bed she would have seen it was still raining outside, but she pulled the blankets over her head and stayed there until noon.

CHAPTER 18

By Sunday morning the torrential spring rains had fallen harder in Redmond than in any of their neighboring towns, splashing heaviest in the downtown area. Main Street ended up getting the worst of it, looking more like a river than a street. In some areas, where the storm drains clogged, the water was a good three to four feet deep or more, making travel by vehicle or foot virtually impossible. Businesses in those areas not only lost business, but some had flooded basements and lost valuable inventory, not to mention the expensive water damages.

The worst of it, however, had yet to be seen. The overflow of rainwater from the downtown area of Main Street ran down the steep embankments, washing muddy soil into the already swollen Abenaki River. The Abenaki was running wild, turning the river's silt and discarded trash and waste into a tumbling brownish-sea, on the verge of overflowing its banks at any moment. The river also threatened to take the downtown bridge, and the other two bridges downstream, with it. It was the worst spring rains the town had seen in almost a century. Some folks wondered if the whole town would be swept away out to sea with the river.

During any normal year the rushing water was an attraction to behold, an annual springtime event brought on by the spring rains and melting snow. People would pull their vehicles over by the side of the road just to take a look at the rushing water as it roared over the falls above the downtown area. Some folks would take pictures of the falls; others just wanted to watch and remember the wonderful sight. Today, however, there were no people snapping pictures. There were no people at all anywhere near the falls. The river was too wild, roaring over the falls with a vengeance, flooding homes and businesses built along the riverbanks. This torrid spring rain that had begun two days earlier was on the verge of being relentless, and if it continued to rain any longer those homes and businesses were going to see the river's full wrath—a destruction beyond their wildest dreams.

While some residents prayed for relief, most everyone held their breath. Thankfully, they didn't have to hold it for very long. By Sunday afternoon the rains finally came to an end, leaving in its wake the violent destruction of property and road damage. It wasn't until later in the afternoon that the sun finally dared to show its face, winking for a brief moment in the western sky as it disappeared below the horizon, ending a disastrous weekend.

By then David Graham was home resting his tired, overworked body in the comfort of his La-Z-Boy recliner, waiting to watch the Red Sox play an afternoon game against the Angels in sunny California. The sun over the Anaheim stadium was still high in the sky, looking wonderful to him. He had been dozing off all afternoon since he'd returned home from another frustrating day at work. Being the lead man for the town's maintenance department was not a rewarding job when age was against you.

The start of the ballgame awoke him from his slumber. He blinked his eyes open and struggled to sit up in a more comfortable position. Before the second inning was over, David was sound asleep again.

A few minutes later, Margaret walked into the living room to see if her husband was awake. Not to her surprise he was still fast asleep. He had staggered into the house in the middle of the afternoon, like a drunk from a day of drinking, and told his wife he wanted to take a nap before dinner. She told her rain soaked husband to change his filthy work clothes before curling up in his recliner.

His stocking-covered feet were stretched out in the recliner and his head tilted, facing the kitchen. If his eyes were open he'd be staring at her knees, but they were closed. To Margaret, he looked more dead than alive. His mouth, slightly open, wrinkled to a frown, and the lids of his eyes had disappeared into a web of crows' feet. He seemed to have aged ten years overnight. His youthful mop of curly brown hair had all but disappeared. The few hairs he had left on the top of his head were now more white than gray, though he hardly noticed or even cared as long as he had something to comb.

Margaret took a few steps closer to make sure he was still breathing. She noticed his heavy chest slowly rise and then quietly regress. She wondered how many more of these long continuous days of hard work his old body could take, not to mention the stress it caused. She had been urging him to retire, but he would not hear of it. He liked his work; it gave himself something to do, and more importantly, made him feel needed.

David must have sensed his wife standing there. He slowly opened one eye, then the other. He took a quick glance at his wife then turned his attention to the ballgame, wondering how many

153

innings had passed.

"The mayor called — wanted to know why you didn't have anyone out removing the street closure signs. He said he went out to inspect the damages and noticed most of the streets were fine, but you still have the roads barricaded."

"I guess he didn't venture downtown. If he bothered to take a closer look he would have seen the roads that way are impassable. Jeepers crow, I was just down there a couple of hours ago, and there was no way anyone was going to get through without a canoe."

"Well, you don't have to jeepers crow me — I believe you, not him. I never did like the mayor and never voted for him. He's your friend, not mine."

"So what did you tell Freddie?"

"I told him you were napping and to go remove them himself. I also told him you're done working for nothing, and were retiring as of today."

"Right. What did you really tell him?"

"You know, Dave, you should really start thinking about retiring. You're not a young man anymore, and with our savings, and the social security you'll be receiving, there'll be plenty for us to live on comfortably."

"Someday, Maggie, I will. For now, I'm going to tell Freddie we need to hire more help, or my wife won't vote for him in the next election."

"Sorry, that will never happen. I strictly vote democratic. And even if Freddie were a democrat, I still wouldn't vote for him. Now, if you're not going to retire, at least take tomorrow off. I'm sure some of the younger guys, like Clay and that new guy you dislike so much, can handle it."

"I fired the new guy yesterday. And as for Clay, if he's

working by himself nothing will get done. Besides, I still have the funeral to take care of. It was postponed until tomorrow, and I'm sure the grave has to be re-dug. I doubt very much the cheap tarp we covered the hole with could have held all that rainwater. It must be full of mud and water by now."

"What am I going to do with you? One of these days you're going to be digging your own grave without you even knowing it." Margaret walked back into the kitchen to get his dinner ready.

David shrugged off his wife's remark, knowing she was only being cautious about his health. Especially after his latest physical, when his doctor had said about the same thing, telling him that if he didn't start taking it easy and not working so hard, he'd wake up dead some morning. When asked how his physical went, David told his wife what the doctor had said and then laughed it off. Margaret told him he should listen to his doctor and left it at that. She knew there was no sense giving him any advice. After all these years of marriage, she knew he was too damn stubborn.

Still feeling tired, David leaned back in his recliner and closed his eyes again, blocking out the ballgame as he tried to focus on the work that had to be done in the morning. He mainly focused his thoughts on the damage near the downtown bridge, where the guardrail leading to the bridge had disappeared into the river. On his drive home earlier, he'd noticed the river had begun to recede enough to see the section of guardrail was completely missing, and the overflow of water was still covering the whole area below the bridge, where most of the stores stood. It was the worst storm damage he had ever seen since taking over the job as the head of the town's maintenance department. He figured it would take a week or more to clean up the mess.

David thought about how best to split up the crews. Since

he'd fired the new guy he was down to six workers, not counting himself. He would need at least three guys to clear all the storm drains again, and one to remove the street closure signs and for other issues that arose. That left only one person for the downtown bridge, and that person would have to construct a temporary barricade for the missing guardrail until a permanent replacement could be installed. The person would also have to fill any holes that had washed out around the bridge with dirt.

The bridge job was really a two-person job but he only had one to spare, and the only one capable to handle the tough job was Clayton Daniels. His other four employees were too old to handle the job alone. It was too bad Malcolm Dangil wasn't still available, but he'd turned out to be a big disappointment.

The problem he had with Clayton working alone, however, was getting him to work. At the cemetery, Clayton was always sitting or leaning against something. Most of the time David would catch him sitting on top of a gravestone with a rake or grass trimmer in his hand, staring out at nothing and most likely thinking what he was going to do that night. That's if he was doing any thinking at all. Clayton was the type of person who needed to be pushed or nothing would get done. Now, thinking of having him do the guardrail job, David could picture Clayton sitting on the downtown bridge abutment, holding a shovel and looking at the women passing by on their way to shop at the downtown stores, if the stores were in any condition to reopen. Some stores, he knew, would take a week or more to repair the water damages the storm had caused.

At least he'd be holding a shovel, David sighed as he slowly drifted off to sleep again. Before he did, however, he wondered who would replace him when he retired. Hopefully, he thought, the town would hire an outsider. There was no one in Redmond

156

he could think of to replace him. Maybe it would be better for everyone if the whole town was swept away by the Abenaki River and out to sea.

As he drifted off to sleep, in his dreams the town did get swept away. The few people who survived stood high on top of the cemetery hill looking down at the raging river. Whole houses and automobiles could be seen floating down the raging river with people struggling to stay afloat, waving their arms for help. The town mayor was one of those, and so was Clayton Daniels, who was standing in the bed of his truck waving for help with one hand and holding a beer in the other.

CHAPTER 19

After three long miserable days of rain the town of Redmond finally awoke to a bright sunny morning. The last time the sun had dawned on this quaint coastal town was four days ago, the same day the weather forecasters incorrectly predicted the rain to last for only one day, with a sunny weekend to follow. "So much for forecasting the weather" was the main consensus among most of the town folks. Some even went as far as to say the weathermen shouldn't be paid. But they only said it in jest, and were happy to see the sun dry out their waterlogged town.

The sun, however, didn't bring the same welcoming relief for Pamela Hays, as a dark cloud hovered over her head. Pamela awoke from a restless night, tossing and turning in her sleep from agonizing dreams, dreaming about Kelsey's whereabouts and what could possibly have happened to her. Theodore, the cat she'd rescued from the animal shelter, was also on her mind. Her two best friends, Kelsey and Theodore, were missing. And to make things worse it was Monday, a workday.

Pamela tried her best to face the day, but Kelsey failed to

show up at work again. It had been three days since she had last seen or heard from her, and she knew something was terribly wrong. So, during her morning break, she nervously called the sheriff's department to report her friend missing.

After telling the deputy on desk duty she was calling to report a missing person, Pamela babbled on nervously about why she knew Kelsey was in trouble. She also told the deputy the name of the person she suspected had something to do with her disappearance. The deputy had not written any of her suspicions down, and suggested it would be best if she could come down to the sheriff's office and fill out the report in person. Pamela obliged and told the deputy she'd drive over after work. It turned out to be one of the longest days at work in her short career as a bank teller, with her glancing at the clock every five minutes, well over a hundred times.

The twenty-mile ride to the sheriff's office didn't help her anxiety any either. When she arrived at the sheriff's office the deputy led Pamela over to a small, unoccupied office and sat her down in a chair next to the desk.

After positioning himself in a chair behind the desk and turning the computer on, the deputy asked her to give him all the personal information she knew about Kelsey. Hearing him ask gave Pamela pause to realize where she was, sitting in the sheriff's office because her best friend was missing. It was something she'd only seen in movies, and never expected to happen to her.

Pamela started with Kelsey's name and address, at first giving the deputy her own address by mistake. She then told him where Kelsey worked and the type of vehicle she drove. Since Pamela had no photograph of Kelsey with her, she gave the deputy a brief description of her physical appearance and the clothes she was last seen wearing to the best of her recollection. She also told him about Kelsey leaving the tavern with Malcolm Dangil, and how Kelsey thought his voice sounded just like the man she'd heard on a radio program—the crazy man who called himself Mister Zero. Not recalling Malcolm's last name, she only told the deputy his first name.

The part about Mister Zero only confused the deputy, who let it go in one ear and out the other, and hadn't typed one word of it on the missing person report form. He couldn't understand what plausible connection there could be between the missing girl and this crazy guy on the radio she was talking about. Sometimes too much information only clouded the problem. He was almost positive the girl had either shacked up with this guy, whose first name Pamela only knew as Malcolm, or was a runaway.

The deputy mentioned, for no reason at all other than to let her know teenagers often did run away, that there had been another young woman reported missing in the neighboring town of Benton. This young woman, however, was considered a runaway, having previously run away the prior year when she was fifteen. He then went on to explain to Pamela that when the girl returned home she got a job working in a variety store making sandwiches, and had mentioned to a coworker how much better off she had been living in the streets of Boston. So it was only logical to assume she'd hitched her way back to Boston.

Pamela told the deputy Kelsey was no runaway; she was nineteen years old. People didn't run away when they were nineteen. This only caused him to lean toward the shacked-up theory.

As the deputy typed the information in the report, Pamela thought about Kelsey telling her the story about her troubled father, how he'd murdered her mother, shooting her in the head and then turning the gun on himself. Kelsey was only three at the

160

time, and even though she was in the same room when her father went berserk, she remembered none of it. The only indication of the incident was a scar she received on her left shoulder when her father pulled her away from her mother's arms, tossing her onto the bed. Kelsey bounced off the bed and into a radiator, breaking her shoulder blade. The bone tore through the skin. An operation left her with a three-inch scar just below her shoulder blade.

Kelsey had moved to Redmond after the horrible incident, living in a small apartment with her grandmother. Her grandmother became sick and died from lung cancer the year Kelsey graduated from high school. Before she died, her grandmother told her everything about her mother's horrible death, and how she received the scar. After Kelsey's grandmother died, she faced the unexpected responsibility of adulthood, having to support herself without the help of family. Fortunately for her, her best friend had grown up in an affluent environment and had a solution.

Kelsey could have stayed in the apartment she shared with her grandmother, who'd rented the two-bedroom apartment for over forty years, but with no inheritance from her grandmother and no savings account of her own, Kelsey couldn't afford to pay the rent by herself. Her part time job just wasn't enough to even cover her basic needs to live on, never mind paying the rent.

Her friend Pamela had saved her from the embarrassment of homelessness by offering her a place to stay in her one-bedroom apartment, which was more of a demand than an offer. There was no way Pamela was going to let her best friend become homeless. Their arrangement, however, only lasted two months.

Sleeping on the living room couch didn't bother Kelsey much; what bothered her was Pamela's boyfriend, Matt Burger, coming over every night, and Kelsey feeling like she was being intrusive. Pamela, on the other hand, could have cared less about Kelsey being there when Matt was over. She felt the three of them were having fun together, drinking margaritas and getting drunk. Anytime she wanted to be alone with Matt the two of them would venture into her bedroom.

The vibrating noises coming from Pamela's bedroom also didn't help matters any, and only added to Kelsey's decision to move out. So, two months after moving in with Pamela, she moved out.

Pamela never mentioned Kelsey's scar to the deputy. Mentioning it never entered her mind, and why would it? Her vehicle and physical description, and the information about the man she'd left the tavern with, were the only important specifics needed, she figured, for the authorities to find her girlfriend. Anything else was insignificant.

When Pamela arrived home from the sheriff's department, she made herself a batch of margaritas to calm her nerves down. She then brought the whole batch and a salted glass to her living room and settled on her couch, with the TV tuned to the local news channel. Though she dreaded the thought of hearing something bad about Kelsey on the news, and having to endure the pain of hearing it alone, she wanted to know as soon as possible. To her relief, all the news stories were about the weekend storm that had ravaged the town.

After the news ended she turned the volume down and sat there, trying to recall what happened Friday evening at the tavern. Maybe if she thought back to that night she'd remember something Kelsey had said to her that might help unravel the mystery of her disappearance, but nothing came to mind. All she could remember and visualize was Kelsey walking out the door with Malcolm. The rest of the night was a complete blur.

She didn't even remember leaving the tavern with Burger, and only remembered waking up in his apartment, trying to push her horny boyfriend off her without much success. She was feeling groggy and sick to her stomach from too much drinking to ward him off, so she just laid still and let him do his thing. Five minutes later she was on her way home, then showered and dishearteningly drove to the bank, bitching about the miserable weather and having to go to work.

Pamela got up from the couch with the intention of making another batch of margaritas, but she suddenly began feeling depressed and sat back down on her couch and cried. With Kelsey nowhere to be found, and Theodore gone and most likely not having survived the storm, Pamela felt she was alone in the world. Then she thought of Burger and called him to come over. Her call, however, went unanswered. She then remembered he said he'd be out of town for a few days. The last time she'd talked to him was Saturday morning when he drove her home from his place to go to work. She'd called him later that morning from work, but Burger didn't answer his phone. He did return her call that night, leaving a brief message telling her he was going to be out of town for a few days. Pamela was already sleeping when he had called, and didn't bother to return the call the next day. She had more important things on her mind.

CHAPTER 20

On Tuesday morning the warm, spring sun crested high over the islands of Craggs Bay, bringing a second day of much needed relief to the coastal communities. With the heavy rains long gone, having moved out over the ocean, things were finally starting to get back to normal. Most of the streets that had been closed since the onslaught of the storm were now cleared for travel, the road closure and detour signs stored away for another day. In a week's time, the damage caused by the torrential rains would be forgotten by most, and the flowering of spring would be the main conversation at the local coffee shops and office water coolers.

It seemed all was well again for most of the towns — that is, with the exception of Redmond. Redmond was still feeling the effects, having received the brunt of the storm's tremendous force. The Abenaki River, which ran right through the downtown area, was still running wild, and some sections of Main Street remained flooded. But the damage from the storm was not the only thing that caused dismay in Redmond. A brutally murdered young teenage girl was finally being buried this morning, and there was the matter of solving the disappearance of a missing young woman. Kelsey Mickelson was still nowhere to be found. She, along with a young man she had recently met, had disappeared into the stormy night.

With the missing person's report sitting on his desk, Sheriff J. J. Foley informed Deputy Finn Bradshaw that they were making a road trip to Redmond, hopefully to quickly resolve the issue. The report had been sitting on his desk since the day before, when he'd called the missing woman's home to see if she had returned. There was no answer, and no answering machine for him to leave a message. His repeated calls also went unanswered. This morning he'd had the same results — no one was at the home to answer his phone call. He now knew he was going to have to make the twenty-mile drive to the woman's home, and waste the morning on what he figured was going to be a false alarm.

Sheriff Foley couldn't remember the last time a person reported missing turned out bad. His memory, however, was deteriorating. The reason for his sudden bout with dementia was the increase of emergency calls into the station caused by the weekend storm. If he had taken the time to think about the recent missing person reports, he would have remembered Callie Webster had been reported missing just over a week ago, and her body was found ripped to shreds and left to rot in an open field outside of town. But unfortunately he had forgotten all about Callie Webster, and went to Redmond on the assumption Kelsey Mickelson was on some kind of holiday, or was a teenage runaway.

The address on the report led the sheriff and his deputy to a brown-shingled one-story bungalow on a dead-end street, overlooking the ocean. The view was nice enough, spectacular even, Foley thought, but the house was too small for his liking.

Years ago Foley had dreamed about living near the ocean, being close enough to hear the roar of the sea. But now he was content living out in the country with his wife and their two dogs. Privacy was his main concern now, and he had plenty of it with fifty acres of fields surrounded by a forest of tall pines.

The first thing Foley noticed when he pulled up to the house was a small compact vehicle sitting in the driveway. The report mentioned the woman's vehicle was missing, which caused Foley to assume the vehicle belonged to the missing woman and she had returned home. His assumption was quickly dismissed when the woman who answered the door informed him she was not Kelsey Mickelson, and the vehicle in the driveway was her vehicle, not Kelsey's red Ford Focus.

***

"I didn't know she was missing," Samantha Stone told the sheriff when asked if she knew anything about her roommate's whereabouts. "I haven't seen Kelsey since last Thursday afternoon, when I left for the weekend to visit my family in Massachusetts."

"You don't have any idea where she may have gone? Any boyfriends she could be staying with?" the sheriff asked.

Samantha hesitated with a confused stare. She was still puzzling over the idea that Kelsey was a missing person. Kelsey never went anywhere that she knew of. If she wasn't at work or at her friend Pamela's apartment, she spent the rest of her time at home, enjoying the ocean. Surely there must be some reasonable explanation for her to be missing; the town was too small for someone to get lost in. She then had a terrible thought that something bad may have happened to Kelsey. She remembered it was just over a week ago a girl had been brutally murdered, and her killer was still out there. The story was all over the news for days. Having been away for the weekend, she had forgotten all about it until now. Now she was being informed Kelsey was missing.

"What about it, do you know of any boyfriends?" he asked again.

"Kelsey doesn't have any boyfriends around here that I know about."

***

Her response was unexpected, causing Foley to hesitate a moment. He had expected her to say yes or no. Saying she didn't have any boyfriends around here meant Kelsey had a boyfriend living outside of town, and that's where she most likely was — shacking up with the guy.

"What do you mean about not around here? Does she have a boyfriend someplace else, and maybe decided on the spur-of-the-moment to pay the guy a visit while you were out of town, and didn't mention it to you?"

"No. I don't believe so. What I meant was I don't know about any boyfriends. I really don't know her that well, or anything about her past life. I've only known her for a couple of months, since she moved in with me. I needed a new roommate — my previous roommate moved out, and I can't afford this place all by myself. She was staying with her girlfriend, Pam, but Pam's place was too small. I believe it was a one-bedroom, but I'm not sure — I've never been there. If Kelsey had a boyfriend before moving in here she never mentioned it to me."

Foley looked at the notes he had taken from the missing person report and at the name of the person who'd reported the woman missing. "Would that person she stayed with be a Pamela Hays?"

***

Samantha only nodded. Her mind was still trying to

167

comprehend the idea that Kelsey was considered a missing person. The longer the two authority figures stood on her doorstep, the gravity of the situation began to weigh heavier on her mind that Kelsey was in trouble.

"Do you have any problem with us coming inside to have a look around? See if anything is missing that you know of, maybe a suitcase, overnight bag. Something that would indicate she might have taken a trip."

"Of course not, please come in." Samantha stepped back to let the two men enter.

***

Standing off to the side near a large picture window with a fantastic view of the ocean, Deputy Bradshaw looked around the living room while Foley asked Samantha some personal questions pertaining to her relationship with Kelsey. To Bradshaw the room definitely looked lived in, with clothes tossed on the backs of the couch and recliner. The coffee table was cluttered, with hardly an open spot to place anything. There was even a plate with the remains of food and a half-filled coffee mug on the table, which Bradshaw assumed were from Samantha's breakfast since it was still morning. On the floor he noticed a pile of dirty clothes next to an open suitcase.

Samantha noticed Bradshaw taking in the room, his eyes stopping on the suitcase. "That's my suitcase. I just got home this morning, and haven't had the time to put things away."

"Yeah, I can see," Bradshaw nodded.

***

Seeing nothing of interest, Foley thought his best bet would be to take a look inside Kelsey's bedroom. If he were going to find something to help locate the missing woman, the bedroom would most likely be the best place to start.

"I'd like to search her bedroom. Which room is Kelsey's?" Foley asked.

Samantha pointed toward a door down the short hallway from the kitchen. "Her door is the one at the end of the hall on the right."

Kelsey's bedroom was uncluttered, not as chaotic as the living room, with only a few clothes laid out on top of the tightly made bed. Several pairs of shoes were lined up against the wall near a closed closet, and a pair of soft, furry sleepers sticking out from under her bed.

Foley open the closet door. Inside was an assortment of lady's clothes on hangers. The shelf above was cluttered with boxes and more clothing. On the floor he noticed two suitcases, a large one for travel and a smaller overnight bag. Leaving the closet door open, he then walked over to her nightstand. There was a gooseneck reading lamp and radio sitting on top. Next to the radio was a graduation picture showing two girls wearing caps and gowns, standing arm-in-arm and smiling as warmly as the sun was shining on their happy faces.

Foley took a good look at the girl on the right, who he suspected must be Kelsey since her hair was blonde and the other girl in the picture was a brunette. Kelsey, he thought, was very pretty, and hoped nothing bad had happened to her.

After setting the picture down, Foley pulled the one drawer open and found some cheap jewelry and a small tray filled with coins. Nothing else. He took one last glance around the room and decided there was nothing that gave him any kind of clue that she may have gone on an excursion. In fact, it looked like she wasn't planning on going anywhere.

Disappointed he hadn't found anything of significance indicating she may have gone on a trip, he walked back to the living room, where he found Samantha sitting on the couch. Bradshaw was staring out the picture window at the ocean, watching the high tide waves crash the rocky shoreline.

After concluding that her cell phone and Ford Focus were the only items missing that belonged to Kelsey, Foley thanked Samantha for her cooperation and told her to call the sheriff's office if she heard from her roommate. He then drove over to Pamela Hays's apartment, and struggled a bit walking up the three flights of stairs. Foley was not a young man anymore, complaining all the way up the stairs about the lack of an elevator. His age wasn't the only issue that hampered his progress; his heavy weight and lack of exercise were the main reasons.

Deputy Bradshaw, on the other hand, was in great shape. He was in the prime of his life, thirty-three years old, and very dedicated to his extreme workout ethic, pumping iron every day before and after work, with an occasional five-mile jog around his neighborhood in the evening. He had no girlfriend — although he was looking — to take up his time. His job of being a deputy and exercise took up all his waking hours.

When Foley finally reached the third floor he found his deputy smiling at him. "What are you so happy about?" Foley asked, knowing full well why.

"Maybe you should have taken the elevator," Bradshaw joked.

"Maybe you should keep your mouth shut if you want to keep your job!"

Bradshaw knocked on Pamela's door several times. The last knock was loud enough for the tenant down the hall to hear, who inquisitively poked his head out his door. Seeing the two uniformed officers, he quickly closed it with a bang.

"Now what?" Bradshaw asked. "See if that guy down the

hall knows where she might be?"

"No. That would be a waste of time. I see from my notes she works at the Redmond Savings Bank," Foley said, looking at the notebook. "Guess we'll pay the bank a visit."

CHAPTER 21

For a Tuesday morning, business at the Redmond Savings bank was unusually brisk. On most Tuesdays a customer could walk right up to the counter for service without having to wait in line. It didn't matter what time of day it was, business was slow on Tuesdays. But not on this Tuesday, a Tuesday following a long spell of stormy weather. By eleven o'clock the line of customers, which at one time wound its way beyond the ropes, had finally dwindled down to one, an elderly woman inappropriately dressed for the warm weather.

Wearing a long dark-colored wool coat and pulling her wire-framed two-wheel cart behind her, Elsie Hermann stood patiently waiting her turn to withdraw money from her savings account with the intent to purchase groceries, including cat food and birdseed. The coat she wore was the only winter coat she owned, and she customarily waited until late spring before having it dry cleaned and packing it away. Her frail, aging body felt comfortably warm wearing the coat, but those who noticed the unusual out-of-season attire looked at her with skepticism, wondering if the old woman was in her right frame of mind. Their opinion, however, caused her no concern. At her age she could care less what other people thought. It was her life and theirs was theirs. No one was going to take care of her, and she wasn't going to give one moment of thought about anybody else.

Pamela Hays was about to motion Elsie toward her window when she noticed two uniformed men entering the bank. One of them was tall, a few years beyond youthfulness, with his whole adult life ahead of him. The other, much older and walking as though age was against him, was on the down slope of his life. The uniforms, Pamela immediately realized, having seen one the day before, were those worn by the sheriff's department.

Seeing them made Pamela a little nervous, thinking they were there for her, coming to give her the bad news about Kelsey's disappearance. She had dreamed about this moment, being confronted with the terrible news that Kelsey was dead, and wondered how she would react to it. Would she break down and cry, or just faint to the floor in front of all her coworkers and anyone else who happened to be present in the bank at that time? Either way it would be an embarrassment.

And here they were, walking through the doorway at her place of employment, the worst place to receive bad news. They would tell her what happened to Kelsey right in front of all her coworkers, who would witness her emotional breakdown. At that moment she wanted to disappear herself, to hide beneath the counter she was standing behind.

Instead of walking toward her, however, the two men disappeared inside Stephen Carr's office. Stephen was one of the loan officers for the bank, no one of any importance to discuss personal matters pertaining to bank employees. If they were there to discuss Kelsey's whereabouts they would have gone directly to the bank manager or the president, Pamela's very own father. Since they'd entered Stephen Carr's office, Pamela at first assumed the two were there to discuss a loan, but then she thought better of it.

If they were coming in for a loan they'd come in on their time off, not during work hours. More likely, it now seemed to Pamela, since Stephen Carr was only a loan officer, they were there to discuss something pertaining to him. Something he may have illegally done, like steal money from the bank. Pamela had heard of loan officers in other banks creating false loans to steal money, only to eventually be caught and have to serve a lengthy prison term, plus having to pay back the money they'd stolen. She herself had had dreams of stealing a few bills, slipping a couple of hundreds in her pocket. But the reality of the consequences, especially the humiliation her father would endure, outweighed the need to enhance her wardrobe with a couple more pairs of expensive shoes she'd probably only wear once in a blue moon.

***

Not having any idea what Pamela Hays looked like, Sheriff Foley and his deputy stepped into Carr's glassed-enclosed loan office. They entered that particular office because it was the first office they came to that wasn't busy with a customer.

***

A man with salt-and-pepper hair and a neatly trimmed beard of the same color occupied the office. Stephen Carr, the man behind the desk, looked up nervously, wondering if they were there for him. Even though he had not committed any crimes, other than not being caught for driving under the influence a few times, seeing an authority figure standing before him gave him an uneasy feeling. Although the town of Redmond's population was too small to have their own police department, it was uncommon to see someone from the sheriff's department enter the bank. Their presence was a first for Carr, who could not muster more than a hollow grunt.

Carr was put to ease at once when Foley wasted no time in asking for Pamela Hays. Carr now began to wonder why on earth they would want to speak to the nice young girl he had been fantasizing about for over a year, ever since the day she'd started working at the bank. He had not heard about the missing person report Pamela had filled out the previous day — it was none of his business. He only thought Kelsey was not scheduled to work or was on vacation. Therefore he had no idea why they wanted to speak to Pamela.

***

"Pam's one of the tellers over there at the counter. Would you like me to go over there and get her? You can use my office if you need privacy," he asked, happy to oblige.

"No, just point her out to me."

"May I ask what's she done? Is she in any kind of trouble?"

"No, she's done nothing wrong, just routine business. We only need to get some information she may be able to help us with," Foley answered the inquisitive man, not wanting to explain their business with Pamela.

"That's good to hear. Pam's a good employee; I'd hate to see her in trouble," Carr added, like he was the bank's human resource person. He then stepped out of his office and pointed in the direction of a tall brunette, who just happened to be staring in their direction.

***

Without being announced she was next, Elsie slowly walked up to Pamela's window and slid her bankbook toward Pamela. She then patiently waited for a response, which was

175

not immediately returned. Pamela was momentarily distracted, seeing Stephen Carr pointing in her direction. The reality of the moment was here, and Pamela braced herself for the bad news. His accusing finger pointing directly at her like she was guilty of some horrible crime.

As customary, except in cases of emergencies, the sheriff politely waited his turn, standing directly behind Elsie. This time the wait was longer than he had expected it to be. Every time he thought the transaction between the two had been completed, Elsie would ask another question, then thank Pamela numerous times for her generous help. When Elsie finally turned to walk away, she nearly bumped into Foley.

Foley politely tipped his cap and gave her a faint smile. Elsie only harrumphed on her way by. His smile widened at the unfriendly retort, giving Elsie praise for her defiance. She reminded him of his grandmother being that way till the day she died.

***

After leaving her window, Pamela escorted Foley and Deputy Bradshaw to a vacant room the employees used for their lunch break. In case the news was bad, she closed the door for privacy, not wanting to break out in hysterics and disrupt the bank's tranquil atmosphere. She then offered them a seat at one of the plastic round tables, with only Foley accepting. Bradshaw stood near the door with his arms folded across his chest.

"I hope you're here to give me some good news, Sheriff. I'm real worried about Kelsey. It's not like her to not call me," Pamela nervously said, hoping for the best. But deep down she expected the worst.

She could not fathom any logical reason why Kelsey had not contacted her by now. It had been four days since she last saw her best friend, and those four long days had also included sleepless nights. If Kelsey were having some kind of romantic fling with the new man in her life, she would have called days ago, Sunday at the very latest.

"Actually, we're here hoping she contacted you by now and told you where she was staying. We've been to her house and spoken to her roommate, but she has no idea where she is or where she had gone. She didn't even know Kelsey was missing until we informed her. She told us she'd been out-of-town since Thursday," Foley said.

Pamela could feel her heart beating faster, and took a deep breath to relax her anxiety. At least for now, in her own mind, Kelsey was still alive. She had a premonition Kelsey was going to knock on the lunchroom door at any moment, laugh, and say, "What's all the fuss about?" The door, however, was as silent as the room she was sitting in.

"No, I don't doubt Samantha didn't know. I tried calling the house all weekend, but no one answered. I knew Samantha was out-of-town visiting relatives, but I wasn't sure when she was expected back."

"Well, if you don't mind, we're going to need some more information from you. The report you filled out was vague, pretty basic, with only her address and a brief physical description. There were a few other details you gave, but nothing to really go on. Can you tell us when the last time was that you saw her? I think you mentioned in the report it was at a nightclub. I'd like to hear more about that night." Foley pulled out his notepad and clicked open his pen to jot the information down.

"Yes, it was Friday night when I last saw her. We went to the Crow's Nest Tavern together. She was hoping to meet this guy there, a customer she'd met here at the bank."

"Was he there?"

"Yes, he was there. He came over and sat down with us at our table. He didn't stay for very long though. After awhile he said he had to leave because he had to work in the morning. It seemed rather abrupt to me, now that I think about it. One minute we're all sitting at the table having a good time, talking and listening to the band, and all of a sudden he said he had to leave. It was raining and he didn't own a car, so Kelsey offered to give him a ride home. That was the last time I saw her, walking out with that guy."

Remembering their last time together, the laughs they'd shared, Pamela started to tear up and grabbed for a tissue from the Kleenex box on the table. She dabbed at her eyes and kept the tissue crumpled in the palm of her hand for the next time.

***

"He just blurted out he had to leave? Did he ask your friend for a ride, or did he tell her to give him a ride?"

After a brief pause, Pamela changed her last comment. "I don't really remember. Now that I think about it, maybe it could have been Kelsey saying she wanted to go home and offered to give Malcolm a ride, but I'm not sure."

"That's okay, but you said she did leave the bar with this guy, and that was the last time you saw her? Is this correct, to your best recollection?"

"Yes, that was the last time I saw her. Do you think maybe he has something to do with her disappearance?"

"He could—he could have plenty to do with it. What about this guy, do you know anything about him? Do you happen to know his name?" Foley asked, and steadied his pen in anticipating of writing down the man's name.

"All I know is his first name, Malcolm. He never mentioned

his last name or where he lived, and I have no idea. I told the deputy all this when I filled out the missing person report."

"Yes, I think I saw it on the report. Now, you mentioned he was a customer. You said Kelsey met him here, at the bank, so he must have an account here."

"Yes, but I have no way of finding out his last name if that's what you're getting at. We'd have to go through all the transactions slips from Friday, and I don't know if my manager would like that—we're very busy. I can give you a description of what he looks like though, if that helps."

Foley knew they could get the bank to find out Malcolm's last name, but he also knew, as Pamela had said, it would take some time. Time wasted. If it became urgent he would request it, but for now he would take a different avenue to finding out his last name and where he lived.

"That's a start. Anything you can remember about him will help," Foley said after writing the name Malcolm in uppercase letters in his notepad.

***

Pamela wanted to tell the sheriff about her first impression of Malcolm, the first time she'd waited on him at the bank, which wasn't very flattering. Except for the jeans he wore, his clothes seemed outdated, like handouts from the local Salvation Army store two blocks down from the bank. His two-toned jacket looked like a leftover from the eighties, or maybe even the seventies. Beneath the jacket she could plainly see the polo logo stitched on a solid, light-green colored shirt. His attire hadn't changed much the next time she remembered seeing him in the bank, wearing the same jacket. That was the day Kelsey met him. He did, however, look much different in the tavern Friday night than he had when he came in the bank earlier in the day.

179

In the bank he looked unsociable, almost threatening in a way, but at the tavern he seemed more nervous than intimidating. After starting to know the person in a different environment, one more relaxing, and with a few margaritas swirling around in her head, she'd changed her perception of him and thought nothing of Kelsey leaving with the guy. Watching them leave together, she'd actually hoped Kelsey had finally found the right guy. Not one that lasted less than a week because the guy turned out to be a jerk. Malcolm seemed to be an okay guy.

Now, sitting across from the sheriff, she began to wonder if Malcolm was just another jerk, or worse.

"He seemed nice and friendly to me. Kind of quiet though, didn't talk much," she told the sheriff, giving Malcolm the benefit of the doubt. There was no sense in misleading the sheriff and causing him to suspect Malcolm of any wrongdoing before he had a chance to question him. For all she knew, Kelsey could have disappeared after she dropped Malcolm off. If that were the case, and she was not off on some romance with Malcolm, it would be the worst scenario. No good ever came to someone who suddenly disappeared.

"How about his appearance; height, weight, color of hair? What was he wearing? That's what we need to know. Put an APB out on him to make him easier to locate. Not too many places you can hide in this town, I imagine."

"Well," she said squinting, trying to remember. "I'd say he was kind of average in height, maybe around five-nine or ten. He was thinly built, probably weighed around a hundred and sixty pounds. I think his hair was brown or maybe light brown. It was dark inside the tavern, hard to tell exactly. Plus he was wearing a hat. He always wore a hat when he came in the bank, so I couldn't tell what color his hair was. He wore the same hat

180

every time I saw him, I think."

"Do you remember what he was wearing besides the hat?"

"He wore a jacket. It was brown with a darker color, one of those two-tone jackets. And I'm pretty sure he was wearing jeans," she said, shaking her head, hoping to remember more about him. "That's all I can recall. He did take his hat off for a few seconds when he first sat down at our table, but he immediately put it back on. I'm thinking it was a polite gesture. Oh, and there was an odd logo on the hat."

"Was it a baseball cap with some professional sports team logo?"

"No, I think it was some kind of a design, maybe letters. I really can't remember. I was going to ask him about it when he put it back on, but I forgot."

"Anything else you can remember about him? Did he say anything that you can remember that might be of importance so we can locate him?"

"No, not really. I can't remember much more than that. My boyfriend came in shortly after Malcolm sat down, and it wasn't long before Kelsey left with him. I watched them walk out together. That's the last time I saw her."

Forgetting she already held a tissue, Pamela grabbed another one out of the box and dabbed her eyes. She then waited for the sheriff to ask her something else. She watched as he paused writing in his notepad, the pen hovering above the page waiting to do its thing. To her the sheriff seemed to be in a trance, like he was picturing Kelsey and Malcolm walking out of the tavern together, like she was, or thinking of other questions to ask her. She was disappointed in her failure to remember more about the man who may be responsible for Kelsey's disappearance.

***

After the odd silence, Deputy Bradshaw spoke up, asking if Malcolm might have mentioned where he worked. He had been quietly standing in the background, taking mental notes and trying to think of a question to ask that his boss might not have thought of. One thing he did know about guys when they were at a bar, they usually talked about their work, something to brag about in front of a girl. Always over exaggerating the importance of their work and the money they were paid.

***

Bradshaw's question jogged Pamela's memory, and she started to recall the creepy guy, Clayton, who had come over to their table. She had seen his approach, his slow ambling walk, confident his quest of scoring would be fulfilled. As he neared her table, Pamela hoped the guy would amble on by, hit on another table, but he'd stopped at the empty chair next to her. She could see his facial features clearer in her head now than she could remember Malcolm's. Clayton had a rough, pockmarked face with a longer than average nose, thin, with hairy nostrils, and teeth the color of whatever foul smell drifted out of his mouth. He had a face one would never forget.

"Yes, he said he worked for the town of Redmond in the maintenance department, with a guy named Clayton. Now that guy was scary looking. He came over to our table and wanted to sit down, but I told him the seat was taken. My boyfriend was coming any minute."

"What did this guy Clayton do next?"

"He walked off and went back and stood at the bar. Every time I looked over I noticed he was staring at us. He just stood there staring at us all night. Kelsey thought he might be that guy she'd heard on a radio program. The guy on the radio who called himself Mister Zero, and said he killed demons who were

182

disguised as teenage girls with green eyes and blonde hair."

"He killed demons?" Sheriff Foley skeptically asked.

"Well, according to Kelsey that's what he said on the radio program. He said he was going out that night to slay another demon. She said the guy had mentioned the demon he was going to slay was somewhere near here."

At the time Pamela hadn't believed any of it, thinking he was some weirdo wanting to be on the radio. Maybe have a little notoriety in his sad life. Kelsey, however, had seemed extremely worried. She truly believed the man calling himself Mister Zero was out there, stalking his next victim. Now Pamela thought Kelsey had a right to be worried, and why not? After all, she had green eyes and blonde hair, and at nineteen, was still a teenager.

"You know, I don't remember seeing him after Kelsey left," she added, thinking maybe Clayton had something to do with Kelsey's disappearance and not Malcolm. If there were anyone who looked the type to harm Kelsey, he'd fit the description—some scary character from out of a horror movie.

"You think this guy, Clayton, and Malcolm were friends?"

"No, I don't think so. Malcolm didn't seem to like him very much. He only said they worked together, but they were standing together at the bar when we first arrived, so I don't know."

***

Now things were beginning to fit together, Foley thought. This information about Clayton possibly being a stalker was something he definitely would consider following up on, but first he wanted to find this guy Malcolm.

They thanked Pamela and headed directly over to the town garage. At the garage they found a note taped to the door with brief information written on it.

—If you need David Graham I'm at the cemetery.—

183

CHAPTER 22

David Graham was patiently standing on top of a slope watching a priest presiding over a funeral burial when he noticed the sheriff's vehicle pull to a stop next to the storage barn. He was standing with Morrie Stover, waiting for the funeral to be over before starting the job of lowering the casket and filling in the grave with the backhoe, when he happened to see the vehicle. After everything was completed at the cemetery he planned on driving back to the town garage to catch up on some emails, and then head home for lunch. Later in the afternoon, he planned on helping his crew with the seemingly never-ending job of cleaning up the roads from the recent storm.

The only reason David could think of for the sheriff's vehicle to be at the cemetery was that they were there for the funeral, running late. The funeral had been scheduled for the previous Saturday morning, but due to the inclement weather they were forced to postpone it until now. He had been wondering why no one was there representing the state police or the sheriff's department. Usually when a person was murdered, not that it happened often in Redmond, someone investigating the crime would be there to show the grieving family they cared. Another reason to be there, especially for this funeral where they had no suspects for the horrific murder, was to glance around at the mourners to see if perhaps the murderer dared to show his ugly face. Sometimes they stood alone, away from the other mourners, sticking out like a scarecrow in a cornfield.

David looked at the mourners surrounding the gravesite to see if anyone stood out. There were at least four dozen, maybe more. Tragedies, especially when the victim was young like the Webster girl being buried this day, turned out most of the town folks who wanted to show their respects for the victim's family. He suspected there would have been even more mourners if the storm hadn't happened and the funeral had been held on the previous Saturday, when most of the local residents had the day off from work.

Up near where the vehicles were parked, lined behind one another on the narrow dirt drive, he noticed several more people standing near parked vehicles looking down as the priest presided over the grave. They were mostly, if not all, high school students paying their respects for a fallen classmate. School had been called off for the funeral. Most of the students were happy for the unexpected no-school day and slept in, not wanting to waste a day off going to a funeral. Callie Webster's closest friends, he was sure, were present.

No one stood out as a likely candidate to be a murderer, David surmised, but he also knew he wasn't versed on the subject of profiling criminals. For all he knew the murderer could be one of the Webster girl's classmates, like the longhaired kid leaning against his vehicle with his arms wrapped around his next victim, a skinny looking girl with too much mascara and hair dyed with

185

blue and purple streaks.

No, he would leave the profiling to the professionals, like to the two uniformed men he noticed getting out of the sheriff's vehicle. Instead of heading over to the funeral, as he had expected they would, the two men walked toward the storage barn and disappeared inside. That was not something he expected they would do, and he wondered what they were up to.

David immediately made a beeline toward the storage barn.

When David entered the barn, he found them milling around inside, looking the place over like they were inspecting it for potential fire hazards. The building was cluttered, and most likely would fail an inspection if the town cared to have it inspected. David knew that would never happen, especially after he complained about needing more space for all the landscaping equipment plus the backhoe, and the old work truck that would someday soon need to be replaced. It was all about money the town didn't have, and anything he requested, he knew, would fall on deaf ears.

"Something I can do for you gentlemen?" David asked, surprising them.

***

Foley and Bradshaw turned around in unison. They were not expecting someone to sneak up on them so easily. Foley was not happy about it, feeling it was unprofessional of them to let their guard down.

"I hope so. Are you David Graham? I was over at the town garage and read the note you left, saying you were over here."

"That would be me—I'm here for every funeral. Dig the graves, and after the service is over, I fill them back in."

"Sounds like a fun job," Foley sarcastically responded.

"I guess maybe you could say I've grown accustomed to the

job, seeing I've been doing it for almost forty years. Usually I don't think about the deceased I'm burying, but this one's going to be especially hard not to have sad feelings. When I saw you guys drive up I thought you were here for the funeral."

***

"Whose funeral is it anyway? Must be an important fellow with all those people attending."

"The Webster girl. Callie Webster. She was the girl who was murdered just over a week ago. Thought that's why you were here, representing the department," David said, slightly irritated the sheriff of Madison County didn't have any idea who was being buried here today.

It was only last week for heaven's sake, David thought, thinking about the day Sheriff J. J. Foley told the whole world on the local news broadcast the murderer would be caught and prosecuted to the fullest. You'd think the very person who vowed to apprehend the murderer would not forget a hideous crime in a week's time. After all, it was the crime of the century for the small town of Redmond, he'd told the news reporter.

David was sure he'd never forget the murder. It was the worst murder he had ever heard of, and he couldn't imagine anyone living in Redmond would disagree. How could anyone ever forget such an awful crime?

There had been other murders in Redmond, although few and mostly in the domestic category, where the husband killed the wife with a butter knife for burning the toast, or vise-versa. This murdered young victim was the most violent of all, having been chopped up in pieces. Her remains, what was left of them after the animals and birds feasted upon her, were found in a field on the outskirts of town. The farmer who happened upon the remains was plowing his field. At first he thought it was a dead

187

animal, most probably a deer. The shredded clothes changed his thinking.

***

"Oh, yeah, the Webster girl. I forgot all about her. With all that's been going on with the weather, and this missing person issue I'm following up on, I forgot all about the funeral. I was planning on sending someone," he was saying, then paused briefly, remembering he had planned to attend the funeral. "Wasn't the funeral supposed to be held last Saturday?"

"Postponed—guess you weren't informed."

"Well, now that I'm here, I guess I can kill two birds with one stone," Foley said, not realizing his unintended adage. It was an adage he used often, and most of the time it went unnoticed. David, however, noticed the untimely remark and raised his eyebrows.

"We'll take a walk over by the gravesite. You mind answering a few questions on the way over?" Foley asked.

"Not at all, but what do you want to know? I only know what I've been hearing on the local news and in the newspaper. I never knew the Webster family until now. I thought I knew everybody in Redmond—guess they moved in without telling me."

"It's not about them. We're looking for a guy that works for you. All I have is his first name, Malcolm."

***

David was expecting to be asked questions about the Webster murder. Maybe asked if he happened to notice someone unexpectedly may have showed up for the funeral, someone that looked out of place. What he wasn't expecting, although he wasn't surprised to be asked about his recently hired employee who was now his newly fired employee, was that Dangil was wanted by the sheriff's department. He hadn't liked him from the beginning, and was still scratching his head over hiring the lazy kid.

"Malcolm Dangil. Fired his lazy ass the other day. He only worked for me one day. Let me take that back—he only worked half a day, if that. Why, what's he wanted for anyway, stealing? He looked the type; never did trust him."

"No, nothing like that. We just need to question him about his whereabouts last Friday night."

"I can tell you where he was Friday night. He was at that bar all night. That's probably why he didn't show up for work the next day. One of my other guys said he saw him there Friday night."

"Do you happen to know where he lives?" Foley asked as he retrieved his notepad, anticipating jotting the address down.

"Sure, but not off the top of my head. I'll need to go back to the garage to look at his application."

"Can you go get it now? We'll follow you over there."

"What about the funeral? Aren't you guys going to stick around till it's over?" David asked just as they reached the exact spot where he was previously standing with Morrie Stover, watching the funeral.

***

Morrie was no longer standing there and had moved over to a gravestone, one tall enough to lean against. His legs were tiring standing still, and he was beginning to feel apprehensive about getting started filling in the grave. He was only scheduled to work the morning to take Clayton Daniels's place. Clayton had a more important job to do down by the Redmond Street Bridge.

***

"Yeah, I think that would be a good idea. How much longer do you suppose it will last?" Foley asked, hoping not long, feeling

189

the empty ache in his stomach. His breakfast had digested long ago, having eaten at five that morning.

They didn't have to stand there for very long. The priest had finished his prayers, and now a friend of the family was playing a guitar and singing one of Callie Webster's favorite tunes. To the trio on the slope, it was a cue to leave.

At the town garage David pulled Dangil's application out from the top drawer of the filling cabinet. Inside the folder was his one page application with his address on the north end of town—Mill Street, a section of town known to the locals as the "ghetto district." Rundown apartment buildings occupied most of the narrow street.

"That's all the information Dangil wrote down, one page worth. Nothing more, other than his name and address, but I guess that's all you need," David said, handing the piece of paper to Foley.

Foley jotted the information down in his notepad and handed Dangil's application back. He thanked David with a nod. No words were needed.

David followed them out the door, not intending to hang around any longer. He had to get back to the cemetery to finish the grave, help Morrie lower the casket, and fill it in. With the unexpected delay, after the grave was completed he planned on heading home for lunch, skipping his earlier plan to check his emails. Those, he figured, could wait until tomorrow.

***

Out in the parking lot, Deputy Bradshaw noticed extensive front-end damage on a truck. The damage looked recent; no rust was showing on the metal where the paint had once been. "What happened to that truck? Looks like it happened recently."

"Oh, that truck belongs to Clay. He damaged it last Friday

night. He said he hit a rock on his way to that bar I mentioned. Supposedly on his way, but I'd beg to differ. He most likely did it on his way home. Now, I'm not saying he was driving home drunk. Just my observation, knowing the guy."

"Clay? Would that be the creepy guy the Hays woman mentioned she encountered at the Crow's Nest Tavern? The guy she didn't like too much," Bradshaw asked his boss.

"Yeah, must be. She said he worked here," Foley said, looking at David for confirmation.

"His name's Clayton Daniels, if that's the guy. Why, what's he done? It must have been one hell of a night," David surmised, thinking about Clayton's droopy-eyed condition the next morning at work, arriving late and looking like hell.

"We're following up on a missing person who was last seen leaving the Crow's Nest Tavern with this Malcolm fella. We also know this guy Clayton left about the same time they did. I'd like to have a talk with him. He may be able to help clear this whole thing up. Is he around someplace?" Foley asked.

"Clay's downtown removing the damaged guardrail and making sure the temporary barrier he put up until the fence company can fix it is still in place. The way that boy works sometimes, I'm thinking he'll be there for a while. It's on Main Street down by the Redmond Street Bridge. It's almost lunchtime though. He might have gone home for lunch."

"Thanks David, we'll check with him later. If you happen to see him before we do, do us a favor and don't mention anything about this."

David nodded, wondering what the hell was going on. The worst storm in years had hit town, and now it looked like he was going to be shorthanded. When it rains it pours. He got in his truck and drove back to the cemetery to bury the dead.

191

CHAPTER 23

Sheriff Foley stood outside his vehicle, staring up at the old dilapidated apartment house, wondering if he had the wrong address. There should have been a property condemned sign posted on the side of the building, not an apartment for rent sign. To him the building looked like it should have been condemned years ago and torn down to make way for a newer design, a place where someone might want to live. His deputy thought the same, saying so as he stood next to his boss, shaking his head in disgust.

The apartment house sat on a quarter-acre lot on the north end of town, near an abandoned boatyard. Unused railroad tracks ran along the side of the dead-end street behind the apartment house, and disappeared beyond the boatyard into an overgrown thicket. There were other apartment buildings on the same street, and even though those buildings were in rough shape, Malcolm Dangil's building was the worst of the lot. New paint and a new roof would have only made a dent in the needed repairs to make the three-story building look respectable. The front porch sagged forward, sinking into the ground, and the rock foundation the house was built on slanted inward, making the house appear to lean forward as well.

Seeing the shape of the building's exterior, one could only expect the interior to be in the same sad condition, or even in worse shape. That's exactly what Foley and Bradshaw thought as they crept up the front porch steps, wondering if it would hold their weight.

The address on Dangil's application only stated the street address, omitting his apartment number, so Foley instinctively knocked on the first door he came to. An elderly man, who looked a few years beyond the age of seventy, answered the knock. The smell of tobacco smoke hung heavy inside the man's apartment, and Foley could also detect the foul smell of body odor.

***

The man was surprised, to say the least, to see men in uniform knocking on his door. In fact, he would have been surprised if anyone knocked on his door. The last time Freddie Rogers had a visitor was Christmas Eve, five months ago, the day his landlord dropped by for his annual holiday visit, wishing all his tenants happy holidays.

***

"I'm looking for a Malcolm Dangil. Do you know what apartment is his?" Foley asked, expecting a quick response and not having to inhale the unpleasant body odor any longer.

"Who?" Rogers asked after pausing a moment trying to comprehend the question. He was still in his pajamas, causing Foley to wonder if he had just woken up.

"Malcolm Dangil; what apartment does he live in?"

"Who?"

"Malcolm Dangil! This is 49 Mills Street, isn't it?" Foley asked, still giving the man the benefit of the doubt, that he was not fully awake and needed a moment to register the question.

"Yeah, that's right. 49 Mills Street," Rogers confirmed.

"Good. Now, this Dangil supposedly lives in one of the apartments in this building. Can you tell me which one is his?"

"Sorry, but there's no one here by that name."

"You sure? What about the other apartments? One of them has to be his."

"Nope. As far as I know there is only one other tenant living in this building. That's Chester Briggs, up on the second floor," Rogers said pointing up the stairs behind Foley and Bradshaw.

Foley was perplexed. Either this guy was mistaken, or he had been given the wrong address. He then wondered if maybe the guy living upstairs shared the apartment with Dangil.

"Does this Chester Briggs have any roommates? Maybe the guy we're looking for shares the place with him," Foley asked, taking out his notepad and jotting Chester Briggs's name down.

"No," Rogers said with a snort. "Chester lives alone, I'm sure. Nobody would want to live with that old coot."

"Let me ask you this question. Have you ever seen anyone else besides this Chester fellow coming and going, someone around the age of twenty or so?"

Rogers didn't have to think about the question for very long. Hardly anyone ventured down Mills Street anymore since the boatyard closed because of the recession, which was eight years ago.

"I haven't seen anyone besides the mailman come up that porch, and I hardly ever see Chester use them. Chester usually sneaks out the back door. Sometimes I catch him hobbling down the drive, heading to town. He uses a cane these days. Next thing you know he'll be using one of them walkers. You'll never see me using one of them damn contraptions."

194

"Is Chester home? Maybe he knows something about this Dangil guy," Foley asked, annoyed. He was getting frustrated with all this runaround looking for Malcolm Dangil. When Pamela Hays told him Dangil worked at the town garage, Foley figured he'd find him there and wrap this missing person case up, but of course that would have been too easy.

"Don't think so. Saw him leaving about a half-hour ago, out the back way, like I said. He's most likely down at the diner having lunch. He got me to go with him one day. Took forever to walk there with that stupid cane of his, but the food was pretty good. The waitress wasn't half bad looking either. I think that's the only reason Chester patronizes the place. He thinks he's going to get some of that. The only thing that woman's going to give him is his food tab. She flirts with him in hopes of getting a bigger tip. Good luck with that."

"I absolutely agree with you, she's just doing her job. Now, I can see this is a large building—there has to be other tenants living here besides you two guys. How many apartments are there in here?"

"Now, let's see now," Rogers said, scratching the gray stubble on his chin to help him remember. "There use to be five, now there's only four. Clifford uses the top floor for storage, so that's why there are only four apartments. Two on each floor."

"Who's Clifford?"

"Clifford's the landlord. He owns the place."

"What about the other two apartments—who lives in those?"

"Nobody, they're vacant. They've been vacant for a couple of months since that nice young couple moved out. I can't remember the last time someone rented the other one. The apartment for rent sign out front doesn't do any good. Nobody drives down this street any more. There's no reason to—it's a dead-end with nothing but that old boatyard down there. Maybe someday they'll reopen the yard, but I doubt it."

"A young couple? You mentioned a young couple lived in one of the apartments. Could one of them have been Malcolm Dangil?"

"I suppose so, never did ask his name. The girl, I talked with her a few times—real nice looking. Her name was Valerie, as I recall. Had a dream or two about her, if you know what I mean," Rogers said with an attempted wink, both eyes closing as though they were connected.

"What did the guy look like?" Foley asked, trying not to visualize the old man standing before him beating-off in his striped pajamas.

"I don't know. Sort of a tall fella, I suppose. He was a big guy with reddish hair. Think that was him, the guy you're looking for?"

"No. The guy I'm looking for is not a big guy. The guy I'm looking for is average size with light-brown hair, in his early twenties. So you're sure you never saw anyone else come to the house?"

"Nope, I'm sure. There's no one like you described been by here that I can recall. Maybe you ought to try asking the old lady that lives in the house out back, down at the end of the drive. I did see some kid walk up there one day a week or so ago. I can't quite remember when; being retired, every day just seems to blend in with one another. I use to work in the boatyard at the end of the street until they closed it down. Doesn't seem that long ago, but it's been at least seven or eight years now. Times go by fast when you're not working. Before you know it Christmas will be coming around again."

"What did he look like?" Foley asked, without much hope of

getting a good description.

"Who?"

"The kid you said you saw walking up back to that old lady's house."

"Oh, yeah," Rogers said, then thought for a moment, trying to picture the guy. "From what I can remember, he was wearing a baseball cap and sunglasses. It looked to me like he was trying to disguise himself. I almost called Clifford but changed my mind, thinking maybe the kid was just going to visit the old lady who lives there. Maybe he was her grandson or something."

"That was a week ago, you said?" Foley asked, thinking about the baseball cap Rogers had mentioned. Pamela had said he wore a cap when she saw him, but wasn't sure if it was a baseball cap or not.

Rogers only nodded, hanging onto the doorknob for balance. "And you're positive you haven't seen him since or before last week?"

"Positive. You think that could be the kid you're looking for?"

"At this time, I have no idea," Foley answered. All he knew was he was beginning to get extremely frustrated. With all the running around they'd done they were no better off than when they'd started that morning. For all he knew they could be on some kind of wild goose chase, wasting valuable time when he could be doing something more important.

Not getting any headway with Rogers, and with this Chester fellow at the diner having his noontime lunch, Foley decided his best course of action would be to try contacting the landlord.

"What did you say your landlord's name was?" Foley asked, pulling out his notepad and pen again, this time anticipating jotting the name down.

"Clifford. He lives over on Deer Hill Drive. Number 28 Deer Hill. I know that's where I send the rent money."

Foley was almost shocked Rogers knew the landlord's address. It was the only positive information he'd gotten out of the old man.

On their way to their vehicle Foley looked up the gravel drive that stretched about a hundred yards, between the two apartment houses, and noticed a small house nestled quietly near a wooded area. Beyond the house he spied someone standing in the yard lifting what looked to him to be a birdfeeder, awkwardly placing it on the pole that held the birdfeeder. Figuring the person must be the old lady Rogers had spoken about, Foley decided to have a talk with her. Find out if she knew anything about this Dangil fellow. Who knows, she just might be the key to finding out where this Dangil fellow lived. She very well could be Malcolm Dangil's grandmother and he lived with her, he surmised.

Before taking a walk up the drive, Foley headed to his cruiser to radio in to the office. He needed to check in with the dispatcher to see if there was anything more crucial than chasing down a missing teenager who most likely was off on a fling. The dispatcher on duty told him it had been quiet all morning, nothing other than the usual complaints about the damaged roads caused by the recent storm.

CHAPTER 24

After returning home from the bank and the grocery store, Elsie went out to her backyard and filled the nearly empty birdfeeder. Normally she only needed to fill the feeder every third day, but lately it's been every other day. Elsie figured the increase in feeding was due to the returning migrating birds, as spring was in full bloom. She had no complaints about filling it other than having to purchase bags of birdseed more often from the store. She would like to buy the larger economy size bags, which would also save her money, but she could only pull so much weight in her cart. The size bags she bought lasted about two weeks. Now, with the increase of bird activity, a bag of birdseed lasted no more than a week. The economy size, she figured, would last a month or more. If she had cared to ask, which she'd never do being too damn stubborn, the owner of Bud's Grocery store would have gladly sent one of his bagboys over to deliver the larger economy size bag of birdseed to her house.

Now, with all her daily chores completed, Elsie was comfortably resting in her rocking chair out on the screen porch sipping on a cup of hot tea. She enjoyed sitting on her porch on warm days, rocking back and forth while gazing out over the backyard of green grass that stretched up to the edge of the woods. Somehow sitting on her back porch made her feel younger, maybe because not much had changed since she first moved into the house with her husband, Claude. The only changes they'd made over the years living there were planting a vegetable garden, which had since turned to weeds, and putting up a couple of birdhouses and the one birdfeeder. Other than those changes, and the trees growing higher, the backyard looked almost the same.

Chubs, the more demanding of her two cats, was also comfortable, softly purring in Elsie's lap, most likely dreaming of snagging one of the songbirds she could hear chirping off in the distance. To Elsie's disappointment, Chubs had snared one of the dainty birds in her mouth once, prancing the half-dead bird around like a trophy. Now neither Chubs nor her adopted sister, Lilly Bell, were allowed outside.

The birds, having filled their bellies with birdseed, were now enjoying the sunny morning in the camouflage of the spring foliage, flying between a grove of sumacs on one side of her yard and the birdhouses on the other. Occasionally Elsie would see one or two of the birds bathing in the large puddle of water left over from the recent storm. She'd often thought of putting in a birdbath, telling her husband it would be a wonderful addition to the backyard, something for them and the birds to enjoy, but Claude had never gotten around to it. Doing so now was beyond her capabilities, so having a birdbath was just an afterthought.

While Elsie sat quietly on her back porch in the solitude of nature, she wondered if she was the only person alive who enjoyed the pleasure of being alone. Being able to just sit in her backyard and listen to the peaceful sounds surrounding her without a care in the world. Her only responsibilities, besides caring for herself, were her two cats and the songbirds. She had no living relatives or friends that she knew of, and that's the way she liked it—no one to worry about.

When she concentrated, like she often did, by closing her eyes and blocking out the light sounds caused by the gentle breezes flowing warmly through the screen porch and the sweet chirping sounds of the songbirds, she could hear faint noises coming from within the forest. Noises, she knew, were those of little feet snapping twigs and playfully scurrying around on the leaf-covered ground.

Hearing these sounds today, she began thinking of the day she spied the young man sneaking around in what she considered her property. Even though she did not own the wooded land, and had no idea who did, she still considered it her property. She felt that whoever owned the land had no interest in it, or they would have done something with the property years ago.

With her eyes closed now, she could picture the young man slowly moving about the forest, stopping occasionally to check his surroundings. When confronted by Elsie the young man politely introduced himself as Malcolm, her neighbor. Elsie had not seen Malcolm since that time, but suspected one day he'd return.

Still absorbed in her thoughts of the day Malcolm was trespassing, Elsie was suddenly awoken from her trance by a loud snapping sound, which was followed by the sounds of crunching footsteps. Elsie opened her eyes and looked nervously toward the woods where she thought the sounds were coming from, thinking maybe Malcolm, or another nosey neighbor, was trespassing on her property. Tensely, she held her breath and waited in silence to see who was invading her privacy.

Elsie's hearing perception was not nearly as good as it had once been. The sounds she was hearing were not coming from the woods, as she had thought. They were instead coming from the other side of her house, up the gravel drive, where a layer of crushed-rock lined her sidewalk leading to the backyard.

To her surprise she saw two men wearing tan uniforms standing on the stoop of her back porch steps. Chubs had already seen them and ran inside the house for cover. Elsie had lost her agility a long time ago, or she would have followed Chubs inside and locked the door behind them.

It took a moment for Elsie to recognize who they were; she remembered seeing them at the bank earlier that morning. She also remembered the awkward encounter, bumping into the heavyset man who was standing directly in her exit path. Her first thoughts were they had followed her home, first from the bank then from Bud's grocery store. She had no idea what they would want from her, but seeing them standing on her porch steps, slowly creaking the screen door open and making a step to enter, she speculated whatever it was they were after was not good.

"Excuse us, ma'am, we're wondering if you could help us out. We're looking for a young man who supposedly lives in the apartment house over there," the heavy man said, pointing in the direction they had just come from.

Elsie was not paying any attention toward where he was pointing, or even what he was asking. She was more concerned with their trespassing, and if they were there to harm her. She couldn't imagine what they would want from an old lady with hardly a penny to her name.

"Unfortunately, the person we're looking for doesn't seem

202

to be at home," the heavyset one said, and continued to explain their purpose for being there. "We talked to the older gentleman who lives in the house, and he told us no one by that description lives there. He did, however, mention he might have seen the guy walking up this way a week or so ago. Up here, to your house."

"Who did you say you were, and what could you possible want from me? You're the same two men that followed me from the bank this morning, aren't you?" Elsie demanded to know.

She was showing no signs of fear even though she felt panic growing inside of her. One reason was the large man's meaty hands were weighing heavy on her thoughts. One hand was still gripping the doorframe, and the other dangled near her neck.

***

"Oh, excuse me, I'm sorry. I'm Sheriff Foley, and this here is Deputy Bradshaw," Foley said, turning toward Bradshaw with a look of surprise. He'd thought his uniform and the shining badge was a good enough introduction.

***

Elsie said nothing in response, as she was still wondering why they were there.

"So, would you happen to know anything about this guy? We could have been given the wrong address. It does happen more often than you'd think. Now, after hearing he was seen walking up this way, we're thinking maybe he might live here. Maybe your grandson or relative?"

"I have no relatives and I live alone. I've lived alone in this house for five years now, since Claude passed away. And if you're asking me about someone who lives in one of those rundown shacks out front, you're out of luck asking me. I don't know anything about them people over there, except the old weirdo Chester."

203

"Well, I guess we were mistaken about that. But maybe you happened to have seen him around. This would be a young fellow, in his early twenties. He was seen coming up this way a few days ago, or maybe a week, wearing a baseball cap and sunglasses."

Elsie paused and set her eyesight beyond the two men standing before her, out toward the woods. She wondered if it could be the young man she'd met they were asking about. The day she had seen him, he was wearing a ball cap but not the sunglasses.

"There was this young man roaming around out there in the woods some day last week. I caught him trespassing and threatened to report him if he didn't leave at once. He apologized. Said he didn't know it was private property." Elsie paused, vaguely remembering he did mention where he lived. "I guess he did tell me he lived in one of those apartment houses, but he didn't tell me which one. Or if he did mention which one, I don't recall now. Is that the person you're looking for? He wore a ball cap but no sunglasses."

"It does sound like it could be him. Is there anything else you can add to his description? Or better yet, did he happen to tell you what his name was?"

"He told me, but I'm not sure. I just can't recall at the moment," Elsie said, lifting her eyes toward the roof to help her remember.

"Let me ask you this. Does the name Malcolm ring a bell? Malcolm Dangil."

The name did ring a bell with Elsie, and not just the first name, which was the only name Malcolm Dangil had given her. It was his last name, Dangil, ringing the loudest.

It had been years since she'd last heard the name Dangil. In fact, it had been twenty-one years. It was the year her baby sister — born after Elsie had moved out on her own and married Claude — married a Dangil, and also the same year her sister was murdered, not long after she gave birth to a baby boy. No one was ever held responsible for her sister's murder, but Elsie had heard her sister's husband moved away with the baby shortly after the funeral. That was the last time Elsie heard anything about them, and she hadn't expected to hear anything. She blamed her sister's death on her husband, but nothing was ever done with it, and then he disappeared.

"Yes, I think he did say his name was Malcolm. What do you want with him? He did seem like a nice young man to me. I can't imagine for the life of me what you would want from him," Elsie said, not wanting to think the person the sheriff was asking about was her nephew. It seemed to be only an odd coincidence that the person she encountered in her backyard and lived in the house next door was her nephew.

"It might not be him, but if it is, I don't want you to worried or anything like that. This guy we're looking for hasn't done anything wrong. We just want to question him about someone he was last seen with. Nothing for you to worry about."

***

Bradshaw was standing on the step listening to the old lady, thinking about Dangil roaming around in the woods. Looking out beyond the backyard, picturing the dense forest, Bradshaw began thinking what the possibilities could be that Malcolm was using the protection of the trees for something devious. The first one that came to mind was digging a grave for a premeditated murder. Was there a serial killer on the loose in this county? The Webster girl murdered last week, and now this missing girl. He then remembered there was also another girl reported missing over the weekend, not too far from Redmond. Maybe, even thought it was farfetched, this Mister Zero guy Pamela Hays had mentioned she heard on the radio was for real, and Dangil was playing the part.

"Did this guy happen to say what he was doing out there in the woods? Was he holding anything in his hand, maybe a shovel?" Bradshaw interrupted, going out on a limb with the shovel question.

"No, maybe a stick but definitely not a shovel. Why would he be holding a shovel? What possible reason on earth could there be for him to be bringing a shovel out there in those woods?" Elise skeptically answered.

Foley fell right in line with his deputy's questioning, adding, "What's on the other side of the woods? Anything beyond?"

"On the other side?" Elsie asked, not sure what he was asking. "It's a forest. It goes a long ways, I suppose."

"I was just wondering. Thought maybe there was a development back there."

"Nope, nothing. If you go far enough, there's a farm out there. But I believe that's located in the next town over. Nothing from here to there."

"The Osborne farm," Bradshaw interrupted again. "I think she's talking about the Osborne farm. That's near where they found the Webster girl, isn't it?"

On their way back to the vehicle, both Foley and Bradshaw looked out toward the forest, and then turned and looked directly at Dangil's apartment house. Both thinking if Kelsey was really missing and Dangil had something to do with it, the forest behind Elsie's house may play a big role in her disappearance. Now their boring morning was beginning to become interesting. They suspected, with a high sense of certainty, they were now on the trail of what could be the town's first serial killer.

CHAPTER 25

Clifford Larson lived across town on Deer Hill Drive, which most of the residents of Redmond considered the affluent section of town, but Larson's home was of modest size, a two-bedroom ranch built on a quarter-acre lot. His home was one of the first to be built on Deer Hill Drive. The other homes, the more elaborate stately homes with trimmed hedges, manicured lawns, and beautiful flower gardens lining the front of their two-story homes, came later. And to add more elegance to their homes, on nice days, like the one they were experiencing today, expensive vehicles could be seen displayed in some driveways for the underprivileged to gawk over.

Driving down the street at a slow moderate speed, not wanting to attract attention and have complaints about driving too fast, Sheriff Foley could see how the better half lived. This neighborhood was definitely a much better neighborhood than the one where Larson's apartment building was located. There were no apartment buildings on this street, or anywhere nearby, only single-family homes with paved sidewalks and tall beautiful maple trees lining both sides of the street.

Larson, an elderly man in his late seventies, answered the door wearing a white terry-cloth bathrobe, the belt hanging loose revealing tan-colored pajamas. After seeing Freddie Rogers and now Larson wearing pajamas in the middle of the day, Foley wondered if every elderly person in Redmond wore the same attire all day. This was something he would never do even if he wanted to. To him it showed a sign of laziness. Besides, he knew his wife would never condone it in the first place.

On his days off, his wife, Olivia, would always find something for him to do whether it was inside the house or outside, and chores required work clothes, not nightwear. If Foley plopped his fat ass down at the breakfast table still wearing his nightwear, Olivia would shake her head and ask if he was sick or something. If he were, she'd let it slide. At night, after dinner, she'd be fine with him wearing his nightwear watching television, which she often did herself, but not during the daylight. You never knew when company would unexpectedly show up, she would say.

Not bothering with introductions to find out if the man standing in the doorway was Larson and owned the apartment building over on Mills Street, Foley got right to the point of his intrusion. He only wanted to know if Malcolm Dangil was living in Larson's apartment building, and if so, which apartment number was his. Time was starting to become important, especially if this was going to be more than a routine missing person case, which it now seemed to be leading in that direction. After hearing what Elsie Hermann had told them about Dangil roaming in the forest behind her house, they expected the worst.

When asked, Larson told the sheriff Dangil has been living in the furnished second floor apartment for almost two months. He'd paid the first and last month's rent. There was no security deposit required. His only complaint with Dangil, so far, was that Dangil still owed this month's rent money.

"Malcolm's a quiet tenant; I can see why Freddie has no idea he is living upstairs from him. As far as I know Malcolm doesn't even own a TV. The apartment is adequately furnished, but the renter has to purchase his own entertainment. If Freddie did know someone was living up stairs from him, he'd probably be calling me every other day, complaining about one thing or another. But don't get me wrong, Sheriff, Freddie is an okay guy. He pays his rent on time, sends me a check the first of the month. He just likes to complain. He likes things nice and quiet. The introverted type, I suppose."

Larson hadn't asked what the sheriff wanted from Dangil — he only asked him to leave the spare key he handed him above the apartment doorframe. The key was in case Dangil wasn't home, and also a way of giving the sheriff permission to enter the premises. He said he'd retrieve the key later, telling Foley he'd been meaning to stop by to see Dangil anyway about the rent money he hadn't received yet.

Foley, anxious to get back to the apartment house with the key, thanked him with a wave, leaving Larson standing at the door still talking about the rent money Dangil owed him. He then hurriedly drove back to the apartment house, hoping to find evidence of a possible crime. Now, thinking that the Webster murder was perhaps linked to the missing person case they were pursuing, time had suddenly become crucial.

After knocking on the door loud enough for the downstairs tenant to hear, making sure Dangil wasn't home, Foley used the spare key Larson had given him to let himself and Bradshaw in. He wasn't sure what he was looking for; he really only wanted to talk with Dangil, ask him if he knew anything about Kelsey

Mickelson's disappearance, find out what happened after they left the Crow's Nest Tavern together. Anything about him being seen roaming in the woods out back of his neighbor's yard, searching for a possible burial site and his involvement in the Webster case, would be questioned later. There was no sense warning him of what crime they suspected he might have committed. Doing so would only give him the opportunity to move the body before the wheels of justice started rolling. That was, if there were a body buried in the forest.

Dangil's apartment was small with only two rooms, not much more than a studio. The door they entered opened to a moldy smelling kitchen. A small, narrow, film-covered window above the sink shed the only natural light. Bradshaw turned the light hanging above the table on by pulling a long dangling string. The low wattage bulb did little to improve the lighting.

The kitchen was confining. A round table with two matching green-painted chairs took up most of the floor space in the kitchen. Moving around became awkward, as the two large men constantly bumped into each other in their attempt to search the kitchen, so they made quick work of it and only checked the cabinets above and below the counter.

There were two cabinets above the counter, one on each side of the sink, and two directly below the sink. Foley checked the two cabinets above the counter and found they only contained a short stack of odd size dishes on one side, and some glassware on the other side. Bradshaw searched the two cabinets below the sink, bending at the knees for a better look, and found nothing but plumbing. There was nothing else below, not even any cleaning supplies. The one narrow drawer below the counter contained a tray of flatware, some forks and spoons, and two butter knives.

The other room, besides the closet-sized bathroom, was a

small living room, but average size for an apartment. A pullout couch and coffee table occupied most of the space, with a three-drawer bureau pushed up against the wall. There were no chairs for guests, only the couch that looked like it had come from a secondhand store or was retrieved from the side of the road. Seeing it, Foley thought about Larson's remark that the apartment was adequately furnished. It sucked to be poor, Foley thought, as he took in the rest of the room in one quick motion.

With the limited amount of space, it didn't take the two of them very long to search the place. Most of what they found belonged to the landlord. Dangil didn't seem to own much if anything besides his clothes, which barely filled the top drawer of the bureau. There were no clothes hanging in the small hallway closet. The closet was completely empty except for a couple of plastic hangers and a thick layer of dust on the shelf. The only items of significance they noticed were Dangil's bankbook, from the Redmond Savings Bank, lying on the coffee table, and a forty-dollar withdrawal slip next to it, dated the same day of Kelsey's disappearance.

The most intriguing item Foley noticed was the long, thin-bladed jackknife sticking out of the bankbook, poking right though the center. It seemed the man had anger issues.

Before thinking about contaminating the evidence, Foley pulled the jackknife out from the bankbook, carefully scrutinizing it as he twirled it in his hand. He was looking for signs of mischief, like dried blood near the handle, where the blood would most likely be overlooked. The jackknife, however, was clean and sharp to the touch.

"Besides this knife," Foley said tossing the jackknife back on top of the coffee table, not bothering to stick it back in the bankbook where he'd found it, "there's not much here to go on. I guess we'll have to come back at another time. I'll ask the old-timer downstairs to give us a call when he sees Dangil, and also inform him there is someone living upstairs from him, and to be more diligent about his surroundings the next time." He had been hoping Dangil was home, and hoping even more that Kelsey was with him.

***

"Where to now? Try to get a search warrant?" Bradshaw asked, looking at his watch. It was nearing one-thirty. He urgently wanted to find this guy Dangil as much as Foley, but his stomach was begging for lunch."

"We could do that, get a search warrant, but we really don't have enough evidence to get one. A judge would tell us all the evidence we have is circumstantial. For all we know, Dangil could have been roaming around out there in the woods looking for a secluded place to grow marijuana. Besides, there isn't anything here to go on — we've searched the whole place."

"Well, I guess there's not much we can do until Dangil pops up. What's next on the agenda?" Bradshaw asked, still hoping for lunch. He had been thinking about it for over an hour. It wasn't like Foley to miss lunch, and he usually ate at about the same time each day, which was noon when most people ate lunch. If Foley ate later in the day he'd become grumpy, not a pleasant person to be working with, especially cooped up in the front seat of a vehicle, frustrated that things weren't going good, like today.

***

"We could go have a talk with the guy at the town garage, see what he knows about Dangil," Foley teasingly answered, knowing Bradshaw was thinking about lunch. He was also getting hungry, and thinking about ordering a chicken-fried steak sandwich and a large side of greasy fries.

212

"Graham? What else can he tell us?"

"No, not him. I mean the guy who owns the damaged truck. Maybe he knows something. After all, he was at that tavern Friday night with Dangil, and they left at about the same time. Maybe these guys are in cahoots."

***

"I guess that's a possibility. There was something suspicious about the guy telling Graham his truck was damaged on the way to the Crow's Nest Tavern, when it most likely happened on his way home, or…." Bradshaw paused thinking about this Daniels fella could have damaged his truck on some old tote road, not running into a rock like he claimed happened. What size of rock could he have possibly hit that would have caused that amount of damage? It would have to have been a boulder at least three feet high.

"Or what? It really doesn't matter if he did it on his way to the tavern or after."

"I don't know, Sheriff. I was thinking he could have damaged it a different way, like taking a drive on some dirt road out in the backwoods and hitting a tree. Maybe taking an unwilling person on some joy ride."

"That's something we're going to have to consider, but I'm starving. What do you say to us going to lunch at that diner the old man mentioned? Maybe we'll find this Chester fellow who lives across the hall. Kill two birds with one stone. I'm sure he must know Dangil is living on the same floor. Maybe he heard some kind of commotion that night. Who knows, maybe he even heard a woman scream."

213

CHAPTER 26

The sign out front of the Redmond Diner stated the food was "home cooked," meaning made from scratch, not pre-made in some large out-of-state factory. The home cooked food prepared in this kitchen most of the time lived up to expectations, and did not disappoint either Foley or Bradshaw as both enjoyed their respective meals, consuming their selection in record time.

Skipping his first choice of ordering a chicken-fried steak sandwich because it wasn't on the menu, Foley ordered a large deep-fried haddock sandwich, topped with lettuce and tomato, and a large side of fries, which he covered with ketchup. He also downed two tall glasses of cola without ice. The health conscious Bradshaw consumed a tuna melt with coleslaw, and a tall glass of iced tea.

Sheriff Foley's only complaint, other than having just missed running into Chester Briggs, was the lack of service. As their order was placed before them, Foley asked the waitress for extra tartar sauce for his haddock sandwich. The waitress smiled at Foley with an acknowledging nod and disappeared into the kitchen.

She arrived sometime later with a small container of tartar sauce just as Foley was about to swallow his last bite.

After paying the tab and leaving a moderate tip, the standard fifteen percent, Foley and Bradshaw exited the diner with a planned attack on how to handle Clayton Daniels when they located him. Mainly what questions to ask Daniels, like what he did after leaving the Crow's Nest on Friday night and, most importantly, what really happened to his truck. The damage was quite extensive. The whole right side of the truck was damaged, from the headlight to the taillight. The damage also made driving the truck at night illegal. If Daniels continued to state that the accident happened on his way to the tavern, and he admitted operating the truck after leaving, then Foley could ticket him with driving an unsafe vehicle. Mentioning this, threatening to pull his license, may worry Daniels enough to cause him to tell the truth, or at least come up with a different scenario contradicting his first story. Usually if someone was lying they were hiding something.

Before pulling out of the diner's parking lot, intending on driving back to the town garage, Foley received a call over the radio from the dispatcher on duty that a woman's body had been found in the neighboring town of Benton, ten miles up the coast from Redmond. Foley told the dispatcher he'd be there in five minutes.

Pushing his vehicle and driving capabilities to the limit, Foley arrived at the scene in just under twelve minutes, parking behind a deputy's vehicle and a lawn maintenance work truck, with the name Burger Landscaping Contractors printed on both sides of the truck. About thirty yards out in a field he could see the deputy standing with a group of four young men, looking down at what he suspected to be the woman's body.

215

"Remind me to remind Hagerman what the basic procedures are when finding a dead body. Anybody with any common sense, especially someone in law enforcement, should know you keep everyone away from the crime scene," Foley angrily told Bradshaw as they made their way toward the group. "Look at them idiots," he continued ranting. "They're probably stepping all over crucial evidence."

Deputy Joe Hagerman stepped aside to let the sheriff have a close look at the mutilated body, telling the others standing with him to move back. Foley looked at his deputy and only shook his head. He then stepped in for a closer look, watching his steps. The grass around the body was matted down and muddied from the vicious activity that must have occurred during the horrific attack. He noticed footprints of different shoe sizes all around the body, as well as animal tracks.

Foley had expected to see the woman stretched out on her back, facing the sky with open arms and legs spread wide. Maybe see her clothes ripped off and her neck sliced open, with a good amount of dried blood covering her torso. What he saw, however, wasn't even close. At first he couldn't tell what he was looking at. If he hadn't heard there was a woman's body found out in the middle of a field, he would have presumed the bloody mess he was staring at was not human, maybe a deer taken down by a pack of wild dogs or coyotes.

"I wouldn't have imagined seeing anything like this when I woke up this morning, Sheriff," Hagerman said. "And such a nice day too."

"What the fuck is it?" Foley rhetorically asked, but still wondered how his deputy, who didn't even know the procedures on securing a crime scene, knew the decomposing body was a woman. Foley could see what he presumed to be the head, and below, what remained of the torso. There was no skin to be seen on the torso, just rib bones and chunks of bloody flesh and guts. The legs had been pulled completely apart from the hip joints. Foley had thought the Webster girl's mutilated body, found in a similar field, was gruesome, but her body didn't begin to match this mutilated pile of mess.

"I'm pretty sure it's the woman who was reported missing, Sheriff. Looks to me like coyotes feasted on her for a while. I found her jacket. Well, actually that fellow right there found her jacket, black with rhinestones across the shoulders," Hagerman said, motioning toward a tall black man, stoically staring at the scene around him like he was visualizing what had taken place. "He found the jacket a few yards over there, by that rock. It looks like it was ripped to shreds, with a knife, I'm sure. Cut in long strips."

Foley glanced over at the man, who was standing mostly by himself, away from his three employees. "Is that so?"

Matt Burger confirmed what the deputy said with a nod. When asked how he spotted the body from the road, Burger told Foley they happened across the body when he stopped the truck to take a leak. With no traffic, he stood behind the truck and looked out over the field while peeing, and noticed what looked like a dead animal.

The answer sounded plausible to Foley, so he turned his attention back to the human remains at his feet. There were about a million flies hovering around the corpse, and about a million more walking on top of it, some crawling around inside. Foley swatted at the nasty buggers, but it did no good and only seemed to attract more.

"Hagerman, how do you know it's the missing woman? I can't even tell if this thing is human."

"Well, if you take a closer look you can see her head is right over there," he said, pointing near the upper torso. "Looks like something was tied around her neck, maybe a rope. You can still see part of it just below where he sliced her throat. And right there, you can see hair. The hair color matches the missing woman's hair."

***

Deputy Bradshaw, who was holding back, stepped forward to make his own examination. The smell was nauseating, enough to make any man vomit. Fortunately, he was able to hold his lunch down. It would have been an embarrassment if he hadn't, and he'd have been the brunt of a few jokes back at the sheriff's office.

Leaning down as close as he dared, Bradshaw could clearly see there was something wrapped around her neck, and suspected it most likely was her shirt, having been pulled up, not a rope as Hagerman thought. The body's midsection was a bloody cavity, with chunks of flesh and broken rib bones. Below, where the legs had been separated from the pelvis, he noticed her pants were wrapped around her feet. If the body hadn't been discovered, in a few days there would have been nothing left to autopsy.

"Yeah, looks like the pervert got a little anxious and was only able to pull her clothes partially off before he raped her. After he was finished he killed her, and then left her body here for the coyotes to feast on," Bradshaw continued, wanting to get his thoughts out. He figured the more opinions mentioned the better.

"Or it was staged to look like she was raped," Foley suggested.

"Why's that?" Bradshaw asked.

"It's kind of hard to rape a woman with her legs together. He'd have to pull her pants off, at least one pant leg anyway. But I guess we won't find that out until we get an autopsy report, if it's possible, which looks impossible to me. And speaking of that, I wonder what's keeping everybody?" Foley said, looking down the road expecting to see the state police crime scene guys arriving. They were usually one of the first to arrive on the scene.

"Should be here any minute, Sheriff. I was told they were dispatched at the same time you were notified," Hagerman informed him.

"Hagerman," Foley said in a demanding tone. "While we're waiting for them to arrive, why don't you take these guys back to your vehicle? I'm sure the crime scene guys will want to talk with them. Finn and I will take a look around till they get here."

After telling Burger and his crew from the lawn company to go wait by their truck, Foley asked Hagerman again how he knew it was the missing woman. He hadn't been paying much attention to what his deputy was telling him at the time he first arrived, because his thoughts were consumed with what he was looking at.

"Her hair color and the jacket she was wearing were a match," he told Foley.

"How can you determine the hair color matches? To me, with all the blood and muddy dirt mixed in, the hair could be any color."

"I don't know, but if you take a closer look, right here...," Hagerman answered, pointing the stick he was holding at an area behind the head. "It looks brunette to me."

"What color hair did you say?"

"Brunette. Why?"

Foley paused, remembering the report for the missing woman, Kelsey Mickelson, listed her hair color was blonde, not brunette. Her graduation picture in her bedroom also confirmed her hair was blonde. Looking closer, toward where Hagerman pointed,

219

the hair definitely looked much darker in color, and there was no way it could be considered blonde. However, he conceded the hair could have been blonde before, but now, mixed with dirt and blood, it appeared to be darker.

"Oh, nothing much. I was just thinking the report mentioned her hair color was blonde, not brunette. But I can understand why you thought it looked darker. It looks like a brunette color to me too. You could almost say the hair was black with all that shit mixed in."

"What do you mean, Sheriff?" Hagerman asked, looking confused.

"You said you thought that her hair was brunette colored. I can understand why you think that. She was most likely dragged out here. Her hair got mixed with dirt, blood, and whatever. So now it looks like her hair is darker, more like a brunette."

"No, Sheriff, the report stated her hair was brunette and she was wearing a rhinestone jacket. This fits the description to a tee."

Foley was now the one confused. "The missing person report listed her hair color as blonde. I have the report sitting on the front seat of my vehicle. I've even seen a recent picture of her when I went to her house this morning. Unless she dyed it recently, her hair was definitely not any shade of brown. Her hair was blonde."

"Which report is that? The report I have has her hair color brunette."

"The Mickelson girl. She was reported missing yesterday over in Redmond."

"I don't know anything about her. The report I'm talking about is for Morgan Spencer. She lived not far from here. You remember the report. The girl was on her way home last Thursday night from the mall, but never made it home. At first we thought she was a runaway since she did it once before. What the hell's going on here, Sheriff? That's two missing girls in one weekend."

Foley had forgotten all about Morgan Spencer, the girl reported missing by her parents. They had mentioned their daughter had run away previously, but insisted that was not the case this time. Foley had assigned one of his other deputies to the case, but had not heard any updates since.

In the distance he could hear the sounds of sirens heading their way. Two state police cruisers pulled to a stop behind his vehicle, followed by the crime-scene R.V. The lull after the weekend storm was short lived. Foley's demanding workload was about to push Kelsey Mickelson's missing person's report to the back burner.

***

Within a week's time the Mickelson report would be buried beneath a pile of paperwork and long forgotten until autumn, when two more bodies were found.

CHAPTER 27

Denial was the stage confronting her now, according to the professional guide to acceptance she'd found on some religious website. Denial was the first stage in the five stages of grief for a lost loved one. The next stage she could look forward to was anger, and after that, a heavy dose of nightly prayers. Then when those failed, depression would set in. The final stage was accepting the fact that she would never see Kelsey Mickelson again—in this lifetime, anyway.

Pamela dismissed the idiotic logic behind the so-called professional guide to acceptance and turned off her computer. She then plodded her way into the kitchen to make a batch of margaritas. Margaritas, she discovered, had a way of easing all her problems, even the most troubling ones. Tonight she added an extra amount of tequila.

While sipping on her third margarita, Pamela started to feel more than just a little buzzed. The extra amount of alcohol she'd added to the mixture was influencing her thoughts, causing her to feel it was her fault for letting Kelsey leave the tavern with someone they hardly knew anything about.

Being an only child, Pamela had always felt like she was Kelsey's older sister, although they were basically the same age, with Pamela being two months older, which meant she was suppose to watch over her, make sure she didn't fall into trouble. Tonight she truly believed she'd failed in her responsibilities to protect Kelsey.

Staring at the near empty glass in her hand, Pamela blamed her failure to protect Kelsey on her drinking. There was no doubt in her mind that if she had not been drinking that night, she never would have let Kelsey leave with Malcolm Dangil.

Despondently, she set the glass down and thought about quitting. After all, she wasn't of legal age to drink alcohol. But after giving it more thought, she felt tonight wasn't a good time for such a drastic measure. By the time she poured the remaining mixture from the blender into her glass, she'd convinced herself Kelsey had only spontaneously decided to go off on some romantic fling. A stupid puppy-love thing with some guy she'd just met. A new boyfriend tops your best friend every time. Pamela, herself, had ditched her friends for a new fling numerous times, although not for more than a night or two.

The thought of Kelsey running off with some guy she'd just met made her laugh for a moment, putting her mind at ease, and she contemplated making another batch of her favorite concoction. Before pulling the tequila bottle back down from the cupboard she glanced at the clock, and noticed it was getting late and she had to work in the morning.

No, another batch of margaritas wasn't a good idea. She didn't want to go to work in the morning with another hangover, like she had the previous Saturday morning. The thought of having to stand behind a counter feeling sick like she had the worst flu ever invented, and confronting disgruntled customers, who obviously would be anxiously waiting for her to count their money, didn't sound very appealing to her. All she could think about was the previous Saturday morning, nursing a monster hangover and wanting to go home and cuddle under the blankets in her nice warm bed, and listen to the comfortable sound of the pouring rain. The only time the rain sounded comfortable to her was when she was in bed and had no place to be. Other than that, she hated the rain.

No, she couldn't deal with another day like that. So tonight she decided she was going to be a good girl and head to bed early for a good night sleep. Something she hadn't been able to do for the last four nights.

As she reached to switch off the kitchen light, Pamela noticed the portable radio sitting on the counter. Seeing the radio reminded her of the Doctor Nancy program Kelsey said she often listened to. Pamela was hoping to catch the program, to see if the sheriff was right about saying the program was most likely one of those syndicated ones. When she'd mentioned Kelsey was worried that the creepy man they met at the tavern, who turned out to be Clayton Daniels, could be Mister Zero, the sheriff told her syndicated programs were broadcast all over the country. The weirdo who called into the program could have been calling from as far away as California. He also mentioned there were probably fifty other towns called Redmond in this country, and the odds of it being this Redmond was as remote as the town itself.

"Yes, but how many are near the coast?" Pamela asked, hoping the sheriff would put some thought into the possibility the man could actually be from around here, and maybe even be the man from the tavern, Clayton Daniels.

224

"Many," he answered, dismissing the idea it was their Redmond. "I'm pretty sure there's a Redmond, California, or maybe even a Redmond, Oregon."

At the time the sheriff's comment had persuaded her to think the creepy man most likely was calling from far away. Now, after giving it some thought, she remembered Kelsey was adamant that he had said he was living in Maine on the coast, near the town of Redmond. Or did Kelsey mention Maine at all? She couldn't remember. Now, seeing the radio, she wanted to find out if this was true, and if the program was indeed a syndicated program.

Pamela wasn't sure which radio station the program was broadcasted on, but the last time the radio was turned on was Friday night when Kelsey had tuned into the program. Since she hardly used the radio herself, she knew Kelsey was the last person to use it. She remembered Kelsey saying the program was on weeknights starting at nine o'clock. Since it was Wednesday and conveniently one minute till nine, she turned on the radio.

To her surprise the radio was tuned to the FM country music station she often listened to. She then remembered Kelsey had changed it back before they left for the tavern.

Remembering Kelsey had mentioned the station was broadcast on AM, either 960 or 980, Pamela turned the knob to AM and quickly found the station. However, instead of the program she expected to hear, there was a recorded message saying the regular programming for the Doctor Nancy radio broadcast would not be aired tonight because Doctor Nancy was taking a much needed vacation. The station then began broadcasting reruns of Casey Kasem's *American Top Forty*. The first song played was "Smoke from a Distant Fire" by the Sanford-Townsend band. She had never heard the song before and thought it was pretty good. The lyrics about a man's girlfriend sneaking around on him reminded her of her own love life.

When the song finished Pamela turned the radio off and decided to call the station. She dialed the number she located in the phonebook, which was answered on the fourth ring, but to her disappointment there was only a message stating the station was running on an automated recording after six in the evening.

On her way to her bedroom Pamela accidentally kicked Theodore's bed-box that was in the living room next to the couch. She hadn't thought she'd miss the four-year old cat if he ever decided to take off, but she was missing him now, more than ever. She wanted to pick him up in her arms and cuddle in his soft black fur, listen to his purring heart. But he was gone, disappeared, just like Kelsey had disappeared into the night. Strange, she thought, that they both disappeared on the same night, and a miserable night at that.

The next morning while getting ready for work, Pamela called the radio station again. This time the receptionist politely answered the phone with a pleasant sounding "good-morning" voice. When asked about the Doctor Nancy program, the woman said it was indeed a syndicated program. Pamela then asked if she knew anything about a caller named Mister Zero. She said no, she never listened to the program, but the receptionist did back up the sheriff's comment by mentioning Mister Zero could be calling from anywhere, from Key West all the way to Los Angeles.

"What about Redmond?" she asked. "He mentioned he was calling from a town near Redmond."

"Could be. He could have called from here, but it's doubtful. Is there anything else I can do for you?" she politely asked.

Pamela thanked the receptionist for the information and contentedly hung up the phone, feeling more confident now that Kelsey's Mister Zero was nowhere near their Redmond, and Kelsey was most likely on some love trip with the new beau in her life, the mysterious Malcolm Dangil. By tomorrow, Pamela thought with a smile, Kelsey would be sitting at her kitchen table drinking margaritas, and laughing about how stupid love really was.

Pamela decided after work she was going to the Redmond Animal Shelter and adopt a new Theodore. Maybe adopt a female this time, one not apt to escape into the night for a one-night jaunt and come home with smoky eyes from a distant fire.

CHAPTER 28

Summer weather arrived uneventfully, warm and dry as expected. The humidity would come later, in July, when the tourists flooded the beaches. Besides the expected weather, summer also arrived with no unexplained deaths. Unless one was to consider the death of an elderly widow lying underneath her birdfeeder, face down in an economy size bag of birdseed, an unexplained death, since the cause of death recorded on her death certificate was asphyxiation.

***

Before her death, Elsie Hermann had thought about researching to see if Malcolm Dangil was a long lost nephew, but wasn't sure how to go about it. She had heard the advertisement on the radio for ancestry searches, but she didn't own a computer and had no idea how to operate one. The Redmond library came to mind. She had been there before to borrow books, but never had any interest in using their computer. The day she went to the library she arrived too early. A sign on the door informed her the library didn't open until ten during the summer months.

She figured she'd try another day, but that day never came as she died soon after doing what she lived for, feeding the songbirds.

***

Because Elsie was old and frail, the explanation — according to the local coroner, who was a licensed medical doctor and not a certified coroner, and only took educated guesses on the causes of deaths when asked — was that she most likely became disoriented and stumbled, falling face first into the open bag she was dragging across her backyard. The old woman also could have experienced a heart attack or a stroke, the doctor went on to explain in a brief paragraph on the death certificate. He also added with a noted asterisk, the only way to determine the exact cause of death, an autopsy, would have to be performed, and one was not forthcoming. The Redmond town council did not want to incur the expense needed to do an autopsy for an old woman no one really cared about, or even knew existed, and voted unanimously against the doctor's recommendation that an autopsy should be performed.

Doing so would be the only way to determine the exact cause of death, the doctor informed the council, but his recommendations did little to change their vote. So, unfortunately, Elsie was buried a couple of days later without an autopsy, and before the rumors that there might have been more to her death than they realized started to spread.

Chester Briggs, Elsie's neighbor, who had a history of sexual abuse, discovered her body three days after her demise. He told the deputy he hadn't seen the old lady in days, and decided to stop over to check on her well-being. The deputy, Finn Bradshaw, thanked the considerate neighbor and closed his notepad. What he didn't know was that Chester Briggs was a man with a history. Some folks around town did know, and rumors quickly began to spread around town that he had more to do with her death than just happening across the body.

Back in the day when Chester was a young adult, a loner roaming around town looking and acting weird, he was known as "Chester the Molester." Back then, before sexual awareness became a hot topic, folks laughed at the accusations instead of acting upon them; therefore, Chester went unnoticed. Now most of the folks around town, after hearing he was once known as "Chester the Molester," believed there was more to the story than what the doctor concluded, and believed an autopsy should have been performed anyway, with or without the town council's approval. Those voices, however, fell on deaf ears. Elsie was buried next to her husband, Claude, in the lower section of the cemetery near the old gnarly pine, and was not going to be exhumed.

There were other rumors spreading through town that summer. Since there were no more murders of young women, most folks felt the person responsible for murdering Callie Webster and Morgan Spencer, and mostly likely Kelsey Mickelson, had left town, and that person was none other than Malcolm Dangil, the mysterious young man last seen leaving the Crow's Nest Tavern with Kelsey. They, of course, were only rumors, no incriminating evidence to support them, so the sheriff's department filed away Kelsey Mickelson's missing person report. The case went cold, left in the filing cabinet next to Callie Webster and Morgan Spencer's unsolved murder cases.

**

The bank hired a replacement for Kelsey's teller position, a young man with an associate's degree in accounting. Richard Robinson gladly accepted the position with the hopes of advancement into the accounting department, an incentive mentioned in his interview in an attempt to persuade him to accept the low paying job. Pamela never got along with Robinson, thinking it should be Kelsey working next to her, not some stocky built, twenty-two year-old smart-ass who thought he knew everything about the banking business, but knew next to nothing.

To add more misery to Pamela's miserable summer, Matt Burger had dumped her for a young, sexy looking waitress working at the Crow's Nest Tavern. Since Pamela had told Burger she never wanted to set foot in the tavern again because it reminded her of Kelsey, and she never felt like going out to any other place, Burger moved on. She got over losing Burger in less than a week, but the pain of losing Kelsey never left her — the new teller was a daily reminder.

CHAPTER 29

On a bright chilly Saturday morning in late September, two young brothers crept along the edges of the Abenaki River under the Redmond Street Bridge, looking for creepy things living beneath rocks and stones that could easily be turned over by the nine and eleven-year old hands. Even though the sun was shining against a background of blue sky, the temperature was still chilly as a wave of cold air drifted down from Canada. The chill did not deter the two boys from wearing short pants and T-shirts, attire not condoned by their mother. Their mother was more of a deterrent for what they wore than the chilly conditions. Today the two boys slid out the back door unseen by their mother.

After losing interest in turning over rocks and finding only slugs and worms, and not the more exciting crawfish and such, the boys began to toss rocks into the river as the water slowly gurgled over boulders and discarded junk that remained stuck in the constantly flowing river. Several yards out from the river's edge, where the river ran the deepest, one of the boys, the older of the two, noticed a large dark object resting just below the surface.

The brothers' world stretched no further than the town limits, and the river was a universe of mystery to their young minds. The discovery of an unknown object was as intriguing to them as the discovery of a new celestial object was to an astronomer. After pointing out the object to his younger brother, both boys inched as close to the edge of the river as they could, without getting their sneakers wet, for a better look at the mysterious object. But even at that close distance they still had no idea what they were looking at.

Noticing several large rocks protruding out of the water, like stepping stones across the universe, the older boy, Donnie, proceeded to venture out to where the object rested below the surface. The first rock he stepped on was relatively easy, flat and dry. The second rock, however, was a bit trickier. When he stepped onto the rock he almost slipped, as all his weight shifted toward the rock when he lifted his other foot off the first rock. After regaining his balance, he cautiously stepped over onto the rock, and then onto the next rock, the rock he thought was the closest to the object.

Leaning his short stature out over the water as far as he dared, Donnie stared into the river, trying to determine what was down there. From where he stood the glare from the sun prohibited him from getting a good look at the object. If he was going to find out what the mysterious object was, he knew he needed to get closer.

Beyond, about a yard from where he stood, he could see another rock looming within a couple of feet of the dark object. The rock surface was relatively flat and seemed reachable, but Donnie dared not chance the leap because the rock looked slippery, only rising an inch above the waterline. Therefore the rock he stood on, he figured, would have to do. That was as close as he was going to get to the object without the possibility of falling in. If he did it would have been a disaster worse than death, according to his mother, if she ever found out he was playing down at the river and fell in.

Donnie turned his sight toward shore, looking for something to poke the object with. There, lying on the shore of the riverbank amongst other debris, he spied a long thin pole, a wooden handle from a broom that had washed downstream from the torrential spring rains.

"Hey Duncan, hand me that wooden stick over there," Donnie said, pointing to the broom handle.

"What stick? I don't see a stick."

"That thing lying right there next you. See it, its right there."

"This thing?" his younger brother, Duncan, asked, pointing at the broom handle.

"Yeah, that's it. Pass it over to me."

"What do you need this for?"

"To find out what this thing down here is, you dumb-ass, so stop asking me questions and hand me that stick," Donnie said, sounding annoyed.

"What is it?" Duncan asked, stretching the broom handle as far as he could without getting his sneakers wet.

"I'm not sure, I can't quite see it. I thought I'd poke it with the stick." He grabbed the broom handle, whose length was nearly equal to his own height.

The rock he stood on was sitting about two inches above the waterline, but just a week or two before it had been completely submerged, and had been since the previous spring when rains ruled the weather. Algae had grown thick and dried to a brown colored powder on top of the rock, but was dangerously slippery below the waterline, with a coating of green slime.

With the broom handle firmly in his hand, Donnie poked the end of it into the slow moving river, testing its depths. From where he stood on the shallow side of the rock, the stick easily touched bottom, but after moving his unsteady legs over to the other side of the rock, where the dark object dug in solid, the river was over six-feet deep, a good foot above the boy's height.

Leaning with the balance of an eleven year old, and trying to keep his weight back from the edge, Donnie reached the stick out as far as he could toward the object, but was unable to reach it.

"Just a few more inches," he said out loud as his younger brother eased his own feet out onto the rock closest to the river's edge.

Hearing Duncan's attempt to join him, Donnie quickly glanced over his shoulder and saw his brother had hopped onto the rock behind him.

"Where do you think you're going?"

"Out with you," he said as he shuffled his feet for a better footing.

"No, there's no room out here for both of us. Besides, you're going to fall in and Mom's going to kill both of us for coming down here. You remember the last time we came down here? We never heard the end of it, and she grounded us for a whole week."

"I remember. But I won't fall in, I swear on Dad's grave," Duncan reassuringly said, as though his deceased father was watching over him like a guardian angel. Their father had died from brain cancer when Duncan was only two and he didn't remember much of him, only what his mother had told him and from the pictures in the family photo album. Donnie was four at the time and still had a few memories, mostly of being tucked in at night and their last Christmas together, three months before

235

his death.

"Yes, you are...look, you're already losing your balance. Now go back."

Duncan held his arms straight out to his sides and intentionally rocked back-and-forth, making like an airplane zooming through the sky, sound effects included. He quickly stopped his playacting when he began losing his balance.

"Okay, I'll stay right here. I just wanted to see what it was."

"Okay then, stay there and don't move," the older boy commanded his brother, then turned and resumed his prodding.

Shuffling his feet with caution, he inched toward the edge of the rock, at the same time poking his stick under the water. "I can almost touch it."

"What is it?"

"I'm not sure, but it's pretty big."

Donnie slid his right foot down the side of the boulder as far as he could without touching the water. He then leaned his body over slightly, just enough to touch the top of the object with the broom handle. From there he was able to poke at it, but just barely. A few more pokes did nothing, so he poked the object harder to see if it would move, but the mysterious object wouldn't budge. It was wedged in tight between the boulders.

"What is it, Donnie?"

"I don't know," he said as he poked it one more time, this time with a little more force. The broom handle skimmed off the top of the algae covered object, causing Donnie to lose his balance. Suddenly he was under the water, shocked with embarrassment that he, and not his baby brother, had been the one to fall in.

Splashing his way to the surface, Donnie grabbed hold of the slimy object and looked at his brother with his eyes wide open. "Shit, I fell in. The damn rock was slippery as hell."

"You're in trouble now. Mom's going to kill you."

"Shut up; don't tell her."

"She'll know anyway—you're all wet."

"Shut up, you rat ball. I'll kill you if you rat on me. All I have to do is change my clothes," he said as he tried climbing up the slippery boulder, with no luck. There was nothing he could grab hold of that wasn't covered with algae. He knew the only way he was going to get out of the water would be to swim to shore.

"Is it cold?"

"Not really. It's cold, but once you're in it's not so bad."

"What was that thing anyway?"

Before swimming toward shore, Donnie looked at his slime covered hands, and then looked over toward the mysterious object. "I don't know, but I think...I think it was a slimy tire."

Instead of climbing out of the water, Donnie swam back over toward it. He then took a deep breath of air and disappeared under the water, opening his eyes in the process. The water was cloudy with silt that he had disturbed previously when he kicked off from the riverbed, but he could see enough to tell the object was definitely a tire, and the tire was attached to an upside-down vehicle.

"It's a car!" he yelled to his younger brother as soon as he surfaced. "Damn, there's a car under here. Holy shit, how did it get down here? I'm going back down to check it out," he said, disappearing beneath the water again.

***

Duncan, staring at the ripples where his brother had disappeared, looked on nervously, with a sense of urgency. He hoped nothing bad was going to happen to his brother, but he was also excited to know there was a car under the water, something exciting he could tell his mother.

237

Fifteen seconds later Donnie resurfaced with a rush of adrenaline, coughing up water and gasping for air. His mad strokes splashed the surface like the flat paddle of an oar, and he scrambled out of the water like it was infested with horrifying creatures.

***

Like a horrible nightmare that shatters your dreams and shakes you awake so violently that you fear falling back to sleep, once again the residents of Redmond were haunted by the horrors of the wet bloody spring that they thought had been washed out to sea with the rains. They were now finding out the horrors were right under their feet—beneath the water that flowed along the edge of their quaint little town.

The upside-down occupied vehicle had gone unnoticed for over four long months. Even after the spring rains came to an end and the river subsided back to its normal depth, the vehicle's dark under carriage kept it from being noticed. By the time the vehicle was discovered by the two brothers, the bodies had bloated beyond recognition. River creatures had also added their bites to the disfigurement. Crawfish, eels, and other tiny underwater beasts had feasted on the flesh and organs until the bodies resembled grotesque open-mouthed eyeless dolls. Their deaths were horrible deaths, even though some said drowning was the best way to go. These deaths, however, were filled with pain and suffering as the water had slowly seeped into the vehicle, and the trapped occupants could only wait for their inevitable deaths that did not come soon enough to end their suffering.

CHAPTER 30

After the two bodies were removed from the Abenaki River and carefully stuffed inside body bags, they were then brought to the basement of the local funeral parlor in the hopes of being identified. From there, the bodies would be transported to the state medical facility in Augusta to have their remains autopsied. The decomposed condition of the bodies, however, made it almost impossible for anyone to positively identify them. This was also the sheriff's assessment when he first glimpsed them. To him, their grotesque bloated facial features resembled inflated balloon cartoon characters, ones he vaguely remembered seeing on Saturday morning television as a kid.

Putting his pessimistic opinion of anyone identifying the corpses with certainly aside, Sheriff J.J. Foley rested his hopes of identifying at least one of the bodies on Pamela Hays. Since the vehicle found in the river was registered to Pamela's best friend, Kelsey Mickelson, he assumed one of the bodies was Kelsey. Foley would rather have had a family member identify the remains, but unfortunately there were none that he knew of living in the area of Redmond, or anywhere in the world for that matter. Therefore, with no known relatives, Pamela was requested to do the honors — a request she seriously frowned upon.

Pamela was reluctant at first, saying no way in hell. She told the sheriff she had never in her entire lifetime seen a dead person, and dreaded the thought of seeing one now, especially a friend whom she still mourned.

For weeks after Kelsey disappeared, Pamela was anguished from depression, and struggled to control her composure at the bank, flashing phony smiles as she waited on customers and holding back her discontentment for Richard Robinson by conversing only when necessary, which was almost never. She had just recently started to see the light at the end of the long dark tunnel of hell, sleeping most of the night without waking up in a sweat and screaming from nightmares. She was even enjoying herself, occasionally going out after work with a few of her coworkers — Richard Robinson not being one of those.

Then the news about Kelsey's vehicle having been found in the river started the nightmares all over again. Only a good amount of margaritas helped to ease her anxiety.

Now, after pleas from the sheriff saying she was their last hope because the dead woman's roommate had vehemently declined, Pamela had no choice but to agree to his request. However, she almost changed her mind when she arrived at the funeral parlor.

Skipping the customary greetings, or even a friendly handshake, the first thing Foley asked Pamela was if she knew of any distinguishing marks Kelsey may have in case the body was too decomposed to make a positive identification. This was the second time since she'd arrived that someone mentioned the word decomposed to her. The first time was the funeral director, and now Foley.

Not quite understanding his inquiry, Pamela gave the sheriff a questioning look. Foley then elaborated by asking if she knew of any tattoos Kelsey may have, or scars from an operation. Pamela said no at first, then mentioned the scar on Kelsey's shoulder.

As for the other body, David Graham had done the honors the night before, but with uncertainty, only saying after a quick disgusting glance that it could be Malcolm Dangil, the guy he'd hired and fired after only working half a day. His "could be" comment also suggested the disfigured corpse could be someone else. But since Dangil was the only one missing, and was last seen leaving the tavern with Kelsey, Sheriff Foley said that was good enough for him.

This verification — or partial verification, as Graham was not one hundred percent sure the grotesque body was Dangil — was also good enough to confirm the theory that Malcolm Dangil was the sole person responsible for the murders of Callie Webster and Morgan Spencer. He also most likely would have killed Kelsey Mickelson if the unfortunate accident hadn't occurred. Blame that on the weather.

Most everyone who voiced an opinion felt Dangil's death was justified, and that he'd hopefully suffering tremendous pain while dying. It was God's answer to those who defied Him and sided with the devil. If they had seen his remains, the hollow eye sockets, they would have felt justice was done.

***

The funeral director, Walter Blais, hesitated for a moment to forewarn Pamela what she was about to see before leading her, along with Sheriff Foley, down into the cool, dry basement where the deceased woman was being stored for the time being. Walter told Pamela to be mentally prepared for what she was about to see, and to try to hold her emotions. He told her the body had

241

been in the water for four months, and the deceased would not look anything like the person she knew and loved. Pamela had already heard his regurgitating words before when she first arrived at the funeral parlor, and didn't need to be reminded again, she told him.

***

Walter said nothing to Foley. He knew Foley would have no problem, as he had already seen both bodies twice before, once when they were freshly pulled from the river, and later that evening when he stood next to David Graham in the basement of the funeral parlor, waiting for him to confirm one of the bodies was Dangil. Walter also knew viewing these corpses would be nothing new to Foley, not after seeing the remains of Morgan Spencer's rotting corpse left in an open field to be feasted upon by any creature that happened by, and Callie Webster's bloody corpse left in almost the same grotesque condition.

Because of the unusually warm autumn weather, Pamela wore a light-colored skirt and a sleeveless blouse. The basement, however, felt cold and oddly eerie to Pamela, giving her goose bumps as she nervously followed Walter and Foley along the tiled floor in relative quiet. The only sounds she could hear were the clicking sounds of the shoes she was following. The room they entered, one of three — the other two reserved for preparing the deceased for viewing — was ill lit, with only two large florescent lights hanging from the ceiling. One of the lights was directly positioned over a steel table spotlighting a black body bag. Dangil's body had already been transported to Augusta earlier that morning.

Walter slowly unzipped the body bag, uncovering only the hideous face and top of the torso, just above the bloated, fleshy breasts. He was hoping it would be enough for Pamela to identify the body, but had his doubts. It was difficult enough for someone to identify a body after only a few weeks of decomposition, never mind four months marinating in a river.

The face was badly swollen, with a light-blue, ghostly hue. The hair had a washed-yellow color and was matted to the scalp, looking like a child's plastic wig. One eyelid lay limp, the other completely gone, showing a hollow eye socket. The mouth, partially open, sagged slightly to one side. Where the skin had worn away, bones could be seen poking out from the neck and upper torso.

Pamela stood a good four feet away, not wanting to come any closer. At first glance she started to cry, placing her trembling hand over her mouth. Foley thought her response was a good sign that she recognized it was her friend, Kelsey Mickelson. He was wrong. She only cried thinking that what she was looking at was definitely not her friend. There was no way the thing stuffed inside the black body bag was Kelsey.

"Is that Kelsey?" Foley asked, expecting an affirmative confirmation.

With Pamela's hand still covering her mouth and tears running down her cheeks, she began to tremble. She wanted to turn and run out the door, outside where there was fresh air to breathe, not stale repulsive air emitting from the dead.

"Can I take that as a yes?" he asked again, this time expecting some kind of gesture like an affirmative nod or wave of her hand. She gave him neither and took a couple of awkward steps backward.

Foley moved over next to her and put his hand on her shoulder, gently rubbing in an effort to console her. "There, there, little darling. You'll be fine. We just need to verify it's Kelsey. I know it must be hard on you seeing your friend like this, trying to remember what she looked like when she was alive."

Pamela shook her head, mumbling an inaudible "no," and pulled away from Foley. She didn't want to be in the cold, clammy basement any longer. Her legs began to wobble, and she felt like she was going to collapse at any moment.

"Did you say no, it's not her? What about the scar you mentioned on her left shoulder? Maybe if you step a little closer, for a better view. That's all we need, any kind of identifying mark will do," Foley said, and put his hand back on Pamela's shoulder, trying to push her forward, closer to the body, where Walter held still, waiting to zip up the body bag.

Even from four feet away Pamela could see it was impossible to identify her scar. There was hardly any skin on her left shoulder. A flap of skin, about two inches wide, was partially covering the open space between the collarbone and her upper chest.

Pamela stood in defiance. There was no way she was going to get any closer to the grotesque body. She saw enough to know she would never be able to identify it as Kelsey. She knew it wouldn't have mattered even if she stood directly over the body. It was impossible for anyone to identify the woman. No one could have, not even the woman's mother.

***

Foley's last hope of someone identifying the body ran out the door. Eventually, after Walter mentioned trying a different avenue, Foley did the smart thing and had her dental records checked with the only dentist practicing in Redmond. To his relief they matched. The bloated decomposed body was indeed Kelsey Mickelson.

***

On her way out of the funeral parlor, after swiftly exiting the basement and taking a moment to regain her composure, Pamela overheard two deputies conversing in the lobby. Hearing them mention Kelsey's vehicle, Pamela inconspicuously paused at the water cooler to listen to the rest of their conversation. She wasn't expecting to hear the cause of death, since an autopsy had not yet been performed. In fact, she wasn't expecting to hear anything new about Kelsey's death—it was more an instinctive curiosity that caused her to eavesdrop.

One of the deputies, the taller of the two, Finn Bradshaw, mentioned the vehicle had probably landed upside-down in the river after slamming into the guardrail during the heavy rainstorm last spring. Joe Hagerman, the other deputy, confirmed Bradshaw's theory with a laugh, saying it was funny how they'd thought at first it was Clayton Daniels who did the damage when he ran his truck into the guardrail. He then added, "Who would have thought it would turn out to be the missing girl's vehicle with that Dangil guy inside next to her? What a way to go."

Hearing this, Pamela walked over to them and asked why no one had bothered to check to see if there was a vehicle in the river when they first noticed the guardrail was damaged, especially after she reported Kelsey missing. Not getting a response from either deputy, she stood defiantly with her hands on her hips, trying to control her temper and not yell at them like she wanted to. She wanted them to know they'd made a big mistake, and should be fired for not doing their job.

***

Not thinking anyone was eavesdropping on their casual conversation, both deputies stared at the young woman, appearing dumbfounded. They knew who she was of course, since that was the only reason for their being there in the funeral parlor. Bradshaw had been standing in the lobby waiting for Foley to come back up from the basement. Deputy Hagerman was hanging around to assist in the delivery of the remaining body up to Augusta. They just never expected her to confront them in a bit of rage, and now wondered if they had said something inappropriate.

"Don't you think someone should have looked in the river?" She asked again, this time with a little more emphasis in her inquiry, demanding a response.

"Well ma'am, we did take a look, but after doing a quick observation we determined no vehicle could have possibly gone into the river," Deputy Bradshaw quickly responded.

"You only did a quick observation? No one actually bothered to go down and check to see if there was a vehicle in the river?" Pamela angrily blurted out.

Wanting to defuse the situation before it got out of hand, Bradshaw's answer to her question was blunt, only saying the damage had been thoroughly checked, and it had been determined that a truck probably ran into the guardrail and drove off during the rainstorm. There was nothing to indicate a vehicle had gone through and landed in the river. He didn't bother to mention to her that all the information they got came from David Graham, the head of Redmond's maintenance department, and that the sheriff's department had not investigated the incident. Telling her now that, after finding out it wasn't Daniels, they had never bothered to investigate who had damaged the guardrail, would have only infuriated her more.

"What do you mean, thoroughly checked? First you said a quick observation was done. Now you're saying it was thoroughly checked. Did anyone actually go down and look in the river?" Pamela angrily asked again.

"I don't remember the specifics, but if you recall we had a torrential rainstorm at the time. The river was overflowing, making it impossible to see anything. Any tire tracks would have been washed away. There were also a lot of other important things to deal with at the time. We had that missing person report to deal with, the woman down in the basement."

"Right. I reported that one. I reported Kelsey was missing, and no one bothered to look for her car in the river. Shame on you and your whole department."

"Look ma'am, I'm sorry, but your friend wasn't the only one missing at the time. We had another girl go missing the same weekend as your friend, over in Benton. She was found dead, murdered. Our priorities changed to find her killer. We wanted to find him before he killed someone else."

"At least she was found! If you had done your job Kelsey's body wouldn't have been in the river for four months, and look like some creature out of a horror movie," Pamela responded, and then started to walk away.

"Your friend would have died that night anyway. It was probably best she drowned — better than being hacked into pieces like the two other girls," Deputy Hagerman blurted out. He had been quietly taking all this in, but at the last minute decided to put in his two-cents worth. Bradshaw wished Hagerman had just kept his mouth shut and let the woman walk away.

Pamela turned back with a scornful expression. "What do you mean by that silly remark? Kelsey's dead, she drowned."

"I'm only saying Dangil would have killed her anyway, just like he killed the Webster girl the week before, and then the Spencer girl the night before the storm. There was no doubt he was planning on killing Kelsey. I was only saying, drowning is a lot better than being hacked to death. It's less painful."

The rumors that Malcolm Dangil had killed Callie Webster and Morgan Spencer started when word spread around town that a deranged man, who called himself Mister Zero, was the person responsible for the murders. No one knew who started the rumors, but Pamela Hays suspected it might have been Sheriff Foley, since he was the only one she had told about the radio program.

***

Pamela had told Foley during their brief interview at the bank, when Kelsey first went missing, that Kelsey had listened to the program the night before when the man mentioned he was going to kill again. Kill another demon that was disguised as a teenage girl with blonde hair and green eyes. The man said the demon he was going to slay lived in Redmond, and it was the same night Kelsey disappeared. Sheriff Foley also told the local newspaper they had a suspect named Malcolm Dangil, but unfortunately they were unable to locate him. Putting two and two together, everyone in town, except Pamela Hays, felt Dangil was the mysterious Mister Zero.

David Graham had also influenced Foley, telling him he remembered Dangil mentioning, in their brief interview when he applied for the job, he enjoyed cemeteries and had dreams of eventually working in one. It sounded morbid to him at the time, he told the sheriff, but he was desperate for help and Dangil was the only one who applied for the job. "If there were anyone else," he continued, trying to explain his reasons for hiring a killer, "I would never had hired the guy."

***

"Malcolm Dangil was not the person who killed those two girls. I can assure you of that," Pamela said, looking straight into Deputy Hagerman's beady eyes. "Malcolm Dangil was a nice young man. There's no way he could have done what you and everyone else in this stupid town are saying. It was some other

248

guy who called himself Mister Zero. You should be out looking for him, not standing around here laughing at your oversight in searching for Kelsey. What about that other guy, Daniels? He's the one you should be suspecting, not Malcolm Dangil."

With that, Pamela walked out the door and disappeared out of their sight. The next time they saw her was at the gravesite the day Kelsey Mickelson was buried, wearing black and hiding behind dark sunglasses.

CHAPTER 31

Two days after returning home from the state medical facility in Augusta for a required autopsy, Kelsey Mickelson was finally being buried in the Redmond Cemetery, on a slope overlooking the tranquil New England coastal town. It was the first week of October, when the autumn foliage was nearing its peak. On this bright cool morning the sunlight, peering low through the leaves of the many hardwood trees, gave brilliance to the baskets of colorful flowers surrounding her grave. Her casket, which was made from the finest oak and shined with layers of dark walnut stain, rose above the open grave. To those in attendance, most felt it was a funeral fit for a queen.

Clutching a prayer book tight in both hands, for the purpose of referencing upcoming passages he knew mostly by heart but nevertheless read from the Good Book to avoid a possible blunder, the priest stood over the casket, recalling Kelsey's loving, short-lived life. The priest began by telling humorous stories which he knew only from her friends and coworkers, as he had never had the pleasure of meeting her in person, or even knowing of her existence before her body was pulled from the Abenaki River. Naming a few of her closest friends, first names only, including the name Pamela, he told the mourners standing silently under the rising sun about the good times they'd shared with Kelsey, and her generosity toward others. Her coworkers at the Redmond Savings Bank and the many customers that came to know her, he said, looking at the many sad faces staring back at him, would miss her warm friendly smile. In closing, before finishing with a prayer, he added that the whole town was there today to send Kelsey off to her new life in Heaven.

Pamela Hays took all this in while standing near the grave. As she listened she thought of her own good times with Kelsey, mostly visualizing the last night they'd spent together at her apartment, and later at the Crow's Nest Tavern watching Kelsey's final exit. She then wondered if what the priest was saying was true for all the people standing around her. She knew a lot of the mourners, but there were many others she had never seen before, and thought they were there only to show their respects or were just there for their own curiosity. Behind her there were many more town folks, standing in sparse groups up and down the slope and along the narrow dirt drive near their parked vehicles. As the priest had said, it did seem the whole town had showed up for Kelsey's funeral. Even some members of the sheriff's department were present, standing together next to their vehicles for a quick exit if need be.

Of the five officers Pamela counted, she recognized three, one being Sheriff J. J. Foley. The other two she recognized from the funeral parlor the prior week. She had no good thoughts of them being there, and no decent words to pass along if a conversation was forthcoming, which she highly doubted since their last conversation didn't go so well, with her just about accusing the sheriff's department of not doing their job.

When the funeral ended Pamela remained behind to say her final goodbye. She tossed the bouquet of flowers she was holding on the casket, and then sadly turned and walked away to let the two men, who were standing in silence, lower the casket and complete the burial.

***

Off to the side, David Graham stood silently next to his backhoe. It had been a sad year for him—too many young deaths. Finally, after thirty-nine years of planting bodies into the good sacred earth, his job was starting to get the best of him. His fragile brain could only withstand so much, no matter how much he tried to suppress the inevitable. It was time for him to retire. Today was the final nail in the coffin, he decided. When he got home, he'd tell his lovely wife he had one more grave to dig, and that would be his last.

At home he found his wife sitting at the kitchen table having tea with her friend, Rose Stover, Morrie Stover's wife. As he walked through the kitchen toward the living room to sit in his recliner, to rest his weary body, he told his wife in few words that he was retiring. Margaret harrumphed at the sudden announcement, only saying to Rose that she'd heard that before.

***

Malcolm Dangil's burial was a complete contrast to Kelsey's. And even though his body was never truly identified, Malcolm was buried assuming it was him, since he was known to have driven off with Kelsey that dreadful night. Besides the cemetery workers, not one single person cared to pay their respects for the man everyone felt was one of Satan's descendants. The only persons to witness Dangil's burial besides the gravedigger, David Graham, were the two cemetery workers who had the menial task

252

of lowering the pine box into the six-foot deep hole. One was the forty-year-old laborer named Clayton Edgar Daniels. The other person was Morrie Stover, now only working part time when David needed the extra help.

Fittingly, it even rained that day, a cold hard rain that partially filled the grave with mud, sliding down the sides of the hole before the cheap pine casket could be lowered. The gravesite's location was as dank as the day. Dangil's grave did not have the prestigious status to rest upon the knoll overlooking the somber town, like Kelsey's. No, this dead rotten soul was to be buried in a lonely place, hidden in the far corner of the cemetery under a veil of unattended landscape. It was located in the low lying section, near the gnarly pine tree, and marked only with an inexpensive stone the radio station paid for as long as it referenced Malcolm was Mister Zero.

There were no flowers adorning the grave; weeds grew in their place, which most folks found fitting for an evil man who had ruined a lot of lives. The man's dead soul would be forever forgotten—only his evil bloody crimes would be remembered. In the years ahead, when most of the folks who'd lived through the violent spring storm that brought terror and destruction to Redmond had expired to their own deaths, exaggerated Mister Zero stories would be told to future generations sitting around campfires.

CHAPTER 32

Headlights flickered like ghosts dancing against gravestones as the fast moving truck bounced and weaved over the uneven gravel road. The driver, who cantankerously steered the old beaten-to-death truck, was impaired, having started drinking well before the sun hit the horizon. It was a Friday night, and Clayton Edgar Daniels began his usual Friday night ritual of drinking as soon as he got off work, and continued to drink at home until it was time to head out for a night at the local tavern. On his way to the tavern he spontaneously decided to pay a visit to an old acquaintance. Someone he knew was falsely accused of doing evil crimes, crimes so horrible only the devil would welcome him into his domain after death.

Clayton parked his truck on the crest of the hill leading down toward the cemetery's lower section, where most of the long forgotten impecunious citizens were buried. One of those buried in a spot least visited, but who probably would never be forgotten like some of the others in graves surrounding his—at least not for a long while—was the reason Clayton decided to visit the gravesite.

He had seen the grave earlier in the day, while standing roughly in the same spot where he now sat in his truck when he'd helped his boss bury another poor soul. He hadn't meant to pay a visit when he stood in the daylight thinking about the man buried down there. It had only come to him as he drove by, making a quick turn onto the road leading to the cemetery.

After finishing the beer, he had been drinking on the way, Clayton grabbed another bottle out of his twelve-pack and took a couple of long gulps. He then exited his vehicle with the bottle in hand and awkwardly made his way down the hill. It was a dark, moonless night. The only lights visible were the headlights he'd purposely left on to guide the way.

Following the path the best he could by sidestepping his way down the hill, Clayton eventually made it to the gravestone without falling. He could not read the name on the stone, for it was too dark to see, but he knew the words carved into the granite stone. There was only the person's name and his alias, no dates or comments.

Standing before the gravestone, Clayton thought about that night at the Crow's Nest Tavern, visualizing Malcolm leaving the tavern with Kelsey and him following them out the door. Even though most of that night was a distant memory, like the conversations he had with Malcolm at the bar and the brunette that made fun of him at the table, there was one thing that he would never forget. It was what happened after leaving the tavern.

***

Out in the parking lot he watched them from the cab of his truck, turning his windshield wipes on for a better view. He watched as they leaned into each other for a quick kiss on the lips.

255

A moment later the two were one, embraced in a hot moment of passion. Before they pulled apart Clayton pounded his fist hard on the dashboard, not feeling any pain. He then followed Kelsey's red Ford Focus out of the parking lot onto Main Street, toward the downtown area.

The rain was coming down hard. Not to lose sight of them, Clayton stayed close behind them. Looking through Kelsey's rear window, Clayton could see Malcolm leaning close to her. He felt his anger rising and switched on his high beams for spite.

***

Kelsey knew someone was following her, but had no idea who the person was—she only knew the truck behind her starting following them when she pulled out of the parking lot. She figured the person was just someone from the tavern who happened to have left at the same time.

The high beams were unwarranted. Driving in the rain at night was bad enough, and to make it worse, the high beams shining in through her rear window blinded the road in front of her. So, like any normal person would do in a situation like that, she flipped him the finger in her rearview mirror, letting it stay there long enough to make sure he got the message. She then slowed to make her turn over the Redmond Street Bridge that crossed the fast flowing Abenaki River.

***

Seeing the finger pushed his anger to another dimension. With his eyes filled with rage, Clayton hit the gas pedal hard and rammed the back of Kelsey's vehicle just as she was making her turn, sending her vehicle into the guardrail and down the embankment.

Clayton drove off feeling vindicated.

"Malcolm Dangil, AKA Mister Zero. Ha," Clayton said out

256

loud with an intoxicated laugh, a spray of foul beer mixed in. "Who would have guessed anyone would suspect a little weasel twerp like you could be a serial killer? Everyone thinks you're Mister Zero. Ha, that's pretty funny. I guess only you and me know the real truth. Lucky for me, Malcolm old buddy, you really were an oddball. Bad luck for you, you ran into me. Or should I say I ran into you, ran into that bitch's car. Good one too, nailed her ass. Sent her right off the road, right into the river. Ha," he laughed again with a little stumble, catching his balance before falling onto the gravestone.

"I guess you were in the wrong place at the wrong time, old buddy boy. If you and that bitch hadn't crashed through that guardrail when I rammed into her car, I was going to rape and murder your little girlfriend just like I did to those other two young bitches. Who knows, maybe you and me could have teamed up. Maybe we could have done both those two bitches at the same time. There's nothing like seeing a girl's terrifying eyes gleaming up at you when you're fucking them hard. Sticking a knife into their soft white flesh is even more exciting. But I guess that doesn't matter now — it's a little too late for you.

"I guess I'll just let things settle down for a while...maybe a long while. Don't want to get anyone suspicious, thinking the wrong way — now do we? Thinking maybe someone else...." He couldn't say him, but he almost did; saying him would only implicate himself, and he didn't want to say that. It was bad enough killing the girls over and over again in his dreams every night. One would think dreaming of the horrible murders he'd committed would keep him awake, but his dreams helped him sleep, seeing every detail from the moment he snatched them away, visualizing the rapes and the unmerciful ending of their young lives.

He then set his beer bottle down on the top of the gravestone and unzipped his pants, whipping out his penis and pissing on the grave. Before he finished urinating, Clayton lost his balance and stumbled backward, wetting his pants. Still standing, he bent and awkwardly retrieved his beer, drinking the rest in one big gulp. He stood staring at the dark grave for a moment, then smashed the bottle against the stone. The loud shattering sound awoke the night.

Before he could turn around to walk back to his truck, he heard loud flapping noises coming from the gnarly pine tree that leaned over him like a giant monster. The noise startled him. Not knowing the exact cause for the commotion, but thinking that somehow his pissing on Malcolm's grave had disturbed the dead man's ghost, Clayton hurriedly stumbled back up the hill to his truck.

After falling into the cab of his truck, Clayton quickly locked both doors and started up the truck. Once inside he felt safe from whatever had spooked him, and opened another beer. With one hand holding the beer bottle and his other on the gearshift, he shifted the truck into the drive position instead of reverse and pushed the gas pedal to the floor, expecting the tires to spin backward. With no time to react other than to attempt to find the brake pedal that seemed to have switched places with the gas pedal, Clayton drunkenly watched the truck as it barreled straight down the hill and plowed into the gnarly pine. His head smashed the windshield hard, knocking him out cold with a deep gash across his forehead, and fracturing his nose and cheekbone. Blackbirds scattered into the night, thinking the tree was being demolished.

***

The next morning, as the sun slowly crested over the hill,

shining a thin ray of light in the lower section of the cemetery, David Graham shook his head at Clayton's truck. Like Clayton the night before, David had spontaneously decided to take a drive through the cemetery on his way to town to meet Morrie Stover at the diner, a regular Saturday morning ritual. Being early, and having another spectacular autumn day to see the sunrise, he decided at the last moment to drive through the cemetery.

From the top of the hill overlooking the town of Redmond and the islands in Craggs Bay, one of the best places for viewing the sunrise, David noticed Clayton's truck smashed into the gnarly pine. From where he sat, he could tell the scene below didn't look good for the truck. It was definitely totaled, beyond repair. He also had a feeling Clayton would be asking for a raise to buy a new one. But that wasn't going to happen any time soon. It just wasn't in the town's budget.

A few minutes later, after yanking the driver's door open, his thoughts about Clayton asking for a raise disappeared completely. Clayton Edgar Daniels was in the same sad condition as his truck, crumpled against the gnarly pine and beyond repair. His face had smashed through the windshield and right into the tree, peeling away his face.

EPILOGUE

The brilliant autumn foliage looked spectacular viewed from the cliff on top of Mount Benton, a popular tourist spot for hikers. From there, ten miles away, one could see all the way to the ocean, where the seaside town of Redmond was in full foliage bloom and looked like a painted scene, a town created by an artist.

On a closer view, a view from a vehicle driving through Redmond, one could almost imagine living in a colorful illustrated world. The most spectacular, magnificent colors came from the trees in the town's cemetery, including the bright evergreens that enhanced the red and orange colors of the hardwood trees. Most of the evergreens, that is, with the gnarly pine, the tree with the large blackbirds resting on the branches that overshadowed Malcolm Dangil's infamous gravestone, being the exception. That tree could not enhance any view, and only soured one's perception when gazed upon.

David Graham had this colorful view as he drove by the cemetery on his way home for a home-cooked lunch break, but unlike most travelers driving the countryside to view the spectacular foliage, David did not notice since he had something else on his mind. He was hungry and only thinking of lunch, and it didn't matter to him what Margaret had made for him. For the last forty-two years they had been married, whatever she set on the table in front of him was good enough.

***

Some things are taken for granted and hardly noticed, like the sun rising every morning. The same could be said for the other side of the country as well — the sunny coast of Southern California.

Even though Los Angeles has no autumn foliage to gawk over, they do have other colorful sights to view, which are year round and not just in the autumn season. The city of angels has their own unique contrasting cast of characteristics. People from different cultures inhabit the city with their odd idiosyncrasies and exotic activities, from roller-skating along beach sidewalks in skimpy, colorful bikinis, to the haughty want-to-be movie stars strutting along the Hollywood boulevards in their elaborate outfits. Tourists, like those visiting the Northeast, often drive these city streets to view what most locals take for granted.

***

If they happened to have been driving on the lower end of Sunset Boulevard on the Monday evening when Redmond was nearing its foliage peak, they may have noticed one of these odd characters strolling into Gold's Pool Hall. This strange looking character was a balding heavy-set man, dressed in a Hawaiian shirt and a pair of outdated checkered shorts.

The man gently opened the glass door to the pool hall and nonchalantly walked to a payphone in the back of the room without saying a word. By his confident entrance one could easily see it was not his first time entering the pool hall, but he always went unnoticed, like the previous night when he'd come in to use the phone. Last night he'd had no luck contacting the person he wanted to speak to. Tonight, he had better luck.

On the other end of the phone the person who answered told him to hold and he would be put on the air when the radio program came back from a commercial break. When the commercial break concluded, the program's host reintroduced the audience to the program, giving them a brief introduction about the show, which included her return after a five month long leave-of-absence for personal reasons. She then keyed in the next person in the queue.

"Good evening," the host politely said. "Who do we have the pleasure to be speaking with?"

"Doctor Nancy, I don't know if you remember me or not, but I called you a few months ago when I was staying in Redmond, just up the coast from here. At that time Redmond was in deep, serious trouble. I have since fixed the problem, but now, since I have arrived here in Los Angeles, it has come to my attention this city is in much more serious trouble than Redmond ever was. So I just wanted to inform you, and all your listeners as well, that I have arrived in Los Angeles to rid this filthy city of demons. You can call me Mister Zero."

ABOUT THE AUTHOR

Geordie still resides in the same southern Maine town where he was born. He has had a variety of interesting jobs and met many strange characters, which have greatly inspired his writing. His passion is writing horror and science fiction stories. Mister Zero is his third novel.